Drawing the Spaces

Drawing the Spaces

Margaret Dyment

ORCA BOOK PUBLISHERS

Copyright © 1994 Margaret Dyment

All rights reserved. No part of this book may be reproduced in any form by any means without the written permission of the publisher, except by a reviewer who may quote brief passages in review.

Canadian Cataloguing in Publication Data
Dyment, Margaret,
    Drawing the spaces

    ISBN 1-55143-015-0
    1. Title.
PS8557.Y54D7 1994   C813'.54   C94-910155-9
PR9199.3D95D7 1994

Publication assistance provided by The Canada Council
Cover design by Susan Fergusson
Cover painting "In the coffee shop" by Phyllis Serota
Printed and bound in Canada

Orca Book Publishers
PO Box 5626, Station B
Victoria, BC Canada
V8R 6S4

Orca Book Publishers
#3028, 1574 Gulf Road
Point Roberts, WA USA
98281

To family and friends, with love

I am grateful for the assistance of an Ontario Arts Council Work-in-Progress grant in the completion of this book.

Thank-you to the many friends who have helped with these stories, and in particular the members of the Wednesday Group: Kristin Reed, Rona Murray, Garry McKevitt, Ally McKay, Sheila Longton, Milton Carman.

Material in this collection has been previously published as follows: "Drawing the Spaces" in *Quarry* and *89: Best Canadian Stories* (Oberon); "Never Seek to Destroy" in *83: Best Canadian Stories* (Oberon); "Sacred Trust" in *Canadian Fiction Magazine* and *The Second Journey Prize Anthology* (McClelland and Stewart); "The Kalil Yaghi Memorial Swim" and "Heinlein's Death" in *Focus on Women*; "Owlgirl" in *Fiddlehead* and *91: Best Canadian Stories* (Oberon); "Sandspit" in *Queen's Quarterly*; "The Personals" in a chapbook by Reference West.

Contents

DRAWING THE SPACES	1
NEVER SEEK TO DESTROY	13
TOXINS	21
SACRED TRUST	29
STAR	56
THE KALIL YAGHI MEMORIAL SWIM	66
SNAPDRAGON	70
STORM OF LIFE	85
SIREN ON THE SHORE	95
HEINLEIN'S DEATH	101
EROTICA	105
THE PERSONALS	115
WHAT REALLY GOES ON BETWEEN MEN AND WOMEN	127
THE IDEAL PLACE	132
OWL GIRL	137
MRS. O'HARA	151
LUCY GRAY	157
VIOLET	165
JOKES	175
NEIGHBOURS	181
THE POEM	186
SANDSPIT	192
MISS H.	201
AN END TO GRIEF	210
LINE OF STONES	218

Drawing The Spaces

When Jennifer was fifteen, she had an art teacher named Aquino who sat his class in the ditch and said don't draw the fence posts or the weeds, draw the spaces in between. He said it was called negative space.

She came to understand this as a symbol for the way we overlook the shape of things, and the lines between them, and see trees and parakeets and people we love as Other, falling into despair.

Twenty-five years later, the art teacher returned to the school reunion and kissed her on the mouth.

Her poem about the French professor who taught his students to stop to look at trees has been read as part of vocal ministry in a Quaker meeting in England.

She has been read in Reading.

The daughter of the professor who taught students to stop for trees came to one of Jennifer's poetry readings, shook her hand and bought a copy of the book with the poem, for her mother.

Jennifer's own daughter met her at the bus terminal, but really wanted her to leave. Anne found her mother's arrival a "hassle."

Hurt, confused, Jennifer finds herself locked out on a cold street in downtown Montreal.

In the morning she hurries, intending to take the first bus

home. But her daughter joins her and they have lunch and talk intensely, about men. Jennifer wishes she had figured out more answers before they reached this moment in both their lives. They had stopped at a second hand store before lunch, where her daughter had bought a plastic duck with a long neck and plastic quoits you are supposed to throw over it: a child's game. The plastic duck sits beside them on the restaurant table. The waiter likes Jennifer's daughter and the duck and hangs around. They make jokes about quoit some duck and about calling it quoits.

Outside the restaurant, an old man with a crooked leg peers in.

And last Wednesday there was a meeting of Quakers interested in problems of the disabled. Jennifer held a baby girl who was whole and perfect, and tipped her back in her hands. The baby laughed out loud. Jennifer startled herself, and her husband, by beginning to weep.

"You have all these marvellous skills, hidden away," says Helen Docherty, signing up Jennifer and her friend Eva to help out in the nursery.

The baby boy who years ago laughed in the tipping of her friend Eva's hands holds himself upright in a metal walking frame beside his hospital bed, his curls starting out around his head, his grin as bright as if he could see his guest clearly, as if she does not appear to him shrouded in fog. His head has been hurt in a motorcycle accident — he was riding up north to visit his brother; the optical nerve is damaged and also, on a possibly permanent basis, he has lost the use of his long legs and his big feet.

Jennifer leaves a space between her visit to him and the visit of his mother. She hopes that he will sleep.

The daughter of the teacher who taught people to stop for trees works at the rehab centre and didn't get along all that well with her dad.

The daughter of someone Jennifer doesn't know dances for money in Sparks Street Mall and pain never leaves her face. She dances her pain and office workers step around her, turning to look over their shoulders. When she finishes, Jennifer puts five dollars in the box the young woman has set out on the concrete. The dancer goes soft and shy: no one, she says, has ever given so much.

Jennifer's daughter at that moment was in Vancouver, panhandling to get past turning seventeen.

How you give to panhandlers is this. On a cold street in Montreal at noon her daughter instructs her, gentle in spite of her shock that Mother has been keeping her spare change to herself. "No matter who it is," the daughter begins, "it feels degrading to ask for money. So of course you will help out if you can."

Now, the dentist's chair is a very vulnerable spot. You tend to forget it when you don't have to be there. "Why have you been so long coming in?" asks Birgit, the pert young hygienist with the very adequate salary.

Jennifer hesitates, then decides to tell the truth. "I couldn't afford it."

Immediately she feels naked. Money is something you don't want to mention in among all these plastic and steel machines. She is supposed to pretend she fits in. She wants to pretend she fits in. But the truth is she couldn't afford it.

And to make it worse she thinks she has bad teeth. Birgit will look into her mouth and find out that Jennifer's parents couldn't afford it either.

"My teeth are terrible," she says.

Now the hygienist will treat her like a bag lady, not as Jennifer would treat a bag lady but the way she thinks people usually treat bag ladies. The hygienist will condescend to her and Jennifer tenses for it, arguments on her own behalf tumbling through her head. She wishes the hygienist would call her Mrs. Mitchell instead of Jennifer, even though a moment ago she was comfortable with her first name.

"You don't have terrible teeth," says the hygienist presently. "They're very good. You must be taking care of them. They are a little — "she comes right up to the word 'crooked' and instead says 'crowded' " — so they will be more difficult to floss than mine." Somehow she makes it sound as if Jennifer is doing a really great thing, taking care of her very interesting teeth while the hygienist is stuck with boring straight ones. That is how Jennifer has come to look at it herself, actually, but the rush of gratitude she feels is the measure of her vulnerability.

It gives her some idea of how it feels to admit you need money on the street.

"What if they are angry with me because I give them too little?" Jennifer asks her experienced kid. It is noon in January on St. Catherine Street.

Her daughter looks at her sideways. "Are you not strong enough to take it if some of the anger they feel about their lives gets deflected onto you?"

Jennifer is strong enough to find a seed of the future in the silence which lengthens between her daughter and herself.

From down the street she sees a man accosting other people. When he turns to her she folds his hand about some coins.

"God Bless You," he says.

A woman with him steps forward and reads the button on her coat: "Every Mother Is a Working Mother." She smiles. Jennifer smiles. It feels as if they are all friends.

The daughter of the man who taught the stopping for trees has never married, but has had years now of knowing all the parts of men in intimacies wives hope never to imagine. Caring for paraplegics requires first and foremost concern for the elimination of bladder and bowel. Catheters, condoms, bags, bedpans, tears. Strong men having to relinquish their strength, learn not to walk, learn not to speak, learn to — she teaches them what they still can do, what they must repeat and work at constantly if they are to reenter what is left to them of life. Some can marry and have children and coach junior hockey from their chairs. Others can roll their eyes and point to a Bliss Board with their tongues.

The handsome man who taught art when Jennifer was in grade eleven did not actually kiss her on the mouth, because she turned her head and took it on her cheek, missing her chance at fulfilment of teenage fantasies. Twenty-five years ago she caught him writing letters during class to someone called "Mary." But the woman standing back laughing as he busses his former students has another name. She is not Mary.

If the connections between us were more evident, I could go on from here and tell you a sad story, or maybe even a triumphant one, about the art teacher and his wife. Eventually you would find yourself seeing again in your imagination the tall young son of Jennifer's friend, clutching the sides of his metal walker, with his curls falling into his eyes, and his grin, and a yellow bruise on the side of one muscled arm where he fell trying to stand beside his bed. The line drawing the spaces moves here between two curly heads: this young man's mop of curls and Jennifer's son Jack's cheerful wild head of hair, braided at the sides now into dreadlocks, and at the front above his high forehead beginning to disappear. The line drawing connections breaks here into curlicues and tendrils as it passes over these two young men in her mind, as if flames erupt into the spaces over their heads.

In his natural state, he is good at fixing things, this boy in the metal walker who cannot move his feet. He knows the zen of motorcycle maintenance. He is interested in how parts interconnect. He takes a technician's interest in the electronic shorts now occurring in his own parts. "Look at this," he instructs Jennifer, pointing to his bare toes, immobile on the hospital tiles. "I tell them to move. Nothing happens. Now put this down on the floor." He hands her a strip of white paper and she sets it so that it touches his toes. He squints at it, concentrates, and the right foot moves, swings forward, crumples the white line. "It's like a computer," he says, wonderingly. "Breaks it down into small bits." Exhausted, he asks her to bring him a chair. "Tomorrow, I'll step over it. Next week I'll be jogging." Jennifer recognizes the amazing optimism of the male creature, who always believes he can hammer together a better world, and that he can do it at once.

Jennifer's father, when he was as young as this lad, was entranced by the opening world of radio. Jennifer's growing up was accompanied by the discordant music of squeals and squawks as her father probed the innards of ever-smaller radios and then mastered mysteries of picture tubes and transistors and modular parts. When his heart raced too fast when he was sixty-nine, the doctor asked him what he thought of having an electronic pacemaker installed inside his own flesh. Of course her father agreed. There is an old joke he has told many times, to do with radios or toasters or vacuum cleaners, and sometimes ailing garden plants, usually not people, and never about himself: "The operation was a success but the patient died."

And he had curly hair, too, thinks Jennifer, suddenly remembering the photographs of him from before she was born. Before the space of his bald pate grew clear across his head, leaving him only sideburns, which in his later years he grew hairily down the sides of his cheeks. He used to hold a mirror to his shining scalp and invite his family to reassure him: "I can still feel hair there, right there, at the back. Take a look." And they would squint, and laugh, and get serious and tell him yes, the fuzz was there. One time he went downtown for a consultation with a company who had published before-and-after photographs in the *Ontario Intelligencer*, promising bald men they could regrow their hair. In the end he didn't sign up. He couldn't afford it. Anyway, his family liked him the way he was.

The undertaker had to explain carefully why there would be

an extra charge for removal of the pacemaker near her father's heart. During cremation, it seems a pacemaker could explode. Jennifer and her balding brother and white-haired mother kept themselves composed, sitting on soft chairs in the undertaker's front room. They agreed the pacemaker must come out.

Television had arrived when Jennifer was eleven. Her father drove the whole family across the Bay to watch the set at Tobe's, a restaurant and dance hall which had become the first public place in their area to have a TV. Later she often watched him carrying great picture tubes in his arms, making his way along the sidewalk beside their house to his workshop, sometimes slipping a little on ice. He was missing toes on one foot, and this made him unsteady. He had explained to her that the picture tube contained a vacuum, making it something like a bomb. He had mentioned at another time that a picture tube breaking could suck in the walls of a house. Through the years she imagined him falling, his chest sucked out of him with the breaking of the tube in his arms. Somehow he was never able to reassure her about this. Perhaps it really was as dangerous as she thought, or perhaps she had not been clear to him how terrified she was that he might die.

You now know all that Jennifer knows about the art teacher and his wife. It's possible the house they bought has the ghost of a young woman in it, or that they are moving to Nova Scotia to raise sheep. These are stories belonging to other people she hardly knows. She does not expect to see the art teacher and his wife again unless they all make it to the fiftieth reunion. If Aquino offers to kiss her again when she is sixty-eight and he is seventy-three, she expects she will manage then not to turn her head. She may be grateful for anyone's survival, in fact, from here on in.

The professor who died young and taught stopping to look at the beauty of a tree taught also that the bomb was going to fall. It was 1959 and he was hard to believe. Now you often see pamphlets in which the mushroom shape of a bomb changes into the spreading branches of a beautiful tree. From Death to Life, it says. Inside is information about what you too can do to stop the bomb. You can start well by kissing someone for whom you feel joy, it doesn't matter whether on the lips or on the cheek. After that, it is learning to live amid space, the long stretches of time and of distance which separate us all and hide from us the interconnecting links. In the silence of this space some call upon God and hear nothing but the echo of their own voice. This echo we often mistake for emptiness.

How far away did Jennifer's friend stand up in Quaker Meeting in Reading, England, and share with them her poem about stopping for trees? Gathering strength in the silence, coming to some kind of orgasm of grace, a woman rose where she had never dared to do so before and somehow brought with her that poem.

Jennifer knows perfectly well the rounded toughening smooth small skin of the hand of Alan, her English friend's eleven-year-old son, now turned twelve. A circle of folk sat together in the Quaker meeting room in Ottawa, Canada, and Jennifer held Alan's hand, thinking about it, how far away we all travel from one another, how small the hand of her own son used to be in hers, and how he is grown, how he strides about Montreal organizing rallies and giving warmth to street people and not always being honest or polite. How he seems to know when to ignore her and wait for her to finish growing up and when to give her a hug and thank her for loving him so much.

What is Alan to Jennifer or she to him. His is the adventure of being a British boy, of growing ever taller, his arms and hands will slope down awkwardly at his sides, he watches his father, who bicycles every day to catch the train to London, where he works, appropriately, on transportation, for the British government.

She had believed that the professor who taught students to stop for trees had also refused to sire children because they might be killed by the bomb. She was told this, she believed it, she thought of it often when her daughter and son were too young to possibly understand. She was terrified that she might have to hold them and be powerless to stop their going blind and the slow peeling off of their soft skin. The bone protruding. The weeping and the vomiting and then the end of the weeping, the silence we all mistake for emptiness.

How foolish of him, she often thought, as her own children waxed beautiful and strong and muscled and grew tall. Why by now his children could be almost as old as I am. His children could be twenty-five. His children could be adults of thirty-three.

And then this imaginary daughter of his walked up to her after the reading, shook her hand, thanked her for writing the poem about her father, with whom this daughter had never quite got along but whom she still missed, and asked if she could buy a copy of the book with the poem so her mother could see it in print. And Jennifer found this daughter was old enough to be teaching survival skills to young men who expect to die of infection and pneumonia and plain old age and probably not of nuclear war.

Later the daughter phoned to convey the mother's gratitude for the book. She telephoned Jennifer on September 15, 1982, happening to call on the first anniversary of the death of Jennifer's father. Jennifer needed comfort, and the phone call from the daughter of the dead professor helped. Jennifer had loved her father, and grieved for him painfully and it seemed without end when he died, on September 15, 1981.

Jennifer's daughter has left her in front of St. Christopher's Community House and she has gone off to spend the night with her boyfriend, in his warm bed.

Jennifer's daughter feels that her mother's arrival is some form of hassle in her life that she wishes to do without. Something between them has cracked. Jennifer missed hearing it. She missed hearing her daughter make any arrangements at all to make the visit from Jennifer easier for all concerned. Maybe she did. Jennifer is not sure. Her suitcase is heavy with David Bowie records and an Emma Goldman book she was bringing to her daughter, but that weight she carries by herself.

"Jack's in there," her daughter says. "You'll find him in the office, straight ahead when you go in."

"You're not coming in?" Jennifer asks, stupidly.

"Not really — we've got some posturing to do. And stuff. It's Saturday night. Jack will take care of you. I'll be at Rick's."

"When will I see you?"

"I'll see you." She kisses her mother, a fast brushing of cheeks. "I don't need any hassle, Jennifer."

The two young people disappear in a swirl of snow down the cold Montreal street.

Jennifer tries to open the unfamiliar door. It is locked.

When is the next bus, she wonders, distressed, starting to talk out loud. I could just get back on the next bus. I can be home in my own bed in two hours.

But she is tired.

And the rush of her adventure has not quite left her. She wants to explore a bit further yet.

She follows a path in the snow around behind the Community House to another locked door, this one with a light. She bangs on it hard. Her son, Jack, lets her in and gives her a large warm hug. St. Christopher's Community House seems to Jennifer the warmest place in all of Montreal. She puts down her case and takes off her coat and boots.

On the phone her daughter Anne had said: "I just want to talk with you for a moment, Jennifer."

She has taken to calling her mother by her first name.

"I was at the Community House again today. There's a woman there called Mary. She's a bag lady. She swears to herself all the time: really violent stuff. I guess she's one of those people they let out from the psychiatric wards. Just dumped on the street. Shit, I feel really useless. I wish I had stayed in school."

What good would that have done? Jennifer could have said, but didn't.

When your kid indicates a desire to go back to school, you as a mother have to encourage it.

And Anne had started to cry.

There was silence on the line because of the tears. Jennifer broke it, chattering into the space between her daughter and herself.

"Listen, you're not in Vancouver anymore, you're in Montreal. I'll come and see you right now. There's a bus at 7 o'clock."

"No wait," Anne had said. "Jennifer, this isn't like you."

"Meet me at nine," Jennifer said.

"Okay." Anne sounded as if she was starting to smile.

What Jennifer hasn't understood is that when her daughter was in Vancouver she was seventeen and now she is twenty and Jennifer's own mother doesn't visit her just because she sounds depressed. Jennifer is forty-seven and for at least twenty-five years now her mother has had to leave space for a spouse, for one thing. Spouse space.

At nine o'clock she says, hugging Anne tight, "I'm not here to take care of you."

Lying.

"Jennifer," her daughter replies, "this is Rick."

Rick is very good-looking and stands close to Anne and flashes Anne's mother a nice grin. He doesn't offer to help carry her case. But she might have refused anyway — she is strong. Her arm aches as under her daughter's instructions she steps off the bus in front of the Community House. Her suitcase is leaden with Bowie records and Emma Goldman's autobiography, debris from her daughter's past life. The night is growing cold.

"That's our friend Mary sleeping in the back," mentions Jack, leading the way across an open space that had once been the nave of a church. Jennifer gets a good look as she passes, and stiffens in surprise. Mary looks normal enough asleep, dark-haired, mouth slack, with an Adidas bag beside her and three plastic bags, stuffed with her possessions. She is curled on an old bean-bag chair. She is snoring. What astonishes Jennifer is that the woman is very young. Maybe twenty-five. A twenty-five-year-old psychiatric-case bag lady, fresh in from panhandling on the streets.

Jack shows her the tuck-shop and goes back to his office to finish off some work. Jennifer sits waiting for him, drinking coffee, eating a muffin, remembering crossly her daughter's tears that very same morning on the phone.

She pulls out her journal to write it all down, then finds herself describing instead what is going on at the table across from hers. A young man has gone off and stuck a quarter into a game of Pac-man, leaving behind a pretty, dark-eyed woman sitting with her donut and absolutely nothing else to do. After a while the boy from behind the counter comes over to the game and sits down and watches, but the young woman sits on at the table by herself, staring blankly and continuously into the space between herself and her man.

Jennifer sits in that space, but all she can do is write down the outside description of what she sees as the young woman's despair. Maybe in actuality the woman is just fine. Maybe the reason she doesn't go to watch the game is that what she most needs right now is that donut and that mug of coffee and a few minutes alone to herself. Silence. Maybe she is praying. Or maybe she is rehearsing the scene for later on, when she will throw it at him, letting anger spill out which right now is invisible behind the mask of her makeup and her unlined face. Maybe she has already left him, only he doesn't know it yet. Maybe she is pausing here, listening for some reassurance that somewhere inside her is still her own self. Maybe she is putting corrals around her fear, the feeling she has that she thinks she wants to cry. He is going to want to make love again, she is thinking, and I should be looking forward to it, if I start to think about it now maybe by the time it happens I will want it to happen, there will be something there for me. Her husband at the Pac-man game has a round face with a moustache and an expression as impassive as hers. Jennifer can't tell if he is winning or losing.

Jack comes. They walk a long time, two tired dots in the darkness, tracing a line across the long space between a house where he has to leave some things and, finally, the house where he lives. After awhile she asks for help carrying her case. Somebody is away, and has said she may sleep in their bed. She puts on her nightgown and wiggles in between somebody's unwashed sheets.

"Don't you know yet," cries her friend Eva later, calling on cosmic verities as she does from time to time. "Don't you know that being a parent is a one-way street?"

Another time she wonders if Jennifer didn't know that every married person wishes for a romantic marriage.

Jennifer feels foolish, asking of the cosmos what it so clearly can never give: grateful children, marital romance.

Wait a minute, she thinks, I do have a romantic marriage. There is a blank space in your universe, my friend. Women receive flowers and still peer around them, dreaming of escape.

The problem is, perhaps, that we have not learned to draw the spaces. We mistake the institution of marriage for the movement of people's souls. Not everything can be said with flowers. We mistake the seed of our own growing for emptiness, for the abyss. It is not enough for Jennifer to kiss her husband in public, on the cheek or on the mouth.

Or that neither one of them ever plays Pac-man.

It may turn out to be enough that they have parented the same children, that they have inhabited the same spaces and drawn between them some of the same lines.

"You're still here!" squeals Anne in delight when her mother phones her at the boyfriend's house next day at noon. Anne wants to be taken out to lunch.

The space between Jennifer's own mother and herself shrinks and expands. Once when the children were little, her mother hugged her and Jennifer embarrassed them both by starting to cry. Neither had anything to say.

In silence grows the seed.

Roots search for water; institutions crack.

"I thought I was very good at letting go," she says to her friend. "What I didn't see coming was the part where they turn to you and say: Go!"

She really thought that they would be different.

At the Quaker meeting she gets to hold the baby, and when

the baby squirms Jennifer remembers one of those little skills we have hidden away, the trick of tipping them back in the safety of your hands, that makes them start to laugh. Her husband comes in from the other room and catches her looking sheepish, with hot tears in the corners of her eyes.

Once again she is mistaking silence for emptiness: echo for the loss of human voice.

Outside the restaurant, an old man with a deformed leg lingers and gazes inside. He turns away from mother and daughter as they come out carrying the plastic duck.

"Wait a minute," says Anne, and goes over to the man.

"Could you use some change?" she wonders politely, fumbling in her pocket to see what she has.

"Oh, it's all right," he says, looking at her scuffed jacket and her old shoes, but brightening under her smile.

"You sure?" she asks kiddingly and their hands meet: he accepts something. "You have a good day now," says Anne.

Across the rush of twenty years Jennifer finds the photograph she and her husband took of their young daughter in her overalls, walking without looking onto the Island ferry, frowning, absorbed, her notebook held in front of her, lost in the unfolding of a poem.

What does she say in Montreal now as she hangs up the phone? She shakes her head: my parents are weird; their responses are so weird. I don't get along with them too well, but I miss them still enough to phone.

"And I'm writing some poems. I'm not going back to school. And Mary? That bag lady? Froze to death. She was just a block from here. By the way, I'm not going to Santiago."

Jennifer listens, uncertain what to say.

At her end, Anne shakes her head, in anger or in tears.

The line between them loops and snarls.

"I'm sorry," Jennifer offers at last, "about Mary."

There are so many other things that are not quite right to say. How young that child was. How terrified Jennifer is her child, too, might slip, might die.

In the space of distance and the space of passing time will come both healing and pain, silence, echo, new seed.

Never Seek To Destroy

Today the news is full of killings, and a week ago I thought there was nothing more serious than the end of love. Nancy hid her golden head in her arms on my desk in the English workroom and she cried. And I felt helpless and angry, as I have before. When my two sisters split up with their husbands. When one of the kids' teachers had a separation and nervous breakdown plunk in the middle of the school year. When Mrs. Hubble, who is sixty-five, left Mr. Hubble, who is seventy. When the Lebanese couple who used to run the grocery store split and sold the business to someone new. All those families are finished, it's over, the bitterness grows and grows, or else there is something numb. Nothing, one sister tells me, there has been nothing, nothing for a long time. It is as if it had never been. She is flying across the country, she is in love for the first time and she gives me her books, too heavy to take with her so far. In the front of Ferlinghetti's poems an inscription: "Something to read when studying gets you down." Looks tender to me. Yet nothing. Never seek to destroy your family, writes her ex-husband, who is the one who did the destroying when it came to it. The one who clumsily abandoned them all: his newborn son, his wife, Gwendolyn my gentle niece, and went off to seek love, not destruction, in another place, with another woman. Something better than the tender emptiness his marriage had become. Yet — never think of it, he says. Signs himself off with love.

Now, I have only a vague idea of where Afghanistan even is. It's on the way to the ocean from Russia, and next in line is Pakistan; I suppose I could eventually find it on a map. There are mountains and children there. People marry, as elsewhere, for one reason or another. Nancy seems more real, sunlight from the broad workroom windows just gilding the crown of her hair and coming to rest in glory on a scarlet thesaurus and a navy-blue *Concise Oxford* at the back of the desk. The workroom is deserted at this moment, fortunately, teachers already in their classes or else down ordering their lunch. In the corridors outside some students are still moving; there is a burst of sudden laughter from a distant class, a door bangs shut. Nancy sniffs and wonders out loud whether I might have a Kleenex. I have two, and she uses up both of them, weeping into one and then daintily blowing her nose in the other. Tendrils of blond hair stick flat to her wet cheeks. She is very beautiful and, in the way of beautiful women, appears to be putting on a show. Our heroine in tears. Betrayed by her lover — no, it is she who has betrayed him, refused and hurt him: either way a pretty cliché. I recognize the pain, though, the things she manages to say. How suddenly it all seemed taken out of her hands, how all her world had stopped and started up again, new colours, new names for new colours. And there were no children to be hurt.

Middle-class sex, as long as it's kept discreet, can add a certain piquancy to staffroom innuendo: it can spice an otherwise dull suburban evening, lend cosmetic sparkle to an already lovely cheek and eye. How to drum up sympathy, however, for the affluent lover capsized into pain? The love itself and all its attendant and exquisite tortures seem artifacts. What is real is that in Afghanistan soldiers are shooting little children. How to take seriously the reality of Nancy's empty womb?

It becomes complex. While my sister talked to the counsellors she had met at the wedding party, the wedding, that is, the marriage of her two good friends who had been living together for three years and had just had a baby, and included among their guests friends of the past two or three years (many of whom in this interim, things being the way they are, have recoupled, so that spouses, ex-spouses, new relationships and new singleships met and intermingled on this joyous occasion), and also the two children, her son by her first marriage and of course the baby — while my sister discussed the possible end of her marriage with another dear friend who has finally definitively finished with her ex-husband, because now she has at last found this very warm male human being (I met him, he is nice, I liked him right away) — a marriage counsellor — "Isn't it ironic that his marriage has broken up too? But then he understands" — while my sister, the wisest person I know, was seeking wisdom from her dear friend and her friend's dear friend, and very serious futures were being decided without anybody feeling very much like laughing at themselves — my niece Gwendolyn and I went for a walk. Gwendolyn wanted to visit the tot lot, because she had lived near it when she was little and her daddy or her mummy had often taken her there. So now she climbed the hill that had once seemed like a mountain and that to a five-year-old is only a hill, she hopped onto the baby swings and clambered up the rope spider's web and nothing fit: she kept taking steps that were too big and reaching for handholds that were too low. And looking about for friends who have long since, like herself, moved away. Gwendolyn explored everything. Then she wanted to go. We held hands and wandered back. Once she stopped me to attend to the colour of the steel sky behind a crimson tree, and again to shuffle back and forth together in a pile of crunchy brown leaves. Then I stopped her when we got as far as Mac's Milk, because I had just enough change in my sweater pocket for a box of maple-leaf cookies; we opened them on the spot and had some as we went along. My niece's charming company brought back memories for me of my daughter at that same age, the wonder of her, the sensitivity to colour and taste and feel, the easy trust of her hand inside mine, the chatter and giggles and silences and scuffing of leaves. Most of the cookies we brought back for Mummy and the people she is talking to: Janet and Harv. They are coming to conclusions: the storm has passed, and Gwendolyn, still unaware, is launched on a new lifeplan that as it happens will take her far away from her daddy. Who in his turn will try to start over, to recouple as he has had in mind to do. To try to grow into something new and not to shrivel up and blow away like a brown leaf on an autumn day without his daughter Gwen. Perhaps his mind has usually been elsewhere anyhow. His mind and heart. Perhaps years from now when his second wife has their second child and he finds he is once again the father of a girl his mind will not turn to a memory of a tot lot with a rope web and baby swings. Nothing. It has meant nothing.

Perhaps.

And Gwen will be all right. Her mother has found a place in this world with pumpkins in the garden and a big back porch and a trip to see the steam engines and friends to play with and a Mummy in love, a Mummy turning beautiful again, laughing, laughing at herself. I love Michael a bit, Gwendolyn whispers in her mother's ear. But don't tell him yet.

My own daughter is twelve.

I have a pair of socks knitted in Afghanistan, heavy, blue, thick-soled, no more draughts in winter from my toes to my knees. I wear them at home all winter long. They were a Christmas present from my brother and they keep me warm. That is my link to Afghanistan: warm feet on a wintry day, family love. I am grateful: how did they come so far, I wonder, and is it cold in the mountains of Afghanistan? In the mirror I remind myself of a guerilla warrior, my slacks tucked into my big socks, the thick stolid line of my calves. On the news we see men in turbans, cloaks and leggings, grizzled men, some smiling for the cameras. We will fight in the hills; we will never give up. Later an Australian reporter writes that the pictures were taken over the border, in Pakistan: there is some deception involved. I hope it is true. That it is all a lie.

That my daughter and her giggling friends did not run out into the streets and shout slogans: where is Jimmy Carter, who says he cares about human rights? Where is he now? Why does he not do anything? Thirty of them, a whole class, dead in the street, bullets in their abdomens and eyes and tearing their breasts just starting to bud and all toppled down like little savage dolls in the street, others home crying, our soldiers refused to shoot but the Russians soldiers opened fire. . . .

How do these reports get out?

Perhaps it is propaganda, vicious propaganda, the Russian embassy announced in a statement to *The Globe and Mail*, a "foul stew."

And my son's your son's high school has not rioted as high schools did here in the sixties, has not been politicized, galvanized into action, cannot have lessons now, cannot learn, our sisters are dead in the street all the youths pouring out the doors and windows we must be men now, we must suddenly be men, and they face the tanks, the kids pouring in from every direction, all the schools.

There is a sound of movement in the corridors. We must go soon to our classes. Our students will be waiting for us, rough-and-tumbling about the room, some outside the door watching for us to arrive: "She's coming, guys!" A scurrying inside the room, some of it mock, to make you wonder: when you get there nearly everyone looks hard at work and full of studied innocence.

So I am staying with him, says Nancy, blowing her nose some more and smiling ruefully at her tears. Right now it's very bad. He sees me shudder when I touch him, I know I'm cold, it's like he's dead, or I'm dead. I am living with him in shadows: all the coloured world has moved out west. I'm staying out of — lethargy, I think. Inertia.

As long as you have a reason, I say. We both laugh, not too shakily.

It's getting better, she tells me next time. We've decided to have a baby.

The woman buying cauliflower in the market, the woman over there in the pink-striped smock, that's Nancy. Nancy downtown in the beginning of August, the baby's due now any day. I watch her choosing vegetables and bread and fruit, dreaming over her choices and not looking around. She is more beautiful than ever with her big belly, and the baby stirs, it frets, I see the smock move where it's pulled tight as she bends over a bin of vegetables. She seems to me to have changed, her gestures slow as if weighed with a kind of bodily grief. I remember the brilliance of her anger and her determination on the committees where I knew her, committees on teenage recreation facilities and on book banning and on school discipline. Even then she never was shrill. I remember her sweetly obstinate, ready to do the research, ask the questions, write the report. She used to mention to me how upset she had felt, but on the outside her anger showed only in the quiet stubbornness with which she would refuse to let a meeting go on until she could "understand." I would see her lean forward and give a little shake, as if to awaken an aggressiveness she needed, and then the politely phrased questions would begin, one after another, where angels fear to tread: Do you think board members are afraid there will be a drug problem? Is

Twelfth Night, would you say, appropriate for a bright child in grade eight? Is there any pleasure, do you think, some sadism, in your continued use of the strap? Naïve like a fox.

Now Nancy dreams. Perhaps she is remembering her lover, the slide of his hands on her bare flesh, the way in their sex the world steadied itself a moment in space, everything balanced, she had no more questions, no one died.

Or perhaps she is heavy still with the thrust of her young husband's pain, the facade he never meant to build crumbling, moving aside as it did before in the first vulnerable times of his love for her, so that their two pains met and joined in the forming of this child. Someone is there, someone she hopes to see, and she could not say if she means the child, whose name is Julia or Brian and who is the seed of their hope, their stake in the terrible future that insists on breaking in and breaking out and in a week or so will split her, coming on without stopping into this specific time, this specific place, having made its choice of parents forever and forever, its choice of country and politics and armament. Or whether she means the other foetus she trembled with the night after her lover and his wife separated and she faced a choice she can never unchoose, never come to again on identical terms.

Well, he is gone; her lover is gone and left no forwarding address. Time moves sluggishly on, bringing with it all the outcomes of all the decisions we have made. It seemed like a mature and adult decision, to try out the sexual things that seemed released into possibility, to switch mates, no one knows, it might be liberating, it might be fun, and she knew him well already, they had worked on committees together! As it turned out it was very easy in the happening, easy to tear one marriage into two — two thousand hopeless shards why there was nothing it was nothing after all, at all — and tear the other one — ah, this was not easy but there was no stopping it like the baby once it had decided to come to break the other on the bedrock of its awful commitment.

So they clung together, she and her young husband, who had thought that all he wanted was a new car and some spare-time sex, swung in time like flies caught in a sticky web: we can't get out; we're growing older; something has been lost and we can't tell if it is something we intended to keep but — we'll have a baby now. It starts as a baby. We'll grow up with this baby for eighteen years and who will we all be then?

There is a single space, a single time. Someone is there, someone she hopes to see, but for all that space and all that time her lover will be far away, not to be met, not to be seen, not to be embraced forever. Is it good, then, this choice, this slow rush through eighteen years to see what must be seen? Sorrow adds love to the lullabies, the way she waits and waits for love's tide to turn, to flow once more through her with all its colours. I could not make the way smooth for you, my children, but I have gone ahead of you and I am waiting for you. When you turn to me you find me here.

On a bloody morning Nancy wakes and her children have suddenly gone ahead. Yesterday was gunfire in the streets and this morning the children are not in their beds. My love, my love, that blood intimacy, your head the shape of my father's head, your curls my curls, your eyes the blue of a young man I chose long ago — who lies still beside me in this bed, we two alone, all the slow maturing of our love now come to this: a man and a woman turn to one another on a morning somewhere in the world and find that after all there is no one else: the bond knit by decision twenty eighteen sixteen years ago has come out to this unity of blood. Whether or not it is our children who have been killed, only we, you and I my beloved, can seed their possibility of a future. We will go to the hills. We will rush the tanks in the streets. We will do all that we can. For we have been a family. And now we have nothing to lose.

Why do you not do anything? WHY HAVE I NOT?

In the night she starts awake from a dream. There is a war and two men have been badly beaten and she feels it as a reality on her block, not an item in the newspaper. Nothing shields her. Her husband is in the dream, and her son, and a man she once knew and let go. All three are in most imminent danger. She comes to where her son sits tensely on the side of his bed, and she holds his hand. She tries to explain to him that she does not wish him to be brave for her sake: that she wishes him to live if he can. Do not die foolishly, O my strong son. I know you are brave. It seems she can see a smear of blood on his face but she goes on. "If the time comes, to be brave" — and suddenly it comes to her that nothing no nothing at all is worth dying for. Not his dying. Not you, my son. Let me die.

At four in the morning Nancy lies awake and it seems to her that children have been gunned down in city streets crying out for life and that she has done nothing. There must be some mistake. In the morning it will not seem so real: she will remember something that eludes her at this hour.

On a morning of sunshine Nancy wakens early in her suburban home. Birds cry outside. In the bedrooms of her house she hears the soft breathing of her children. No one is dead; no one has left. The beloved whom she meets each day stirs beside her in the bed, wakes a little, smiles in his sleep and touches her. For a moment in time the world is steadied on its axis, the chaos of newspaper accounts rights itself, falls silent. Sorrow that lies within her now like the membrane of her cells rouses to deep wordless joy. Something is here that is called a family: never seek to destroy.

From this moment flows the rest, the confusions and restlessness and fears of everyday. Just then, as one time before, Nancy has no questions.

Good morning, my daughter. It's time to go to school. Wake, wake, my son, my tall boy.

You do not need to go to war today.

Toxins

Martha came home on a dark winter afternoon when her daughter Kate was supposed to be in school and found her in tears on her bed. Kate sat up, sniffling and rubbing her face and saying she felt foolish. The story was fairly simple. She'd gone out on her noonhour by herself, head full of English class and looking forward to going back because next was Drama, her favourite subject. She was having a good day: no Math until Tuesday. Maybe if she wasn't trying this accelerated thing she would have been with her friends and she wouldn't have noticed the headlines.

"Have you seen the paper?" she asked, rubbing at her nose. Her face was blotchy and it didn't help that yesterday she had hennaed what was left of her hair a red that Martha associated with cheap women. Kate had gone on about how good henna was for the hair, how organic. Martha tried to readjust her prejudices about henna, and about heavy eye makeup, for that matter. Her daughter chose to wear to school thick black eyeliner and mascara that just now had pooled under her eyes and run down her cheeks. The combination of black-circled eyes, the shock of red hair and the shaved sides was, to say the least, disturbing. Her scalp showed through over her ears, a grey colour. Was there some rule nowadays, Martha wondered, that a girl couldn't be political and pretty at the same time? Actually she suspected that there was. And boys still hung around: that in fact was one of the problems. The current boy lived out in the suburbs — part of the attraction was probably that Kate so clearly did not — and one of the things there was tension about was the number of nights recently that Kate had been phoning home to say that she was stranded out there and would stay over with a girlfriend. Still Martha believed that her daughter hadn't yet Done It: that a mother would know.

Kate had come home and evidently just thrown herself on the bed. She was wearing the same ratty blue jeans she had left in that morning, and the pink rumpled man's shirt with the collar taken off. Martha missed again the brown string necklace that had been a part of Kate since she'd been a little girl. A policeman had yanked it off her neck the last time she was arrested, spat "Garbage!" and tossed it away. She supposes that he includes her daughter in his idea of garbage. The necklace had bugged Martha when Kate insisted on wearing it even to bed, and maybe had not always washed her neck properly because of it, but at least she had had the sense to respect it. Respect was what was apparently lacking in this policeman supposedly trained to handle difficult people. If they behaved like this with white-skinned, middle-class kids, she shuddered to imagine how they must handle black people or native people or street people. She thinks the answer may be in changing the way we train our police.

But Kate was telling her news. She said that the Israeli army had somehow let Christian Phalangists into a Palestinian camp called Shatila that was under Israeli protection in Lebanon. There had been a terrible massacre.

Martha tried to think about this event that had upset her daughter so much. To her it seemed vague and very far away. It went through her head to ask her daughter whether her period was due.

"It's just that I couldn't go to Drama and stand on one leg as a heron — that was what I was going to do — I just couldn't, Martha."

When had Kate stopped calling her "Mom" and begun calling her by her first name? Had she ever called her "Mom"? She must have, when she was little.

There were piles of papers on the floor all over the room. Kate had been up till all hours working on a mailing to about twenty people: the minutes of the last meeting of the Alliance for Non-Violent Action, an article about prisoners and copies of political cartoons.

Something about the woebegone mask created by the makeup brought to the surface an old pet name. "Katybelle, you were up late last night." She was fairly sure that Kate hated that name, but once it had slipped out she didn't like to make it worse by apologizing. It belonged with the memories of her daughter's younger self: that bright-eyed mischief with long brown-blond braids. "Maybe you could have coped today if you'd got more sleep. I do wish you'd get yourself onto a regular — "

"Marthaaa! Really, I don't need that shit right now."

Martha sighed. She felt offended, but four-letter words didn't seem to pack the same punch for her daughter as they still did for her. Her gaze dropped to Kate's bare feet on the bed. Almost absent-mindedly, she reached for one foot and began massaging it. They sat in silence, her thumbs making circles, pushing, probing, manipulating the base of each toe, down the instep and against the tough callus of the heel. Under the toes were blisters, nearly healed. That was from the long walk she had gone on the month before, a march over the Ivy Lea Bridge to Griffis Air Base.

Martha had a theory that the way to keep your kids out of trouble was to go with them to things. This had worked very well for baseball games and school plays and community picnics. Theoretically, the things that Kate was now choosing to do were open to the public, too, but practically speaking her parents recognized they'd been left behind. They were not going to take workshops in civil disobedience and go to sit-ins and marches and blockades. When Kate walked over the Ivy Lea Bridge, her parents watched it on television, a clip on the evening news. There had been an aerial view of a flowing mass of heads moving over the bridge and then a voice-over which stopped their hearts by asserting that the guards had standing orders about trespassers on the base, to shoot to kill.

"Ouch."

Martha had pushed too hard.

"Sorry."

Kate made no move to pull away — some intimacy between them held. Martha stroked the top of Kate's foot, set it down and started on the other one: wiggle each rosy, smooth toe, dig into the shape of the bones.

"Katie, do you remember that guy in Herb and Spice who

was so excited about footrubs?"

Kate smiled. "Reflexology, they call it."

"Yeah. Remember he said he slept for hours after somebody rubbed his feet, because all the toxins had been released out of his system?"

"Where did they go, I wonder? Did he wet the bed?"

They both laughed.

"Anyway, watch it. I'm getting your toxins out. Starting with that massacre."

The girl stiffened and her foot jerked, but Martha caught it and went on with the massage. There was anger in her, too, anger at this kid who thought she knew it all, who should be right now in school standing on this very foot. Martha channelled her feelings into scaled-down pummelling, trying out the idea about the toxins, even though really she thought it was foolishness. The toxins in herself were bitter. That handsome policeman, tall, blue-eyed.

"Your daughter was throwing bags of red dye at President Reagan's car."

Martha had believed him.

On the morning of the visit of the U.S. president to town she had been wakened by the throb of helicopters. Days like this in the capital city always made her feel restless anyway, and then she came upon her daughter at the kitchen sink. Drops of vegetable colouring were going into each one of a pile of baggies and they were blossoming red as Kate added water. Already a number were filled and sealed and waiting on the draining board.

"Kate, dear, this isn't okay. What exactly are you planning to do? You *must not* throw anything at Reagan. He's the president of the United States; he's surrounded by guards and they have guns. It doesn't matter what it is you throw; how do they know it isn't a bomb? This is dangerous! Tell me what you're doing!"

"Calm down, Martha. It's a group action, and we agree with you. We're not going to throw anything. We're going to use these to dye the snow red around wherever he makes his speeches, but we'll do it afterwards, not during. We won't do a thing at the procession except hold up the banner. But I have to take these along. They're for after."

That afternoon, Martha was busy in the store with a customer when the phone rang.

"This is Sergeant Don Stewart of the Ottawa Police. We have your daughter Kathleen in custody here. I'm sorry to say that there was an incident. Some bags of red dye were thrown at the car of President Reagan."

"No. She promised me that she wouldn't throw anything."

His voice went careful, as if he were making clear the facts, not as if he were lying in his teeth. "Now I must say that they didn't actually get any dye on the president's car. But they did get some on some other cars, including a police car."

She had thought she had a category for being set up, but somehow it hadn't occurred to her that he could sound quite as guileless as that and actually be lying. When she got down to the police station (she was very angry with Kate, because it meant she had to close the store on a busy Saturday to get there) he still looked as if he were telling the truth. We adults, siding together understandingly to control these disruptive kids, was his attitude. As they walked down the corridor to the room where Kate was being held, he plied her with friendly, intelligent-sounding questions about Kate's activities. She told him what little she knew. Later it made some sense. The guy had arrested an underage minor, thinking he was getting one of the leaders. In fact Kate had done nothing, but she could have. He would like it if, even for a day or so, they got some chargeable leads from the mother.

Still, she thought, and said to Kate later on, what can you expect if you go out to demonstrations dressed like a punk and carry with you a bag full of packs of red dye? It had been a demo against U.S. and Canadian complicity in genocide in East Timor — this Kate had tried to explain. But where is East Timor anyway? Some unknown country these children had decided suddenly to be so upset about. Who was their leader, the blue-eyed police officer had wanted to know. But there was no leader; she knew that, and she told him that. They just worked together, finding out stuff, taking turns calling the meetings and sending out the minutes.

Like this mailing Kate was working on now. Part of it was about a couple of prisoners. One was a mentally retarded man named Jimmy who was on death row somewhere in the States for a crime it sounded like he probably didn't commit. The other was a woman named Linda somebody, again a story from the U.S. She apparently was in jail basically because she was a lesbian. Martha had read the handout. It didn't seem likely to her that this was the whole story, but certainly the woman sounded convincing. In spite of some disillusioning brushes with certain police officers, she was still not convinced that the entire system was wrong. Police officers had somehow got the idea that acting brutal to kids would keep them out of jail but, at least in Kate's case, it had made matters worse. When Kate was just starting to go out to alternative music nightclubs, she had run onto the stage one night in reaction to a song called "More Dead Cops" and grabbed the microphone and announced passionately that genocide for any group was wrong, including cops. Now when Martha mentioned this her daughter winced or became angry; she'd been young, she said, and didn't want to be reminded.

The foot massage was going on automatically now in a rhythm. She was getting the hang of it. The afternoon was closing in already and streetlights came on outside the bedroom window. Kate seemed settled down. Her voice and Martha's voice came and went in the shadows, reweaving the fragile bond: homework, the massacre, that mailing to do, the prisoners, the school play (Kate had two parts), the new band playing tonight that Kate wanted to go to (but it's a school night; we had an agreement! Martha said), the boyfriend, some amusing and disturbing stories about customers from Martha's morning in the store, the children, the children, the dead ordinary families with children from that massacre the day before in Lebanon.

The phone rang. Kate leapt to answer it. "Patricia!" she said, and her voice rose with pleasure.

Martha stood up and thought about the other nurturing she still knew how to do: getting a meal. Even that was harder now that Kate had become an adamant vegetarian.

This Patricia was one of the group of women who had been arrested with Kate at Litton. Their idea had been to enter the building and to place a citizen's arrest on the president for endangering the human race. Apparently Litton manufactured guidance systems for cruise missiles. They had poured vials of their own blood over themselves to dramatize the seriousness of what they felt. Martha has photographs of this. Kate had explained to her that the demonstrators try to document what happens, because then there is less police violence. So Martha has colour pictures of her daughter with her curls sticky with her own blood. Just the idea of their preparing their blood this way terrifies her.

"It was a nurse, Martha. An accredited nurse. We did it the night before."

She pulls things out of the fridge and listens to the way Kate's voice has suddenly opened up as she talks with Patricia, has lost its guarded quality. She is only the mother: she has spent a lot of her life over the past sixteen years trying to keep her child safe and the instinct is still upon her, but events are outrunning it. Her daughter has found out about the world, and has drawn her own conclusions. Other women have to help to nurture her now: teachers, her aunts, women like Patricia in these "affinity groups" which form when she goes to the demonstrations against uranium mining, against the building of the Darlington reactor, against the buildup of a nuclear arsenal, on behalf of forests and native people and taking back the night. Martha is grateful for these women who care for her daughter and at the same time she feels annoyed, sidetracked. When is letting go the right thing to do and when is it irresponsible? What is left of her job? At sixteen her grandmother was a young wife on the prairies with her first child on the way. But Martha herself at sixteen was in grade twelve and was memorizing dates of old wars for her next history test. And treaties: that came with it. Treaties and wars.

She feels changes going on inside her. She wishes she could find the right place to pick it up, to explain it to, for instance, that young policeman, or to her smiling friends. Can it be that they all are seeing it wrong? If we are wrong, thinks Martha, then we are wrong about the very issue Kate was arrested about the first time: the one about uranium mining. When she indulges in memories now of her perfect baby girl, she has to remember also that Kate has radioactive toxins built into her bones and teeth that weren't there for Martha's generation. How long ago did she first hear that story about the women who were employed to paint luminous watch dials and licked their brushes to keep them pointed, to do a good job? Martha sorts the plates from the bowls and puts all the cutlery in one heap in the sink. Before they can eat, there are dishes to do. She turns on the tap. It's like an evil fairy tale, she thinks. We haven't cared enough: I think that's it. Even the mindless task of doing these dishes is losing its obscure comfort: she knows she can get them clean, but does not know what the detergent is doing when she lets it go down the drain. Things are not necessarily turning out right.

Kate finishes on the phone and comes to the kitchen. Martha hands her a towel.

For a few minutes, neither of them says anything. Then Kate starts to speak and stops. The guarded note is back, and something else: a vulnerability. She is polishing a glass more than she needs to.

"I was... I was making a list before you came home of things I have to do. Martha — Mom — I don't have time anymore for school. I don't want to go back."

In the dishpan, Martha's hands grow still.

The clock ticks sharply. Once. Again. All the arguments Martha has made before go through her head again but this time none seems enough. Suddenly she knows that she, Martha, is about to break a very important rule. She looks away and, neutrally, just putting the words out there into the space between them, she says:

"What exactly would you do — supposing you did drop out?"

Kate puts down her towel.

She pulls a paper out of her jeans pocket and reads her list: East Timor, Lebanon, Meares Island, Big Mountain, Black Rose prisoners' support, Alliance for Non-Violent Action, poetry, learn more about publishing, Against Cruise Testing (who have some money to hire somebody to organize and work at the desk....) In the mask of smeared makeup, her eyes look bigger than ever, full of dreams.

Martha sees her daughter standing there on the cold kitchen tiles in her bare feet. She thinks about toxins. She has rubbed and rubbed and rubbed and it has not come right.

SACRED TRUST

This journey began twenty-five years ago, when I stood in a church in Avebury, Wiltshire, surrounded by circles of stones. Avebury is near Stonehenge, but is a village, a place where people live. Like Stonehenge, it is surrounded by a prehistoric bank and ditch and, in the fields round about and on what we assume are ancient sight lines leading in, are standing stones, some weighing forty tons. Through a prodigious effort we can only partly imagine, these stones were cut and dressed elsewhere and dragged on frozen ground to this place, where they were erected in a circle a third of a mile across. In Saskatchewan and Alberta the circles and sightlines are made with cairns and rows of loose prairie stone: people call them medicine wheels. In Avebury I stood stock-still in a wheel within wheels. In early Christian times a little Saxon church was built, square and rough. Its floor then was covered with rushes. People stood or sat on that floor when they gathered to recognize mystery, and to worship it in whatever way they understood. One imagines their heads full of barbaric monsters and heroes, overlaid with the new hero, Christ. Later generations added a Norman slit window to the church; the Tudors, I think, added pews, the Victorians the carved pulpit and choir. These details and more are tersely outlined on an unpretentious typed sheet kept for visitors to read on a table just inside the door. The British are comfortable with their long past. I am not; daughter of the new world, accustomed as I am to clean air and a clean slate, an expectation of future with virtually no hold on the past — in Avebury, abruptly, mystery rooted me. I saw the long long lines of men and women pulled from their warm beds on a Sunday morning and brought one step after another to the door of this church and then into its shell, caring for it, changing the rushes, carving the wood, adding whole sections, attempting over and over again to give shape to what cannot be expressed, but which far back before anything was written drew other men and women to move stones, strain, grunt, sometimes burst in pulling them erect, to plant them deep in that circle in the fields.

The museum at Avebury has a pair of scissors, notable for being one of the earliest scissors extant in Great Britain. They were in the pocket of a barber who was crushed by one of the stones, at a time when local farming people, fearing the pagan powers of these giants on their land, used to dig a pit at the foot of one, fill the pit with fire, and then upset the stone, where it would crack in the heat and could be broken and dispersed as small, safe rocks along fence lines and in foundations of local barns. This barber was perhaps inspecting the pit, or even lending a hand to help dig, when the loosened menhir fell. It must have seemed an awful reaching-out of vengeance from dead gods, at the time.

Avebury changed me. I found I desired to seek out the sacred spaces of the earth. Slowly I created for myself the position I now hold, halfway between Anthropology and the Department of Religion, in a small university of long tradition and little repute, in a Maritime province of Canada. Mine has not been a brilliant career; neither has it gone unnoticed. I have done what I intended to do: to visit sacred spots, and report.

I have climbed the pyramids, which are the same age as some of the medicine wheels of the west. I have been lucky enough to enter the Ajanta caves in India and to walk and take measurements in Java, at the nine stupa of Barabudur. Last summer I tramped through Irish countryside to visit Cairn L and Cairn U, and the Mound of the Hostages at Tara. Yet also last summer, later on, I visited Israel, ignoring politics and following the Way of the Cross through Jerusalem's noisy streets. After that I stood in the place where Mohammed ascended into the heavens and received his vision of life after death.

In a word, I have collected these places. I bring back my coloured slides, my careful measurements and, in academic journals, my brief, dry accounts. Every few years, illustrated by the photographs, written for the general public, a book comes out. A coffee-table book, full of speculative theory untrammelled by proof, a Christmas gift for dabblers in the mysterious and the occult. The books hold my position for me at this university, and they prevent me from ever going anywhere else. I am that uncomfortable populist, that suspect theoretician, Harriet Dixon Ross.

Next week, in time for June 21, I am on my way to collect one more place, a medicine wheel I haven't yet seen, Moose Mountain, southeastern Saskatchewan. We will take measurements at solstice.

Suddenly I don't care.

One plus one plus one plus one has not equalled Avebury, and has not equalled Avebury Plus. I expected something else — what was it? To come closer, perhaps, to the mystery's heart. On the academic level, to find patterns — but patterns I have found: my books attest to that. My classes are well attended. Every day I turn down invitations on the lecture circuit. The patterns I sought, perhaps, were ones that would be so convincing, so compelling, would so speak to the archetypal templates of the human psyche that people would know it was true, and as a consequence live more happily, or at least more certainly, from that time on.

Did I want to be a preacher, then, for heaven's sake — a TV evangelist — was this my secret plan? To say to the world: behold the moon, behold the three stars, Aldebaran, Rigel, Sirius, behold the carven spirals on the entrance stone at Newgrange, Ireland — and to have my listeners fall at my feet? Not my feet, actually, but the feet of Truth. I think I wanted to help make Truth irresistible.

If so, I was wrong.

Even to myself, truth is entirely too resistible. The more of these places I see, the more alternative explanations I invent. Definitely we have proved and we are proving again that early peoples were much more sophisticated astronomically than used to be believed. And certainly if we in the present times connect wind-swept hilltops and sunlit caves with the presence of the ineffable, no doubt so did they.

I — I, though, am going missing. I have lost my focus, or never had one. I do not know why I am taking this trip to collect one more once-sacred place.

And I hate the idea, I find to my chagrin, that I have set myself up for ridicule. At my age it should make no difference. But age is part of the problem. I am over fifty. Some people I respect begin to pity my life: "Poor old Harriet. She could have done so much more. But she went off half-cocked on the semi-occult. Never even focused on, say, one developmental period. If she'd stuck to the Stone Age, perhaps, but she didn't; what a mish-mash she has made of it. Not anthropology. Not history of religion. She must have had something in mind when she started, but it looks as if she never thought it all out. She has a good mind, but unfortunately she has let it go. She can still pull out sensational connections for the untrained minds of undergraduates, but academically let's face it: her work is just plain fuzzy."

I wince: I hear Bernard's voice, saying those words. Bernard is the head of anthropology in this university. If I want a more exciting post somewhere else, he is the person who must recommend me. Instead he is hinting early retirement, the golden handshake. He would like to divert my salary to two or three of the sweet young things crowding the carrels in Graduate Studies.

"And she surrounds herself with bright young men."

The young men come without my invitation. I am glad to have their work but I do not set out to draw them in. One of them, Jonathan Wollner, will come with me on this trip. He is my choice for the usual reasons: I need help, there's money left from my grant for the Holy Land, he's keen. I can see he adores me as well, but not to the loss of his good sense. He has invited his wife to accompany us, at their own expense. I am vaguely aware that part of his reasoning is to share this wonderful treasure, me, with her. This neither warms me nor offends me. It is an error which belongs to the young. With it goes enthusiasm, which I do like, and which does warm me, particularly at this time in my life. Jonathan will get over his idolization of me, and meanwhile, partly because he wants to please me, he is turning in good work.

The one person I have made a point of recruiting for this trip is Eileen Simmons, a first-year graduate student who joined us last fall. She was in one of my classes as an undergraduate, and it is obvious that she is still deeply unhappy since the collapse of her marriage last year. She still turns in her work, as prompt and thoughtful as ever, but several times when I have come upon her unexpectedly, her eyes have been filled with tears. She spends no time with the other students, does most of her work at home on her own. I like Eileen. I think this trip might do her good. So I have insisted I need her to take my notes. I would be glad to be there when the sparkle comes back into her eyes and her body begins to move again as it used to, in confidence and an openness to her sexual power. I remember Eileen as a delight when I first knew her, and scarcely recognize what she has become, this dull-eyed, dull-haired mouse.

So.

Those are the outlines of this part of the strange journey my life has become. We fly to Regina next Tuesday: right-hand man Jonathan, his wife Kathryn (an unknown entity so far to me), recorder Eileen and me. We will rent a van to take us all to the town of Kisbey. I have a letter of reassurance and introduction from Bernard in case it is needed in obtaining permission from the native people in the area for us to visit the wheel. But there should be no problem: our intentions are benign. We will take photographs, measure distances, camp nearby and be on hand for several days at the rising and setting of the moon and the rising and setting of the sun. We will line up cairns and see if it is true that these hunters and gatherers who did not need to plant took the trouble to determine the beginning of summer, this longest day of the year. There are many circles of stones on the prairies; some are also burial mounds, although why and the exact connections with their astronomical uses need much more work.

We will make notes. It will fall to Eileen to collate.

I guess what I want to ask is: so what? Why do this? Another set of measurements; another set of slides. Another breathless expectancy (nothing, it seems, can spoil this) while we wait in darkness for the first rays of moon or of sun. And then we will go home. Jonathan will have a story to tell. I will change my lectures to include whatever it is we have found — becoming predictable now, although such a short time ago it was all wildly new. There will be some unexpected finding, some puzzle or pattern that has so far proven elusive and now begins to promise results. I am still interested.

But for myself, although literally we will be on the move, increasingly I have the sense of standing still.

Kate, are you awake?

Kathryn stirs against his shoulder.

Definitely — no way I'd be asleep on a plane. I was practising deep breathing.

You were very convincing.

Kathryn's lips twitch in a sardonic smile. She leans past him, blond hair parting at the nape of her neck and falling smoothly across her cheeks. Jonathan catches his breath, runs a finger up the back of her neck. Kathryn turns slowly to give him an arch glance.

Yes? What? There is something to see?

Oh. Yes. There. I wish you had taken the window seat.

Love, the view from the window means much more to you. It would have been wasted on me. I've been quite happy here, lost in my P.D. James novel and in controlling my inner fears.

He covers her hand with his as he points to the grid pattern below.

Thought you'd like to know about Chief Piapot.

She slides her hand free, swings her hair back from her face.

Pee-a-pot?

Well, I don't know how it's pronounced.

I thought they pee-aed behind bushes?

They may have done, but Piapot also pitched his teepee in the way of the CPR tracks, trying to stop the train.

Right down there?

Further along, actually. It says here it was Saskatchewan's first sit-in. Hey — 1882 — Kate, that's not very long ago at all. My Grandpop was born in 1896.

My sense of time gets all confused out here, doesn't yours? We go through a time warp coming out here from the east coast. Think what they went through, though, your lovely grandparents, coming to no history, from all that noise in downtown London.

No history except the native peoples who had been here all along!

Right. So these native people we're supposed to meet to get permission to explore the medicine wheel — their grandparents, maybe even their parents, were living the original nomadic life, weren't they? Are you sure they aren't going to mind if we look at their wheel? I'd be touchy if it were me. Why should they believe we won't take away arrowheads and stuff?

Maybe we will.

Jonathan — you wouldn't, would you? They'll be letting us in on trust.

We certainly won't take apart the cairns — it's sad the way even some of the wheels that have been discovered just in the past fifteen years have already disappeared. People don't realize what it is they've got on their land. They just see that it's in the way of the tractor. But as for picking up the odd arrowhead or darthead — we'll see. That hill is probably rich: there's a point where one more doesn't tell us anything new. We may be able to bring home a souvenir.

Kathryn shrinks into her seat.

I think it's a matter of trust.

Hey, Kate, I'm the guy who went with Martin to the sweat lodge....

I know: you were purified. Then why set out to steal from the Indians — you're going to tell me about their different ideas about property. The earth is the Lord's, I mean Manitou's — we only borrow it.

Yeah — something like that. We don't realize how much our heads have been affected by our training in a materialist, capitalist society.

And some of your best friends are Indians.

Kate, that's shitty.

She glances about her, meets the eyes of Eileen across the aisle. Eileen smiles politely, drops her gaze.

Kathryn leans back against the seat, practising deep breathing again. A quarrel 35,000 feet up. Just what she needs to take her mind off her fears. She thinks, as she breathes, how to approach this with Jonathan, what it is she really meant to say. Then remembers that the breathing won't work when she's still stewing over whatever has upset her. For a few minutes she tries to empty her mind of all the pros and cons. In. Out. In. Out. At the corner of her eye she sees clouds piled like solid mashed potatoes in the blue air. Jonathan follows her glance and for a few minutes the two of them are like children, entranced by the clouds as the 747 hurtles through the sky.

EILEEN'S NOTES: Harriet is asleep, I think. She seems to be looking out the window but her eyes fluttered awhile, then closed, and her head is drooping. I'll risk taking a few notes here, writing small and disguising it inside my copy of *In Flight*, the airplane magazine. Decided at home to make two sets of notes, inner and outer. Harriet talks as if these are the same: "To the Amerindians all was sacred and nothing was sacred." But not to us, that's the thing. We make these distinctions; Harriet calls it "fragmentation." Some people would call it other names: "progress," "civilization."

The official notes I am to take for this trip are not, as far as I have been informed, to include either poems or prayers. And maybe this journal won't either. But I can try to record what is happening to me, and I can guess at what is happening to the others.

The lines on Harriet's face now: the light from the sky outside etches the fan of soft lines starting at the corner of her eye, and the corners of her mouth turn down when she is asleep, in bitterness or sadness that is impossible to see when she is awake and sparkling as she does, full of a kind of electricity, making connections, jumping to conclusions, ready or not, and pulling everyone who comes across her path, even the office personnel, into her excitement. At such times she seems as young as her students, but right now you can see that time has passed.

She looks, of course, much like a child, curled away from me in an airplane seat which for most of us is cramped but for her leaves lots of room. It is always the first thing you notice about Harriet, her tininess. Later it becomes the last thing: you remember instead her vivacity, that excitement. I remember the day she heard she had the grant to go to India; the whole department got caught up in her plans. You forget that her feet don't touch the floor when she sits in a normal chair. You see instead a giant with flashing eyes who can and will scour the world for what she wants to find: India, Antarctica, Lebanon, Israel, Ireland, Colorado, Montana, the Caspian Sea!

I don't know why I agreed to come. Something about Harriet moves me, maybe her size, as if she needs taking care of, although obviously she does not. More likely I want to get a little closer to whatever it is that drives her on. If she is finding something, then I want it too. This is not a good moment in my life. (Self-pity wells up so easily, even when I write that one line. Steady on, here.) What I mean to say is: This trip right now in this plane is a lot like the rest of my life. That is, I'm moving very fast, pretty high up, and I don't know where the fuck I'm going. (And it may turn out to be someplace very small.) The ground has disappeared from under my feet: I'm winging it. Well, to continue the metaphor (this is cheering me up!), both the airplane and I are made of strong stuff and probably won't crash. We both have a definite destination or two before us, the city of Regina for the plane, back to my thesis for me. It's the larger journey that has become problematical.

"Eileen," said my mother, intending comfort, "look at it this way. At least you got out of a bad marriage before it was complicated by kids."

Wrong, mother. Wrong and wrong. It was not a bad marriage but it was very complicated, and the complicating — and terminating — factor was kids.

Why do I still say, even here, where I am trying to write the truth, that it was not a bad marriage? For me it was bad, bad times. I have been jerked around, I have been treated by my beloved as if I were a piece of slime which he had to pick off his person. When all my sin was that I loved him and wanted to bear our child. I am the normal one, not him, with his visions of saving the world. It is incredible to me that for so long I believed it was my fault, that somehow I had harmed him, had tempted him from his noble path. Early and late I loved Daniel because he was a guy who gave a damn, about the world, about everything he saw. He fought all the way to keep from becoming one more person who could switch it all off. I remember the excitement with which he came to me with what he felt was the key: helping people to empower themselves. I watched him learn patience as if overnight, my impatient man, to listen and to be still; I thought we would raise our children to learn these things and in some way we would make up for the baby we had given away.

Then I found out that I myself had not been treated with respect. My idea of empowerment is not his. I thought you give the other person your power, and then they don't use it, that is what it is all about: in the light of that free decision we grow together into trust. Anybody, I thought, understands that. But Daniel operates on some other system. I found out he'd made it permanent: he's found the work he has to do and he and I will never have another child.

I am still wracked as I remember this, as I let it into my gut.

Why, then, do I still think of him?

Those two across the aisle are having a fight. I saw it just now in her — Kathryn's — eyes. What do they have to fight about — they look so beautiful together. And I like Jonathan. It's easy to see he's one of the satellites around Harriet, but he's not the only one to go through that. He has a similar kind of electricity to Harriet anyway. I know the other female students pay attention when Jonathan walks through — and he's a nice guy, he bothers to get to know us, treats us right — which is more than you can say for some of the others finishing their PhD's: on the make, pompous nerds, expecting to be kowtowed to as if they're full professors when they're still sweating over their footnotes same as us.

So there are tensions in that marriage. What else is new.

At the beginning of this trip, then, I set down these inner notes: something tense between Jonathan and his wife, something sad or bitter about Harriet, something hollow about me.

HARRIET: We begin the descent to Regina. I wake with a start. My ears hurt. A baby has begun to wail. I was having an anxiety dream about the rented van: in the dream it became a red bus. The rental people assured me that there are bound to be vans available for a midweek trip and that the best thing to do is to wait until we arrive, but now that seems like madness. We really do need a van; I ought to have made certain we had one. In my bag is a list of what we need to buy before we start out, which will have to be tomorrow by the time we pull everything together. Already it's past noon, even allowing for the hours we have gained.

With guilt I remember Alana Podessky, my colleague in the Anthropology Department in Regina. I probably ought to have told her we were coming. But we parted last time on such bad terms: I just want to quickly pass through! I see Eileen stowing away her notebook; I wonder what she decided to write down so early in the trip. Across the aisle, Jonathan's wife is looking white-lipped as we descend. Jonathan is holding her hand. He catches my eye and grins, welcoming me back awake. Hello, Jonathan. Pay attention to your wife. But he is now, I see, being quite solicitous. I don't know about that young woman yet. Jon shows her off as if she were this precious, fragile creature, and she seems to play up to that, but my sense is there's more to her. She teaches grade seven and eight: that's not a quiet, easy job: that's the horrible in-between age when the hormones come in. I must ask her about her class.

The plane is making a turn coming down to the runway now; I catch a glimpse past the wing and my neighbour's head of a grid of residential streets, and then the rush of terminal outbuildings and now, here we are on the ground. I would have liked to have caught the pattern of the runways from the air. I am interested in the patterns modern men — they *are* mostly men — find useful; it's sometimes illuminating to compare them with ancient ideas of intersections and highways. But on this trip I never did get an overview — and I need one, I definitely do!

We're taxiing straight over to the terminal. Good. I guess I could ask Jon to pick up our gear while I go see about this blessed van.

Eileen turns to me, smiling. "Welcome back, Harriet."

"I've been back a while. What were you writing — letters?"

It would have been very easy for her to agree. Instead she hesitates and says — "No, I was taking notes."

"Well, that's what you're here for! Keep it up! But what is there to take down so soon? The make of the plane? The map of our flight?"

And then she tells me, this brown-eyed young woman I am choosing to fuss over a bit; tells me what she has decided to do — the inner journey and the outer one. "I know what you will say," says Eileen.

"You do? What will I say?"

"About the sacred and the profane being a modern error; that everything is sacred and one set of notes will suffice."

"I think — it will be an interesting thing for us to talk about while we're waiting for the dawn on that hill."

As we scrabble for bags and jackets and find our way into the aisle, I am caught in a surge of happiness. Because *that* surprised me; *that* I did not expect.

Jonathan's wife looks pink-cheeked again, now she has both feet on terra firma. She walks beside me as we go up the long ramp. She confesses this was her first flight. I am astonished, then remember that both she and Jonathan grew up in the same town as our university, and do not need to have travelled very far. I am still feeling lifted on a moment of hope and unpredictability when I see Alana Podessky waving vigorously to us from across the mezzanine. We are being met.

There are times when there is no one else I know who can make the speeches this woman Alana makes, arrange the grant money, beat the bushes for the right grad students, find a place on a program for a bizarre idea whose time has almost come. At other times, and most recently, she has been a pain in the ass. In fairness, I expect it must be hard to maintain that rather wonderful Rumanian flair here in the midst of the Canadian prairies, but Alana tries. I see now she has also put on a few pounds. At fifty or so, the fiery Alana is taking on the unmistakable élan of a hefty Jewish mama. Her grey hair stands out in little curls all over her head. Before I know it, I am enveloped in a bosomy hug.

"Welcome to Regina, Harriet!"

We step back from each other, both aware, I think, this was not quite an academic hello. But I've never come to Regina before, and I suppose she is pleased. Or else she is pleased with herself that she caught me out.

"Yesterday I phoned Bernard about something else and he told me you were coming and which flight you were all on. So Lance and I decided to come down and meet you."

I become aware of a young boy, maybe thirteen years, who has been hanging back. Dark-skinned, sloe-eyed. Alana introduces us. Lance Starblanket.

"He and I have a favour to ask. But what are you people going to do first? You're not leaving for Moose Mountain today? Let's find your luggage."

Chattering, laughing, Alana takes us in tow. I decide that, after all, it is much nicer to be met than not to be met. I arrange as I had planned for the others to pluck our gear off the carousel. Kathryn seems to have taken a shine to Lance, and he stays with them as they wait for the luggage. Alana and I go off to the vehicle-rental booths. She could and would pull a few strings for me if necessary and I begin to relax. In fact there is no problem: they will deliver a van to the airport from downtown within half an hour. Just time for us all to get a cup of coffee, if the luggage has arrived, and find out what it is Alana wants. I'm a little nervous about that. But I seem to be trusting her. Probably it will be all right.

EILEEN'S NOTES: The first night. Alone in a motel room on the edge of Regina. Jonathan and Kathryn are somewhere else in this same place. Harriet accepted the invitation of a colleague to stay in her spare room. This colleague has a protégé, a boy named Lance Starblanket, who is to accompany us and be of some help to us, in return for a visit to see his folks. He is a Plains Cree whose family lives near the Moose Mountain medicine wheel. But those are exterior notes. What I want to say here is the inner journey, as much as I can. I told Harriet today on the plane what I am doing and she seemed pleased where I expected her to be annoyed. Now I feel inhibited, worried she is going to demand to see these scribblings, afraid that will keep me from writing what seems to be truth. I have to decide just to go ahead, edit them or something later on.

As I go back over this day of travel by air and then by van and of busy buying and arranging for tomorrow, four moments rise to the surface: I feel as if they were all moments of meeting in some sense or another.

The first was Harriet's response to my admitting to her about these notes. She looked into my face for a moment and seemed to really see me. How seldom people do that ordinarily — and how little of it there has been lately in my life.

The second was that unexpected meeting with Dr. Podessky. I think Harriet was caught off-guard by that hug. Maybe it wouldn't have happened at all if she weren't so small, so easy for even a short woman like Dr. Podessky to reach!

The third was the very special way both Jonathan and Kathryn took to young Lance. The boy was shy initially but in no time at all he was happily telling them about the band he plays in in Regina. He's interested in music and it seems that's why he's come to the city to finish grade eight and why Dr. Podessky has taken him under her wing, although he lives with an uncle. He has been learning native drumming from the uncle — the uncle has been "sharing" it, he says — but also is going through the usual teenage phase of forming a band. They call theirs Better Red Than Dead, and according to Dr. Podessky it takes a lot of nerve to make a point about being a native here in Regina. I liked the way Jonathan talked to him, mainly about music (it turns out that Jonathan knows a lot about modern music — something I didn't know.) But it was Kathryn who got him talking about his loneliness away from his family — it seems he's the eldest, at thirteen, of seven or eight kids — she had him admitting that Dr. Podessky seems "old," and that around her he minds his p's and q's. You could see, though, that the fact that she lets him practise his drums in her basement was pretty special.

I don't know what to say about that conversation between Kathryn and young Lance. There was love in it, I want to say. But they had just met.

This is what I see: when you are travelling, you are in a heightened state of mind. You leave behind the familiar and you act out an exploration into the unknown. So this makes for different possibilities — emotionally one feels somewhat skinned without the usual excuses and support systems. That must be why strangers in the seat beside you so often relate the story of their life.

Harriet informed us this evening, as she drove us over here in the van, that young Lance's father is in jail, I don't know what for or for how long. This makes more poignant a moment this afternoon when Jonathan and Lance and I were in a stationery store buying notepads and extra pens and coloured pencils. (The others were a block away, stocking up on groceries.) Lance is a small, serious-looking kid. He was supposed to be helping us carry things, but wasn't in fact much help. He kept wandering off, eyeing pencils, erasers, loose-leaf binders and things, and I remembered how much I enjoyed stationery stores when I was a kid — still do. After awhile we found out what it was he coveted. He wanted the long boxes some of the coloured pencils came in.

"Do you think you could buy these, and could I have the boxes?"

"It costs more. What do you want the boxes for?"

"I can make neat whistles out of them to give tomorrow to the kids at home."

I saw Jonathan capitulate instantly. "Sure, son," he said.

"I'm not your son, actually," said Lance; I wasn't certain whether he was explaining or protesting. Up till then he'd been extremely polite.

Jonathan could have said the wrong thing, I expect, right then, but he was very relaxed in his reply.

"Hey, I wasn't taking you over, Lance, don't worry: it's just an expression where I come from. I hope I do have a son some day, though. A person can always use another drummer, not to mention someone to fetch and carry. Here." He grinned and thrust the paper bag of supplies into Lance's arms.

I was smiling. "I could use that kind of son, too," I said.

Suddenly Lance dropped his superpolite stance and became a normal inquisitive nuisance kid.

"Don't you have any boys?" he asked me.

"No," I said, "or girls either."

"You don't have a husband?"

"Not at the moment."

He thought a moment.

"You did have?"

"Yes."

"Where is he now?"

I was becoming embarrassed: we were in a crowded store and people could overhear. I glanced at Jonathan and caught him looking amused. I think he was interested in my answers and didn't want to stop the kid if I could handle it.

I said that my ex-husband lived in the same city that I do but that I don't see him anymore.

"Why don't you?"

I'd had enough and decided to be evasive and then if necessary tell him to lay off. "He's busy," I said.

"What does he do?"

I hesitated. He helps out people like you, was the irresponsible answer that came to mind. But before I said anything, Jon spoke:

"He thinks of Eileen."

Lance glanced at me as if to see if this were right, but Jonathan thrust an arm across his shoulders and steered him away. "You guys out here ever heard of a group called the Dead Candies?"

Lance had. Clearly Jonathan was "in." Before we left the store, we checked further into Lance's plans for gifts for next day, and then brought him back over to the crayons and colouring books and coloured notepads. We decided Harriet's grant can extend to a few gifts for the current residents and possible descendants of the land once inhabited by the people who built the wheel. It began to seem more real to us that we were going to meet Lance's mother and his brothers and sisters. It seems there are six younger Starblankets, which is almost impossible. As Lance tells it, his family implements the band's decisions about visitors to the wheel. For awhile the band had lost control of it, but recently, with land claims, it is back where it belongs. Alana's idea in adding this boy to our trip is becoming easier to understand.

Now I could write some emotion if I dare touch a bit more of the truth. Son. It scares me to use the word, even inside my head, in case somehow I pull you off centre, distort your straight growing wherever you are. Or let out my hurt. I allow myself this for you: the cool light of my love like a great white balloon, no strings attached. Son — I must box this back in. I can see Daniel's seventeen-year-old face, white, tense, sitting across the table from me as I filled in the form and we both signed our names. It isn't as if he forced me: we both thought at the time it was the right thing to do.

Not for Harriet, this, but interesting for me: after so many years it is all still so strong. And brought back so fast by the questions of one young boy.

"Not all of the prairies is this flat."

"So say you. I bet we can see for thirty miles."

"I love all that texture in the fields, and all those different shades of brown and green."

"Did you see the prairie sunrise?"

"I was up, but my eyes weren't open."

"It's a good thing Harriet is driving, that's all I can say."

They laughed.

"We won't be there for a while yet," announced Harriet, "but sometime this afternoon we'll be into the Moose Mountains."

"They're not really mountains?"

"No. Just a low ridge. But they call it the Moose Mountain range. What we do is we go to the town of Kisbey and ask directions."

"No, you don't have to," said Lance. "Ask me. I'll get you there."

Harriet glanced into the rearview mirror and caught the boy's excitement as he bounced in his seat a little, gazing at the road ahead.

"How long have you been away?"

"I was home for Christmas."

"That's quite a long while. You'll notice some changes."

"I expect so," replied Lance politely, and Harriet smiled to herself. There was a pause, and then he offered suddenly: "You'll know we're getting close when you really do start to see some hills."

"Okay, Lance, but we're not used to the west: you might have to tell us when what we're looking at really is a hill."

Miles rolled by. Eileen had bought a guidebook when they stopped for lunch in Regina, and was regaling them with facts. Kathryn and Lance had their heads together over the road map.

"These towns were all named after railway men!" reported Eileen. "Sedley, Osage, Creelman — oh here — Kisbey was named after a mailman. What a relief!"

"Where are the Indian names?" murmured Kathryn.

"Kenosee?" offered Harriet. "I saw a sign for Lake Kenosee. Is that Cree, Lance?"

The boy sounded doubtful: "It sounds a bit like 'waiting' but a bit like 'fish' — not really like anything at all."

Jonathan hooted. "Is there a tourist bureau in Lake Kenosee? Seems like they could do something with 'wait and fish!'"

"It's one or the other," said Lance, again seeming to explain carefully. "So they couldn't use both. Maybe it's neither one."

The flat prairie near Regina had given way to rolling hills. Lance pointed out small oil rigs nodding in fields near the road. He was enjoying the navigating. As they came closer to his home, he stopped looking at the map and directed Harriet onto a grid road which Kathryn stopped trying to find on the map. Harriet found she trusted the boy's directions, and she liked the feeling of rocking across the prairie as if they knew where they were going. She was glad she had insisted on driving. Even the cushion she was sitting on, which brought her high enough to see out comfortably, she had thought of in advance and brought along in her bag. All the items on her list had been duly checked off: pup tents, sleeping bags, transits, tripods, tape, cameras, Coleman stove, gas, food, plates, cups, cutlery.... At this moment the journey had its own momentum. She was content with road maps, placenames, and the constellation of young people gathered in the van. Suddenly she noticed a bump on a nearby hill that did not appear to be bushes or low trees. Lance said nothing, however, but in a few minutes directed her onto a gravel road, buffalo grass growing in at the sides. Harriet drew to a stop.

"What's this?"

"It's the road to my house."

"No, Lance — I mean the thing on the road."

"Oh, that's a Texas gate. It's safe to drive over."

On either side of the road the land was fenced. The boy explained quickly to these easterners that the bars laid in across the road over a dug ditch let traffic through but kept cattle in.

"We had them when I grew up, too, in P.E.I.," announced Eileen, unexpectedly. "The cows won't go across because they're scared. But it's safe to drive over, or it should be."

"It's safe, Lance?" asked Harriet as she started the car moving again.

"Sure it's safe."

"I could get you a drum, Lance, maybe," they heard Jonathan say suddenly. In the mirror, Harriet saw Kathryn look at her husband with a frown. She looks like she did on the plane, Harriet thought.

"I have a drum, thanks. Dr. Podessky helped me get a set of

drums. You saw them, Jon."

"I guess I meant a native drum. Don't you need something special for that stuff?"

"I'd have to ask my uncle. Usually one of our people makes the drum."

"Yeah, I suppose so. It was just an idea." He paused. "I took part last summer in a sweat lodge ceremony — " he began.

Kathryn cut in awkwardly. "Does your mother know you're coming, Lance?"

———

Kathryn is holding onto the edge of the back seat of the van with her hands. Dust blows in at the windows; everyone else exclaims and rolls them up. Kathryn is in the middle, balancing: there is no seat belt for her space. She has been trying not to meet Harriet's eyes in the rearview mirror, and to cope with feelings of frustration and anger that are running out of control. What is the matter with me, she wonders, unhappily. I just want out. Beside her, Jonathan is growing more and more excited, pointing at things outside and peppering Lance with inane questions — at least, Kathryn thinks, to me they seem inane; nobody else seems worried. She realizes she might be overreacting and does a swift calculation: yes, her period is nearly due; yes, she does have tampons in her luggage. Okay, the world is not so black as it seems but, dammit, premenstrual insights are true, too, and important to hang onto when the flow of Pollyanna cheerful hormones clicks in three days from now, and masks what she is seeing clearly right now.

What she sees is a group of self-indulgent middle-class whites, herself included, blithely driving themselves (as they have money and transportation and the ability to do this) to a place that this child beside her, with all his emotional and practical ties to the place, has not been able to get to in six months. She resents the academic confidence Harriet displays, as if she knows what they are going to do. She feels increasingly uncomfortable and put out with her young husband, who seems to her in his exuberance and boyish bumptiousness to be putting on a kind of show, for Lance, for Harriet, certainly for herself and maybe even for Eileen, and to be missing, maybe, the whole point. Which is? she asks herself, and feels irritation again. How should I know? Just that we are going for a visit, it can't be understood and planned for in advance because this isn't our place: it is the boy's place, and the place of the people who placed those fieldstones in peculiar formations on one of these hills. But she, Kathryn, would rather be in her classroom. She shouldn't have come. It was Jonathan's idea, this trip — he had been so sure she would love these people he works with, she had seen that it meant a lot to him and, because of some work she'd done last summer, she did have the possibility of a week off. So she had yielded to his excitement, and now she thinks it was a mistake. In her mind's eye she sees the face of her favourite and most difficult student, bent, flushed, over the basic algebra that keeps defeating him, trying to make sense of it under the hostile gaze of the supply teacher. It's the end of school; they're mostly into field trips, but last time his response to a supply landed him with the vice principal in charge of discipline. And that young girl, new to the class so late in term, still making her way through the inevitable testing kids do to each other, having to face it this week without the support of her teacher. There was final marking not quite done, promotion meetings next week, report cards looming — Jonathan couldn't understand why she wasn't happy just to leave it all behind.

Lance is explaining about the "Texas gate." What Kathryn hears is a metaphor for her own life: you can't see the fences but you feel that they're there. Am I afraid to step outside, she wonders, for fear it might hurt? Look at Eileen: I see the hurt on her face, in the way she hunches her shoulders, the way she walks and talks and holds her notes close to her body. Jonathan, when I am in a better mood, still stirs me. There are times when I love to be with him. What am I missing, then, what is it seems so dead wrong, like a missed turning, about my whole life and this particular trip?

Lance, who has been holding the road map in front of him, folds it and puts it between them.

"There's my place," he says. Harriet stops the van.

Kathryn sees a house that reminds her of the pavilion at Long Lake where she used to go as a teenager to dance on a summer night. In summer all the windows were open to the weather and the lake, and she and her boyfriends danced on the board floor to music from a jukebox left over from the fifties. In winter the glass windows were on and the doors locked, the store closed down, and the building looked a lot like this, like Lance's home.

The boy leaps out and runs to the door. In another moment, children emerge from everywhere, some from where they have been playing under a stoop beside the concrete steps. His mother appears.

At least, she must be Lance's mother. She doesn't look any older than me, thinks Kathryn. The woman is thin, long hair pulled back, but bright-eyed, full of smiles, laughing a lot with surprise and possibly embarrassment. Round-faced children stand shyly near her. An older girl whispers in Lance's ear. The woman smiles.

"Thanks a lot for bringing Lance out. I had a message he might be coming, but I wasn't sure. You folks from Regina?"

Lance breaks in. "No, no, Mum: they're from the east! They want to measure the medicine wheel and stay up there overnight! They've brought tents and food and survey stuff. Do you think it's going to be okay?"

The woman hesitates. "You couldn't build a campfire up there," she begins, and laughs a bit. "We found out we had to make that a rule when they first started bringing groups out here a few years ago. They was going to move stones around to make a fire. But you know about that, don't you? You won't move nothing?"

Harriet takes over, explaining, reassuring, bringing out Bernard's letter and spreading it out. The woman points back down the road they have come; Kathryn understands that they have already passed the medicine wheel, and will need to drive back a mile or so to park and then walk up. She notices again how Harriet's small stature helps her to seem more trustable. Behaviour that in a tall woman would seem dominating and controlling, in Harriet looks almost cute. I expect it's a nuisance in other cases, thinks Kathryn, striving to be fair. But finds she still feels upset: "I bet she knows how to use cuteness too."

Suddenly Kathryn knows she genuinely does not want to go on with this: she does not want to identify herself with these people going up to measure and quantify what is clearly to the native people a very special place. She looks at Lance's mother as she bends to scoop up a toddler who is pulling at her. She is not even certain that the woman can read the letter Harriet is waving in front of her. Kathryn can see that the woman wishes to be polite, but she is also aware of the tension in Lance, and that they have not been invited into the house.

"May I hold her?" She walks to the woman and holds out her arms. She realizes at once that likely the child won't come, but like a gift she does: the chubby brown arms let go of her mother and she settles against Kathryn. From a place she doesn't know she has, she suddenly finds words.

"Listen, I'm not really part of this expedition. I know I'd really be putting you out, Mrs. Starblanket, but I wonder if I could stay down here in return for some helping out? I've got my own sleeping bag — and lots of experience with kids!" She feels rather than sees Jonathan's start of dismay.

"She's a teacher!" says Lance, and Kathryn is afraid that might make it harder for the woman to agree. So she speaks again fast, not thinking it out.

"Are you staying here, Lance? You're not going up on the hill?" From the brightness that flares in his face she sees that she is right: he was waiting to be asked.

"You're staying for supper, Lance," says his mother firmly. "I'm not letting you go again that soon! He could go up later on if you want him to — but won't he be in the way?" She smiles at Kathryn. "Sure you can stay with me if you want to, and you don't need to help out none neither. I'll be glad for somebody to talk to."

Kathryn doesn't dare turn her head for fear the look on Jonathan's face will make her change her mind. She knows he will be bitterly disappointed.

But inside herself, a little bird begins to sing. This is what I wanted to do, it says. With it comes a spurt of hope: maybe after all Jon understands — he did do that sweat lodge thing and .... But as the groups quickly separate, the anthropologists preparing to drive the van back to a spot near the hill, and she goes to him for a quick kiss good-bye, over the little girl's head, his face is bleak. He sets her bedroll and bag on the ground and gets back into the van.

"Good riddance," she says defiantly under her breath, as the vehicle disappears down the lane. With the child beginning to squirm in her arms, she whirls round and round, twirling among white and yellow flowers on the low windswept grass. Children run to her, crying, "My turn! My turn!"

In a moment they are all down in a laughing, tumbling heap, and the two dogs are barking as well.

This feels all right, thinks Kathryn, deliberately ignoring the view from behind the house, where two anthropologists and one notetaker may be seen in the distance, starting to move slowly toward one particular hill.

"We don't realize how high we've come because the slope was so gradual," remarked Eileen. "Look how far we can see!"

They stood catching their breath after the long climb, between two of the spokes of the great wheel.

"Of course, you don't have to be very high on the prairies to be able to see for miles," answered Harriet dryly.

Still, it was impressive. Jonathan gazed into the distance, smiled at Eileen's moment of excitement. Uncharacteristically he said nothing.

Drat that woman, thought Harriet. It was so obvious how much he has been looking forward to sharing this.

They set to work. For the first few hours they were busy. Then, basic measurements made and their tripods set up, the three of them sat together on the grass, drinking cups of hot soup and looking out over their bit of the world.

"I'm so glad I came!" exclaimed Eileen. "I thought these things would be like archaeological sites, which I think would be boring places unless you know where to look. I didn't expect this" — she waved her hand at the lines of fieldstones laid out in neat spokes from where they sat — "and definitely not this!" She gestured at the fieldstones piled high in the centre. "It must be twenty feet across! And almost as tall as me!"

"Depends on where you measure it from," said Jonathan appraisingly. "The ground has come up over it a bit."

"Why didn't you tell me it was this big?"

Jonathan laughed. "We didn't mean to keep it from you. I guess we thought you knew. They say this cairn weighs sixty-four tons."

"Wow! And was put here — "

"John Eddy from Colorado figured out this wheel worked as an astronomical instrument from 150 BC to 300 AD, isn't that right, Harriet? Some of the stars they used then are other places now, so it's hard to figure out. Maybe they used it earlier too. The Majorville wheel in Alberta seems to be at least a thousand years older than this one, and that's a lot of time to account for. It's possible people used them for different things at different times. That cairn over there seems to be lined up with where a star named Capella was at the time of Christ. They think the Majorville wheel is as old as the building of the pyramids. This baby is old, too, but probably not that old."

"It's so fragile," said Eileen. "So easy to destroy. Just stones, in the grass. But people have respected them, and left them in place, through all this time." She cupped her palm over one of the stones, and smiled. "It's warm."

For a while they sat in silence, the wind lifting their hair. Then Harriet got up. The student and the notetaker followed her instructions as they finished preparations for a long, wakeful night.

Moonrise came and went. Harriet was right: no amount of cynicism or academic frigidity could spoil that moment when the moon rose and they marked its place halfway between two of the spokes in a line with the central cairn.

They took it in turns to nap as they waited for dawn. By 4 AM all were again awake. Eileen spent time with Harriet at her outpost, taking notes using the penlight Harriet had provided, then walked across the wheel to where Jon crouched at his transit, sighting at stars.

HARRIET: I see patterns here, in this moment on top of the world. I see this wheel, the stones glimmering white under the moon, the cairn like a sleeping woman at the centre, a goddess lying close to the earth. There is a light in that house across the fields where Kathryn snagged and left us, its windows looking out round about, like a minor turret guarding the sacred place. Lance's mother said that local folk hold this hill in respect. You would think young people would drive up from the village on the other side, and use that access as a lovers' lane. In fact, I rather like the idea. The woman said they don't; she volunteered this information, looking guarded. It was obvious she didn't expect us to understand. People come here just as we did, to sit at the top and find out how far they can see. It seems to me that the taking of measurements, far from being a desecration, is almost a religious rite. It is exactly what the ancients intended for this place. And now in the middle of a June night under an enormous prairie sky I see very far: the stars wheel in the sky; we have measured tonight one cycle of the moon and at dawn we will see the rising of the solstitial sun. The ancients understood this hill to be rooted in the planet, and tonight I feel those roots tugging at me, holding me to this place.

Am I too discovering a cycle I didn't know about before, dark into light, light into dark? Alana wants me to return, return and stay. She has an opening for a full professor, tenure, graduate students, no golden handshake for some time to come. A chance to publish in a different way. What would it be like here in this flat part of the world, so newly inhabited by people like us, prehistoric artifacts still around to be discovered, arrowheads, spear points, atlatl weights, dinosaur bones? What would it be like to live in the tension of the square grid of Regina's new streets and the circling swirl that is the ambience of my friend Alana? The Bernards and Jonathans of our lives will still be there, but we could, I think, now work together here. Alana is sometimes like a force of nature, but I could navigate those storms. Why believe in this now when all these years of living have told me how impossible it is? Yet I did begin to believe the moment I saw her waiting for me. As if I had lived my life so far in order to see Alana Podessky standing there in the Regina terminal with her grey curls tousled, and that hug. But what an odd place this is on the face of the earth, to come home.

EILEEN'S NOTES: Harriet says she'll be fine by herself for a while, a nice way of saying she wants to be alone. I have moved away from her, physically and, I feel, psychologically. But I don't want to go back to Jonathan just yet. Something happened over there on my last visit, something I need to think about some more. Probably he does too. I have sat down halfway between them, between the woman who brought me to this place and the man who unexpectedly has moved and confused me on the night of all nights when I would like to be clear and to know my own mind.

Jonathan is responsible for the sighting between the large cairn, one small cairn and the brightest of the pre-dawn stars. He explained to me this afternoon that the stars have moved since this wheel was built, and at least one is now hidden in the light of the sun. However, he's had his transit lined up for hours, and has been using binoculars to look at other stars. I asked him if he could see anything through the transit in the pitch dark, and he said yes, the glimmer of starlight did make a shape. I bent my head to take a look, and as he reached to adjust the thing I found his hand instead in my hair and I was being kissed for the first time since I left Daniel. What I felt were two things: absolute trust — I hardly know him, but my body warmed (how fast it warmed) without the least problem about what was going on, about who he is or I am or where was Kathryn, his wife. That was the first thing. The second is a lot harder, and not new, but as solid to me right now as this stone is under my hand, and I do not know what to do. I knew this was the wrong man. I knew the right man is Daniel. I am crying as I write this, because I think it is stupid and wrong for me to go back. What could we build across this bitter abyss? I am still so angry, I still feel so profoundly puzzled and betrayed, so bruised in my sex. I don't think it's possible to let that much hurt just go.

    I stand beside this cairn, built so long ago by the hands of people I have difficulty picturing at all. It stands beside me like a companion. It really is on the highest point of land. Jonathan told me this afternoon about his experience in the Mohawk sweat lodge, and about vision quests: how a high point of land was used as a place to seek one's identity, in oneself and in relation to the tribe. We whites tend to look overhead for our metaphors of meaning, he said, but native people look more to the ground under their feet. Jonathan said some people believe now as well that there are lines of force under the earth, magnetic or other mysteries that influence the course of our events, and are much closer to us than the stars. I see the hills a little now; I couldn't before. Surely the sky is beginning to grow bright. We will soon be at dawn. The wind has risen, and makes me feel as if I am alone, no longer linked to the others in our common task. I try to imagine the people of so long ago, coming up here as we have come, carrying stones from the fields; later, carrying confidence and knowledge and power as they found they had succeeded in predicting the moment when summer begins.

    Something is moving out there: I seem to see what I've been imagining, dark shapes . . . .

Someone touched her hand. Eileen jumped hard.

    "Lance!"

    "Hey, Eileen, I didn't mean to scare you!"

    It was obvious from the mischief in his voice that he had, and was delighted with himself that with the wind in her ears she hadn't heard him creep to her side.

She sent him to talk with Harriet. "Don't scare her now! The sun is going to come up any minute and she has to pay attention!" Eileen made her way to where Jonathan stood tensely at his post. In spite of her better judgement, she laid her palms on his shoulders and began to massage his upper back.

"That feels good," he said. "Were you talking to someone? Did Lance come up the way he said he might?"

"Yes, and he nearly scared me out of my wits. I've sent him to watch the sunrise with Harriet. Jon, Kathryn is coming up the hill, with Lance's mother and all the children. They drove partway across the fields in their truck. They're bringing breakfast: a feast, Lance says. It's supposed to be a surprise. Kathryn learned last night how to make bannock, and they have Saskatoon berry jam."

"So Kate isn't going to miss the sunrise after all!" She heard the cheerful lilt in his voice, and for a moment felt alone. She dropped her hands from his shoulders and stepped away.

"Eileen, something happened last night."

She found herself smiling. "Something nice. And so is this, this is a nice moment, your wife coming back up that hill and bringing all those little Amerindians with her. She's awfully good with kids, Jon."

"Is she? Maybe you're right. I thought she hated kids. She doesn't want to start our family, keeps putting it off. But now I think of it, she's so damned involved with those students of hers that she doesn't — "

He stopped.

"Doesn't have time for you, is that what you were going to say?"

"Yes. But if she's so good with kids, why doesn't she want to have one of her own?"

Eileen kept her voice steady. There are zillions of possible reasons, she thought, and only one Daniel. Kathryn's reason was probably standing right here in front of her. Neutrally she drawled, "Yeah, think again, Jonathan." You big sap.

The sun arrived, a ball of fire seeming to zoom into the sky, blazing across the cairns into their eyes, right where it was supposed to be. Frenziedly Jonathan and Harriet took sightings, shot film, called out numbers to Eileen. As light blazed in the sky, the children rushed up the last part of the hill, shouting their delight. Behind them came the two women, Kathryn with a bulging knapsack, Lance's mother carrying a basket and a cloth bag. Jonathan stretched his tape one more time, to the edge of a shadow, called a last measurement to Eileen, and went to meet his wife. She was glowing with exertion and excitement. He was reminded of the way she had looked when he had danced with her first in the pavilion at Long Lake. Impulsively, he dug into his jeans pocket.

"Here, I had an idea I'd give you this when we got home," he grinned, "but I just figured out you were right. You wouldn't appreciate it." He brought out an exquisitely chiselled, small white arrowhead, and laid it in her hand.

"As a matter of fact, since you did give it to me here, I appreciate it very much." Kathryn smiled; the sun shone gold in her hair. "The kids say that in spring this whole mountain is purple with crocuses. They call them prairie tulips, they're so tall. It must be beautiful here, the whole hillside moving with purple flowers."

"We'll come back," Jonathan said with conviction. "We'll come back with our kid."

Kathryn looked at him. "That will give you a chance to bring back that other stolen stuff you have in your other pants pocket."

Jonathan looked sheepish, but made no move to take anything else out.

Kathryn glanced about her, then went over to the central cairn and carefully, in an almost ceremonial gesture, laid her gift at its base.

"Hurry up!" Eileen was calling. "Harriet says we can't start without you two. Sit down here, make up the circle. We're into ritual here; Harriet says we're on sacred land."

"Well, as much as anywhere," smiled Harriet, looking about at their faces and the long distances behind and before them, new this day as every day since before these hills were made, and bright under the morning sun.

STAR

Star is running. One moment he was asleep, the next he knew that something had moved on the other side of the wall. This is the fifth day Star has slept in the empty apartment in the big brick house. When he wakes now, he knows at once where he is: curled on a carpet on the floor of an empty living room, a few blocks from downtown Ottawa. Beside him glow the orange coils of an old electric heater he found in the front hall the first night. He has been warm, he has been comfortable. His long jacket serves as a blanket, his pillow is his jeans bunched under his head.

This morning, at the sound next door, Star rose at once to his feet, slid into his jeans, unplugged the heater, glided to the front window and quietly pulled aside the blind. Overhead the sky was still dark, but behind the houses a pale light was starting to show. Water rushed in the pipes in the next suite; he took the opportunity to wash his face and to flush the toilet while the sound was masked. Breathing softly, he laced up his running shoes, shrugged into the jacket, and hung his drum around his neck, stuffing sticks and rattles into pockets. There was a soft crackle as peas inside the rattles brushed past the paper muffles. The night before he had unlocked the back door, as an emergency exit. Very carefully he returned it to the lock. He placed the heater as he had found it, eased the Yale lock open, eased it closed again. Then Star was gone, running through dark city streets.

His drum bumps lightly against him, like a friend. It is not a true native drum, although he made it, but one all of wood, with intricate shapes designed and tested and cut with a jigsaw while he was still at school. He finished it in the autobody shop with bands of chrome. It's called a tongue-drum, and he likes the idea of wood speaking, and likes not to have to worry about a hide drumhead splitting in the cold. "Star" had been the name of a local band for which he had been drummer, singer and then, as an added attraction, had done a juggling act. "Star" is the name he has brought with him to this new life in the city. He foresees a future for his drum when summer comes: he will drum up a crowd to watch his juggling, and some magic tricks, too, that he knows, and intends to have ready by then.

Now, though, he's heading downtown. On his first day in the city, he drummed for his breakfast on the market, and it took until nearly noon. Then one of the market vendors told him about the Shepherds of Good Hope and he has eaten breakfast there every morning since. Each day he's learning his way around better. He knew all along he could survive, but now he's becoming confident that he can bring off his emerging plan: big money on the market in Ottawa in just a few months! He feels like writing to his mother to tell her this, but it's too soon. Anyway, among the things he hasn't yet acquired are paper or pen or stamps. Would she accept the charges, he wonders, if he phoned home? He wants it to be the other way around: he wants to send money to her. He has been here less than a week, but he's finding his feet. This could be his lucky day.

In spite of the cold. He left his one pair of gloves behind in a warm car, when he was hitchhiking down.

When he reaches the soup kitchen, he is glad to get back inside, doesn't mind the slow, shuffling camaraderie of the long line. As usual, people express interest in the drum. He taps a brief tattoo. Michael looks up from behind the counter and gives him the high sign. This is exactly how they met five days ago, Star drumming a tattoo and Michael, who was one of the servers that day, too, just having to take a closer look at that drum. Star collects his scrambled eggs and toast and looks around for Pedro and Luke. They're over by the windows and he joins them. Michael detaches himself from his job and comes over.

"Man, let me look again at that drum."

Star grins and hands it over.

Michael raps experimentally and expertly across the wooden drumhead. "You take this to Oka, man? You coulda cheered up the troops."

"I'm no warrior," says Star. "I'm a hunter. I hunted a warm place to sleep, and thanks to you I found it. We were all up a little early this morning. But from what I hear, it's got the hostel beat to hell."

Michael makes him explain about getting up early. "Jesus, it all comes back. You can hear everybody piss. I'm sorry now I gave you that key."

"Hey, no way. It's the fucking Ramada Inn compared to the street. I'm happy. I *want* your key."

"Well, it's my apartment. I may not have paid the rent, but there's that month I paid in advance, so it's still my key. You guys catch the Sandbird gig at San Antonio Rose?"

Michael and Pedro play on the market in the summer; they feel mingled admiration and contempt that Star hustles at thirty below. Luke listens silently, a small, wiry kid, hair almost as dark as Star's, but he is white. Italian, maybe. Star suspects that Luke is new to town too.

Breakfast over, Star stands and says, "I've got to get to work." No one laughs, and he appreciates that.

"I'm to unload a truck at ten," Luke says abruptly. "You want I should come by and pick you up? You want paid work?"

Star laughs happily and makes the arrangements. It's his lucky day all right.

Outside, he runs again, to warm himself and in a sense of excitement. The doorway he'd picked out yesterday as giving some protection from the wind is available. He sets down his drum, pulls the muffles out of the turtle-shell rattles, and looks around him. He needs something to put out for coins. The other days he'd used a milkshake container or styrofoam coffee cup he'd found on the street, but today the city cleaners must have gone through. Reluctantly, he pulls off his cap and sets it out. He feels around in his pockets, locates a dime and a penny left from the day before and tosses them into the cap to seed it. An icy gust blows around the corner, sprays his long hair out wildly, invades the collar of his jacket. Already his hands are raw and numb. Star squats in the shelter of the doorway and starts to drum. He remembers a song his grandfather taught him, a song about midwinter, the beginning of the return of light on the darkest day of the year. He picks up the rattles and they chatter while he drums, drums with the flat of one hand. He throws back his head: the old song echoes off plate-glass windows, a wail of grief arcing into defiant joy.

A woman in a fur coat passes, walking a dog.

You could give me tranquillizers. Corinne's own voice, going round and round in her head. Explanations, she doesn't know to whom. Like I had before. The nightmares might stop. You could say: Corinne, I think you're well again. We could all believe it. And then something like that could happen again.

There were only two small things I wanted to do that day. I wanted to go down to the market to get some salad stuff, and I wanted to walk the dog. So I thought I'd do both those things in one trip. Then I would go back home and strip more wallpaper. We're renovating. An endless job.

Down on the market, sitting in a doorway, there was a street musician — strange — too early in the morning, and the middle of January! I noticed him because he had a drum. I've never seen a drummer there before. Also he had hair down to his shoulders, which made me think of my son David. There he was, chanting some Indian song, more like a howl, but he wasn't threatening-looking. He looked very young, maybe sixteen or seventeen. He looked cold. Still maybe I wouldn't have noticed, but Mootma, the dog, started to pull back on his leash. When Mootma was a pup, Hal insisted that David train him as a guard dog, but by nature malamutes are friendly. I was never sure he'd really attack anyone, even if I gave him the command. Partly because of the dog, I saw this boy, and I did an out-of-the-way thing for me — went back after I was past and put some money into something he had out. He looked like David. He looked like David. I gave him some money; I bought vegetables and fruit; I went home.

The trouble is, when a boy disappears like David, even though there is something like that empty canoe, no one ever knows for certain he's dead. He's just gone. Even the police had the nerve to hint about that. Kids take off: they make a break from their parents; sometimes they even fake suicide or accidental death. What would I do, what would I do if after all this time he just walked in the door?

"Hi, Mom. Hi, Dad. It was just something I had to do."

Whistling. David would be whistling as he came down the walk: he always was. Half the time I think he didn't know it. The day he left, I stood at the window crying, indulging in letting-go tears, but our son was whistling as he set off down the street, carrying his great oversize duffle bag with his tent and his tree-planting gear. He expected to be back in three months — sooner if the blackflies got too bad. Instead he drowned. At least, they found the upside-down canoe.

So what if he did just walk in the door?

I was unprepared for the anger. It hit me like a storm. I was nearly two storeys up, where we're putting in the cathedral ceiling. I ripped at a strip of wallpaper and it came off the wall too fast in a great broad swath that threw me over to one side. The ladder started to slide. I was terrified, grabbing, slapping at the wall. The ladder caught. On a gouge where another time like this I'd sliced through all five layers. I got down, very slowly, sweating, lowering my foot to the next rung, then the next, trying not to jiggle anything but keep perfectly steady, not start the ladder sliding again. I made it all the way down. For a while I just stood there, staring at the wall.

For the rest of the day I worked more carefully. At five I stopped, took a shower in the carmine bathroom that cost us more than I care to remember but pleases me every time I step into it. I changed to clean sweater and slacks to look presentable for when Hal would arrive home.

Perhaps this really is grieving I'm doing. But why does it go on and on and on?

"You coming, man?" It is Luke, waiting for him across the street.

The two boys set out briskly to walk to their job, partway across town.

"You been here long?"

It turns out Star's hunch is right. Luke had come into Ottawa from Toronto only two weeks before.

"I had steady work as a dishwasher. Man, I shouldn't have left it but this big cookee, man, he was dangerous. There's always sharp knives in a kitchen, eh? and this one day he had a fight going with the cook's assistant and, shit, I was sure's certain somebody was going to leave there without his balls. I was scared, man. I quit."

Luke has quite a lot to say now that he is away from the rest. He's anxious to work and to earn money, but Star still doesn't quite understand why. Something about Luke's dad, some energy he is bringing from his having to leave home. He respects the fact that Luke doesn't want to talk about it, and doesn't push. He wants to tell his new friend about his own plan, but feels shy in his turn.

As they are passing the Y, Luke leads him around a corner. They warm themselves in the blast of hot air from a grate.

"Good place to know about on a cold night," comments Luke.

They find the truck. Both boys lapse happily into silence as they work.

By the end of the day, they have cash for their suppers and the promise of some snow-shovelling work for next day. Star forgets about the hostel meal and maybe a hostel bed and in an expansive mood invites Luke to come back after they buy something to eat and spend the night at his "squat."

"Gotta be quiet," Star warns.

They have to put in time, too, and neither one feels like spending their first day's cash on beer. They hang about in the warm mall downtown and then walk over to where Star has been sleeping. They circle the block until finally the lights go out on the owner's side. Once more around the block, and then Star digs out the key and they glide into the darkened apartment. Luke's a quiet guy in any case, but Star repeats the ground rules in a low voice as he sets his drum down with care and goes back to the hall to bring in the heater. They lay their cold hands on it until it's too hot to touch. Star thinks proudly of the folded ten dollar bill still in his jeans pocket, with small change. Gloves tomorrow, he thinks, and I won't have to hustle before we go over to see about shovelling snow. Might do it anyways, though; we can't sleep in.

They have closed the doors to other rooms, and the living room, with its carpet and with the heater going, becomes cosy and warm. Star creeps out to the kitchen door and takes it off the lock. Then, overwhelmed with fatigue, he peels off his jeans, folds them under his head, and huddles in under the jacket. Luke hits the ground with a little thud; they both laugh sleepily. It has been a long day. Star spirals down into sleep.

This at least I can do, Corinne says to herself, getting her husband a drink, setting the table, taking the casserole out of the oven. This stuff at least is under control. She sees that Hal is tired from his day. Only later, after he has gone up to bed, does she suddenly feel how weary she is herself. Mootma comes to her, whining, wanting his ears scratched.

On an impulse, she goes back down with the dog to the darkened living room. She perches on a stepstool she was using during the day, and sits there for what turns out to be a long time, one hand rubbing the dog's head. Moonlight washes in the window opposite the corner she sits in, and paints a long line of shadow behind a broom left leaning against the wall. The layers of wallpaper hang off in artistic tatters, as though someone were trying to say something about death and decay, or maybe just the passing of time. Other families have lived here, she thinks; other women have thought those layers of coloured wallpaper were each one, in its turn, just what she wanted. The dog sighs and stretches out on the floor at her feet.

Outside the window, two young fellows walk by. Corinne notices them a little because one is carrying something bulky under his arm. The next part seems unlikely, but she has the impression that they turn in at the apartment next door. But there's nobody there. She gets up and looks out. They have disappeared. She listens. Her heart beats. Mootma catches her tension, and sits up again, ears cocked. After a while she hears it: low laughter, a very faint thud.

> *Hal?*
> *Huh?*
> *Are you up?*
> *I'm asleep.*
> *There's somebody next door.*
> *Bring the dog.*

Star wakes in a flash of terror as the light floods on. A wolf-like dog stares at him from the hallway. He has no time to make connections with the dog he sang to this morning in the market. The dog looks mean, looks and sounds ready to attack, a low growl in its throat. Star moves slowly, staring at the animal, rising to his feet and then remembering his pants. He reaches for them and clumsily pulls them on. A large man moves into the room. Star sees that a woman is holding the dog on a leash. He looks around for Luke. His buddy is lying there on the floor with his jacket over his head. Maybe he's still asleep.

"Luke! Let's go, buddy!" A movement under the jacket lets him know his friend is awake.

"Oh no you don't," says the man, in a voice that makes the skin on the back of Star's neck prickle. "We've called the police. Stay right where you are." He is a big man, but something vague about the way he moves suggests that he, too, has just awakened from sleep.

Star scoops up his drum. The dog growls. The man speaks to the woman. Out of the corner of his eye, Star sees the woman bend forward, he thinks to calm the dog, then he realizes she is unsnapping the leash.

"Sic'em, Mootma," says the man, and a white fur missile launches at Star's face. His reaction is instinctive. He steps aside, crashes the drum sideways in the place, he knows, a dog is vulnerable. He hears a click, he hears a gut-wrenching sound of bone breaking and of wood cracking, a shadow beside him steps forward, fades back, and a flower of bright blood spreads quickly in white fur, slick, shiny, soaking out into the carpet around the body of the dog. That was Luke, that was a switchblade, that's what a man carries who is afraid of knives. A blast of cold air lets him know that Luke is gone. Star feels calm and clear as he backs toward the open kitchen door. As in a picture he sees the woman drop to the floor beside the dog. She says something. The man starts after him, but the thing his wife says makes him turn back: he kneels beside her, stopping her, taking her hands, which are red with the dog's blood.

Star stands at the door in the bitter cold. His precious drum is cracked. His jacket is in the living room, and his ten-dollar bill. I am not going to make it, he thinks. He feels oddly detached. He sees the man hold his wife's hands, then sees the sudden movement with which the man jumps to his feet and kicks the broken tongue-drum, hard. Wood splinters again as it slams into the hall.

"Goddammit! Those little pricks . . ." He jerks out the cord of the heater. "Stealing hydro . . . how long has this . . . by God, if I ever see that little shit anywhere around this neighbourhood again . . . ." Still Star stands outside the door, looking in. The woman is dark-haired like his mother. The woman has picked up his jacket from the floor. He sees her look now from it to himself. There is blood splashed on his sweatshirt, and he shivers in the cold. He stands straight. His long hair shadows his face.

"I'm sorry about the dog...."

Hal begins to move toward him.

Corinne steps between her husband and the boy. Wordlessly she thrusts the jacket at the intruder, gives him a shove to make him hurry, and bangs shut the door. For a second she stands there with her back against the outside door, then walks forward into the room, turning to her husband as if she hears something.

"Hal, is that the police?"

Confused, the man heads for the front door. His wife follows him, stepping around the white dog's body as if it weren't there. "Will we need to change the locks, Hal?" She sees now that he is going to answer: they will talk about locks. And about the new tenants, and how to clean the floor.

Outside, Star pulls on his jacket. He ought to get out of here, but the will to run has disappeared. He is out, he is alive. It is a bright night. Trees crack in the cold.

Luke's footprints show long strides, breaking through snow up to his knees, long steps, getting the hell away. Star feels he has done his duty, going back like that. At least now he isn't going to freeze. And he took nothing, nothing but a little power to run that heater. He has left behind much more: his broken drum, his cap, his chance at a warm night. For a moment he almost feels he can knock and go in again, ask politely could he please have his cap too? He grins. No, buddy, don't push your luck. He is not quite all the way back to where he started this morning. Quite probably he'll find Luke again tomorrow, at the hostel for breakfast. Or maybe he'll find him right now, where he is heading himself, over to that grate with the hot air. Star thrusts his hands deep into his pockets, rediscovering the ten-dollar bill, and Michael's now-useless key. He starts off, breaking way slowly behind Luke's long leaps. They could use some snow shovelling back here. That reminds him of his job for next day. I'll get me a stash, Star thinks, one way or another I'll get me a stash. I'll team up again with Luke, or with somebody else. Come summer, right on that corner at George and the market building, we'll put on a show. I'll make another drum. He begins to whistle, that tune from the midwinter ceremonies that his grandfather taught him when he was small. The clear, wild notes carry in the quiet night.

To Corinne, it seemed she could bear almost everything. She had borne her grief, she could bear the hard work of the renovations to her house, she could bear remembering what Hal could hear and what things Hal never could hear. She would make the arrangements to have blood cleaned from the carpet of this floor. The broken drum and the body of her son's dog were, in some odd way she could not yet identify, comforting.

It was only that whistle like a cry of grief, sliding into defiance and then glee, clear notes arcing then fading in the strange, cold night, it was only the boy's whistle which suddenly was more than she could bear.

The Kalil Yaghi Memorial Swim

When Paul and I married, old Mr. Kokesh shaped for us a wedding gift — a slightly crooked small staircase with toothpick railings glued to a romantic crescent moon. It has hung in all our kitchens, crowded with photographs and bills and notes to ourselves, its dusty steps inhabited by salt and pepper shakers and other treasures: shells, china animals found in boxes of tea. But the old man died after making that gift: they carried him out of his house on a stretcher a few days before the wedding, overcome by the fumes of carbon tetrachloride. They got him to the hospital but it was too late: he had ascended his own stairway, gone wherever old men go who shape wood with their hands.

Over and over we tell these tales, as if there is magic in them, some mystery that reassures us even though the stories circle about death. We tell about Kalil Yaghi too.

Another old man living across another street. In his old age he has taken over the bench in the front window of the local laundromat, which is owned by his son, and gives orders to people who used to believe that without him they could manage perfectly well to get their coins in and their clothes in and out. We have grown accustomed to being instructed as to which washers are free, and even to finding Yaghi ringing our doorbell if we are too slow getting back after the wash is done.

Mornings he stands on our corner, smiling and shaking his head as Paul and I leave for our swim. The colder the weather, the more humorous Yaghi finds this early-morning trek to the pool. Today we didn't see him and that was one more bad sign. We were fairly certain he must be dead.

Paul said, "Let's make this a swim in honour of Yaghi."

We neither one of us wanted to say "the Kalil Yaghi Memorial Swim," in case he was still all right. We were not even certain that the person on the stretcher the night before had been him. His son has been ill lately; Yaghi himself always seems well. He attributes this to the constant wearing of two sweaters: in winter to keep off the cold, in summer to keep off the heat. When no one is doing a wash, he sits for hours in the window, telling rosary beads, squinting with his one good eye at a little New Testament written in Arabic. He and I have difficulty carrying on a conversation, my Arabic being non-existent and his English not much better, but one day he drew me a sketch with a pencil, on the edge of a newspaper, showing how one goes about making a wooden plough. From this I gathered that he used to be a farmer in Lebanon, before they came here and he ran a grocery store where our bookstore now is, then moved on to the family store on Somerset, returning in his old age to keep tabs on the laundromat and the corner.

Paul and I swam well, not overdoing it. We've just got over Christmas: we haven't been swimming, we're out of shape. We went to the cafeteria for breakfast, and there was Anh-Lu, the friendly young Vietnamese woman who takes care of the till. Paul gave her a New Year's hug.

"I hope I wasn't too forward."

"She probably didn't know who you were without your beard."

We both giggled.

"Well, she was willing," Paul said.

All this was in honour of Kalil Yaghi, and we hoped it wasn't in memoriam. His wife has been in hospital for several years, senile, unaware of her surroundings. It would have had some horror for him to find he was going in himself. We walked home in the intense cold, thinking of this. It seemed we might make tomorrow's swim, when we would be able to last longer, in memory of Barbara, my mother's cousin, who died suddenly of a heart attack two days ago in England. We remembered how, on her last visit here, she helped us move our bookstore, filling and carrying boxes as if she were much younger. Later when she was up on a chair, delightedly shelving and organizing and exclaiming over the technology section, we had to insist that she take a break. It is hard to imagine she is dead.

We returned to our preoccupation with the drama of the night before: the rising wail and abrupt stop of the ambulance siren in the night, flashing lights, the short, stocky form on a stretcher under a yellow blanket, people bobbing about in the Yaghi's lighted living room, then Sarah, Yaghi's daughter-in-law, and somebody else dashing out with their coats on and riding off with whoever it was who had been struck down. It seemed a bad sign that the ambulance had stopped flashing its lights, as if there were now no reason to rush.

"How will we find out what happened?"

"The girls will tell us."

The twins, Yaghi's grandchildren, standing solemnly at the window last night, watching the ambulance go off down the street. It would be sad not to see Kalil Yaghi again.

"Look who's here."

It is Kalil himself. He advances along the sidewalk toward us, wine-coloured tuque pulled over his ears, brown winter jacket on top of his two sweaters. Squinting with his good eye, and no doubt about to prolong his joke about our swimming in cold weather, but we beseige him with questions. "Who went to the hospital last night? Why did the ambulance come?" We wave our hands, make ambulance shapes, repeat words. In a moment he understands.

"Boy," he says. He mimes choking, losing air.

"Is he all right?"

"Okay," announces Kalil. "Go to school!"

We all grin.

Paul and I cross the street, smiling, still bemused. So next clotheswash — and we really must do one soon — Kalil will be still there.

"Too much!" he will order as we fill the dryers. "Break machine!"

"Here," he will offer afterwards, insisting on holding one end of my sheets as I fold them up, directing the whole process. Discreetly looking away as I stuff my underwear into the bag, returning to organize the socks. "Shirts!" he will cry again, an old joke. He wipes his face with his hand, always pretending surprise at our great quantity of shirts. "How many?"

And next summer, when Paul sets in to repair the newest cracks in the stucco of this building which once belonged to Kalil, the old man will still be there, looking over Paul's shoulder, shaking his head. In August he will be found in our grape arbour, unabashed, wearing his sweaters, picking off the big grape leaves from these vines he once planted, to take to Sarah, his daughter-in-law, who will be making supper. He will act out advice to us about pruning back the grapes. When we go out for walks, we will meet him coming down the other side of the street. He will catch our eye, lift his hand in greeting, go his way.

"A good job we did that swim," I say. "I didn't think it would work. We'll go on with our plans for tomorrow, but I'm afraid it's too late for Cousin Barbara."

We are sad and smiling at the same time.

"Dying seems easier, knowing that Barbara has done it," Paul says softly.

For Barbara, because when she was here she was so alive, tomorrow I will swim an extra length.

Afterwards we will meet Kalil, still standing on the corner outside the laundromat, his one eye dead and staring straight ahead, his good eye squinting with laughter, and with having to keep us all in line.

Snapdragon

At the back of the parsonage there was an old summer kitchen, and this was the space which Helen used as her studio. Most mornings she spent an hour or two there, separate yet not separate from the needs of her husband and her two teenage sons, and the constant flow of visitors and telephone calls which went with her husband's job. She could hear the doorbell from where she sat on a stool, facing her latest canvas, and when Gary was out she carried the telephone with her and plugged it in near her work.

This morning she again had a vision of flame. It started with Judith, her sister, and bridges, then turned into flame. A letter had arrived yesterday from Vancouver, saying that Judith and Michael and the twins are coming for Christmas. In it was a photograph of Judith with her kids, taken three months ago at the end of summer, and posed against a backdrop of Lion's Gate Bridge. In the picture Judy is in shorts and looking great, her long legs still slim, red hair pulled back in a knot and curly tendrils escaping all around her face. The twins are eight and growing up. It looks as if they have inherited that tall, easy grace.

Sisters are lost selves. That was the thought that hit her as she studied the photograph. Or maybe alternate selves — I'd make all those choices again, probably, Helen thought.

Always up until now, when things went wrong in her marriage or her motherhood, she envied the lives of her sisters: Judith, with the career and the high-paying job; Deborah, baby of the family, at thirty still unencumbered, still living near home. With Judy out west, it was usually herself and Deborah who got together to compare notes, so that she knew that life had not been easy for Deborah, but neither had it been boring: nearly always there was news of a new lover, a new job. When Helen's boys were young and her husband stuck in a strait-laced rural charge, Deborah's life had looked glamorous and free.

It is Judith's life which challenges both of her sisters. Judith is the middle one, the one who burned her bridges, travelled clear across the country and there proceeded to build a useful, and now brilliant, career. Judith has everything. True, she is on her second husband, but that happened nine years ago, and it seemed she shed that first marriage painlessly, an outgrown skin. The one thing Helen remembers from her sister's first marriage that seems too bad is that Judith was a photographer, and her first husband built her a darkroom. She even had a couple of successful shows. Since the marriage with Michael, not to mention the arrival of the twins and now this promotion, she has had no time for this or any other creative pursuit. At least, if she has, she hasn't mentioned it. Husband number two is an architect, very good-looking, and they seem still to be in love. Judith waited until Michael and her thirties to have children and had promptly managed twins, boy and girl.

Helen feels soft and formless when she thinks of Judith's life. Her own world is one of dreaming inside her studio in the mornings, interrupted by the small, detailed concerns of church work and women's groups, keeping things going, and then the slow pace of volunteer work she does in a home for seniors. Friends often buy her paintings, but she never feels organized about marketing her work. She has an apologetic feeling about her whole life.

Then came this vision of fire. She wants to try to paint it, and not for the first time. She first painted this particular flame when she was a child in grade six, working feverishly with a box of watercolour paints under the surprised gaze of her teacher, who taught all subjects and was no artist and who had assigned them to draw a picture of a house on a street. Orange, red, yellow overlaid had leapt higher and higher at the top of her page, black houses in flames, black treacherous pits that must be made by bombs. In the foreground, in bare feet, blanket clutched about her, the girl.

The outside world as it was brought to Helen as a child was full of pain and loss. Yet surely her own life had not been like that. Her own life was full of warmth and family love and singing over the dishes and laughing at her father's corny jokes — and endless chores, too: she remembers the intricate dusting of stairs, the scary job of fetching horse and cow from the back pasture, then straddling the dangerous well to let down the bucket on its long thin rope. And she took care of her brother and her sisters after school, mainly Judith, but sometimes her mother asked her to walk the baby, or to please amuse Tommy for a while. All this was good for her, she's certain of it: it taught her maternal feelings, a sense of her serious responsibility in the scheme of things. The story of the "Judy-jitney-jumps" she remembers with pleasure even if it may not always have been much fun at the time. She had liked the sound of the name she invented almost as much as the game itself: "jitney" she had found in a book of her mother's — it was some kind of cart. She still can feel Judy's bony knees dug into her back, and hear her sister's shaken laughter as she, Helen, tore about the yard, bumping Judy on her back. And Tommy wanted jitney jumps too, she remembers, smiling, but even then he didn't hang on well.

Out of sight of her mother and the endless list of jobs, she learned to find what corners she could to be alone with her sketchpad and her dreams. Very occasionally she was able to get away from the house, and then what she loved to do was to trek back into the fields and make detailed sketches of silk-laden milkweed pods, or moss and stones in the dry creek bed.

Even then, usually Judy had to tag along.

Their mother was busy, with a house to be cleaned from top to bottom every week, beds that had to be changed, the garden, the baby, and young Tom wandering in and out and competing with Deborah for space on her crowded lap. He was the boy and had his own identity, but the three girls as they grew learned to divide up turf.

Helen reaches for dark colours, getting in the houses now, houses bursting into flames. When she just up and left for university, was that hard on Jude, then? But by then Judy was almost twelve. When Helen came home for holidays, Jude had become the big sister. She remembers their mother had made the younger girls matching tartan skirts, and Deb followed Judy around wherever she went. If anyone was excluded then, it was Helen. Judy, monkey in the middle, grew up wise beyond her years. Deb needed advice about boys earlier than either one of her older sisters, and Jude was there to hand it out. Then she turned around and gave support and advice to her older sister, a young mother then, and giving up on her art. It was Judith who kept that flame alight. When she got her first office, the first thing she did was commission a painting from Helen for her wall. Even their mother consulted her in those last years of their father's illness. Judith acted like a social worker long before she took the course. Then suddenly, the break. She took a job at the other end of the country and hadn't come home since. At first it was supposed to be because she couldn't afford it, and they all had to chip in or else she wouldn't even have seen their mother. But for some time now she's had the salary to let her come. She's been busy. But has she really needed to stay away this long?

Poor Tom; no brothers, thinks Helen. He misses all this. The thought of her own two sons makes her smile: the one so dark, the other so fair. The engineer and the artist. Yes, alternate selves. She remembers when they were little how much their interests were alike. At some point one began designing engine parts and the other filled his sketchbooks with cartoons. Will they miss the parts of themselves they've left behind?

She finishes with the dark colours and starts in on the child. Then she finds herself still going back for dark tones on the brush.

So there were four of them; their parents loved them; they lived in the country and they were poor but they were happy. The idea of giving rides she learned from bumping joyfully on her father's broad back (she remembers a blue work shirt, the fabric warm and sweaty as she clung); the idea of care she learned from the busy hands of their mother, cleaning, sweeping, wiping noses, brushing hair, setting out endless plates of food. Within the circle of their family they were safe.

But the lives of children in other lands were not safe. Their faces stared out from the six sides of her Mission Band box: black and brown and Oriental faces and native kids and then one white child like herself, or more like Judith because of the curls. The children on the box needed children like Helen to fill the box with pennies. Then those children could smile, they would have blankets and food. Perhaps they would even find their parents or big sisters once again after whatever fiery war. But at best that was temporary. Children the world over, except for ones she personally knew, children of every colour-and-creed, were wandering forsaken, orphaned, hungry, shaking with cold.

Helen's mother taught her to divide her allowance into four parts: Jesus, Others, Yourself and Savings. The first letters spelled out JOYS. Her allowance by grade six was twenty-five cents, which left one extra nickel for Others; it took a long time to collect enough for a blanket, which cost five dollars through the Mission Band fund. Helen saved and saved. She was a conscientious child. It was not like her to go against her teacher's wishes and draw the scene of fire, but something had pulled from her this unbearable idea: her own little sister stumbling across the frozen stubble of November fields like the ones she passed on her way to school. Cold bare feet on the freezing ground. What would it be like for Judy, then, with no mother, no father, no big sister to keep her warm?

Helen sits on her stool in the sunshine in the old summer kitchen and wonders why she spends her time this way, why this very minute she is not out helping the poor. It's not as if she doesn't know where to find them now. As a minister's wife she is only too aware of every good cause for country miles around. She returns to her flames and does something different with the colours coming from the burning house.

Perhaps at Christmas she can talk with her sisters about this question of alternate selves. Christmas is still two weeks away. It will be at Mother's, as usual: their mother is still in the red brick house with many rooms where they all grew up. Lately Helen has found herself reading articles on Alzheimer's or on Parkinson's disease with sharp, concentrated interest. She supposes the others might be doing this too. Perhaps at Christmas they can have a family conference on what is going on; perhaps not. It will be very difficult to raise. But with Judith there, all sorts of things might straighten out.

In the midst of bright fire, something dark. Smoke. Shadow. About noon she comes to the face of the child. All this time she had assumed the girl would have the face of Judith. As she washes her brushes and prepares to go make lunch, suddenly Helen knows that when she comes to it, however incongruous it may be, that child will be painted with long neat brown braids. The lost child is herself.

She heads for the kitchen, but stops again by the photograph posted on the bulletin board beside her studio door. My little sister, she thinks, in a far-off land. At least, British Columbia seems far away right now. But maybe if the church session sees its way clear to giving Gary a raise, maybe we'll get out there ourselves. Here we are, both in our forties, and neither one of us has ever seen a mountain. She looks affectionately at the way her sister smiles at the invisible guy with the camera, and the way the twins cuddle close. No, not forsaken. Just far away.

As it turns out, Judith and her family arrive early and are the first into the old house. Helen is not surprised when Deborah calls the very next day to announce a change in arrangements.

"What do you think of this, Sis? I'm moving in with Mom in the New Year! I didn't want to get you worried before, but several times lately I've gone over there and she's out and left all the doors wide open, I mean open, not just unlocked, and one day she forgot to turn off the taps in the laundry room and the basement flooded — I guess you did hear about that one. But you know how it is: she's independent and so am I. I've got a life of my own I don't think she wants to be too close to." She laughs briefly. "You know what I mean. And Mom's a going concern herself, of course, what with all those old ladies coming in to tea and her Ladies' Aid and the Horticultural whatsit. But good old Michael the architect just took one look and he's gone crazy with all the possibilities in Mom's house. Somebody has put up the cash, maybe Judy, maybe Mom, I don't know, but when it's done I'll have my own space and my own entrance — "

Helen interrupts the excited account, asking for details.

"Yeah — through the old coal chute, you're right, that's it, except you're not going to believe how fancy — and I'll pay Mom half the rent I pay now here, and we'll eat supper together most nights — you know, keep an eye on each other — this is really going to help. Helen, I'm going to save money on this."

"Does this mean you'll get through your course a little faster?"

"I doubt it. As long as I'm doing it in the evenings after work, I'm kinda locked in. No, but maybe some trips, eh? Some short ones. I could get a buddy in there in my place to be company for Mom from time to time. We can both come and go. But it'll be a better setup. Good old Jude, eh?"

"How is she?"

There is an instant's hesitation before her sister replies: "Oh — it's so great to see her. She gives out nice hugs. It takes a little while to get back on track, of course, after all this time. It's been ages, eh? And you know — there's something about being back in the house, and Christmas — it's practically as bad as a wedding for stirring up old stuff."

Helen laughs. "Debby, I don't know what you're talking about!"

"Hah! Well, you soon will. And maybe it's this business of planning change around the house too? And me moving in? I don't know. Maybe it's something from her work."

"You think she's tense about something."

"Oh, just a bit. She's fine. And you should see the kids — they're growing like weeds. . . . "

A few days later, they are all together. Their mother strings a clothesline at the side of the stairs, which is where they "always" hang their stockings now. This year there are eleven, all sizes and shapes, from Deborah's stretchy one that elicits groans and snide remarks from the people trying to fill it, to Mother's useful-looking little white sock that she wears when she gardens. It seems important to put names on the socks, and Mother sets about looking for her roll of masking tape. Eventually, with Deborah's help, she locates it, and people begin sticking on their names. Deborah has permanently embroidered DESPERATE DEB on hers. Helen shyly decides to add HELPFUL above her own name, and then one of her sons sticks in HARPY as well, which bothers her, but she pretends not to care. It is difficult to persuade Judith and her husband to put up stockings at all, since in their separate family tradition stockings have been only for kids; they think they know that Santa has not come prepared. Then there is a tense moment when Judith is still hanging up their socks and everyone is pretending not to look at what anyone else is doing, the teenagers are dumping in candies and oddments alongside the adults, and Judith's young twins decide to creep up the stairs for a sneak preview. Mother, coming along the row beside Judith, pauses and slips a second, special gift into the sock marked Desperate Deb.

Judith's voice makes everyone jump: "You kids get down from there and mind your own business! You'll spoil everything! You're not supposed to look!"

There is a startled silence — everyone can hear the nuts hitting each other as they roll into the socks. Then Mother calls kids and stray husbands out to the kitchen to decorate cookies. In her kitchen she still knows where things are. Later she sends them up the back stairs to bed. Helen slips in to check.

"Mother, did you realize this element's still on?"

"Oh, that's where I was boiling the icing. I got distracted, what with all the kids. I would have noticed it, dear." Her mother fusses a little more about the kitchen, setting out breakfast dishes for the morning, then says she is going to set them a good example and go to bed. "And if you kids know what's good for you, you'll turn in soon as well!"

Helen laughs and gives her a kiss.

"We'll try to be quiet, Momma. It's been so long since we were under the same roof."

What with one thing and another, and after a lot of other words have gone by, it is about midnight when Judith spells out BRIDGES in the Scrabble game beside the Christmas tree, Tom cries Excellent! and notes down 65 points. The four siblings are sitting together around the old dining room table. Tom had gone off earlier and reappeared wearing a dramatic white robe one of his friends had made for him. After that they all changed into pyjamas and dressing gowns, but no one seems in a hurry to go to bed. Helen is feeling relaxed and cheerful in her worn viyella dressing gown left over from university days. Deb has been putting on weight, and has pulled around her an ancient red bathrobe that they all recognize as having belonged to their father. Judith is stylish in a high-necked green silk lounging outfit that looks good enough for the office. For a reason that has to do with the hour, the cream whisky that Deb has produced and also, probably, the occasion, the game slows down.

"'Bridges' always makes me think of your first boyfriend, Helen," Deborah remarks. "Do you remember?"

"The guy with the glass eye," reminisces Tom. "I remember! He used to take it out and roll it around in his hand."

"You were just little! Are you sure you didn't make that up? It's true, though, that my first boyfriend was a guy named Bob Bridges, and he did have a glass eye. Do you remember the story of how he lost his eye?"

"Yes," says Judith, too quickly.

"Do I want to know?" Deborah addresses her question to

her brother, a minor conspiracy against older sisters, but Helen won't be stopped.

"No, listen, I've got to tell you this if you don't know: it's important for whenever you're going through the bush. He and his dad were out in their woodlot one day when Bob Bridges was just a little tyke — and his dad held a branch forward and wasn't careful and he let go too soon, and the branch snapped back into his kid's eye. Ugh. I've always remembered that: it's one of my main 'be careful' stories."

"You did a painting one time of that eye," murmurs Judith. "I remember. It was a good picture."

Helen glances at her, liking that she remembers, but also suddenly feeling vulnerable.

"Yuck. Did it really rip right out like that?" Deb shudders and tries to top up the glasses, but Helen holds a hand over hers. "Can that happen? I guess I really don't want to know."

Judith sighs. "Well, 'bridging' is just a technical word for me, guys. I don't see Helen's old boyfriend and his bloody eye and I don't see bridges over rivers either, mainly. I spend my days anymore trying to get social services groups to think 'bridging.'"

She watches speculatively as Deborah slowly spells EAT from the E in BRIDGES. She fingers her own tiles.

"What are bridges in your job, then? For me after this many years in music it's always going to be part of a violin." Tom smiles around the table at his three sisters. He's in love, thinks Helen, or else very happy about Christmas. Or dear me, could it be the whisky? Tom turns to Judith: "You want them to bridge their clients, Jude, is it, with what? Or who?"

"Whom," corrects Helen, and covers her embarrassment by passing the fudge. Damned schoolmarm, she scolds herself.

"Well, with the community in general. Individuals, sometimes organizations. For one example, the Rehab Centre has a guy who was brain-damaged in a diving accident. Before that he was just an ordinary jock — a nice kid. Star of his school basketball team. But no artistic talent, so far as anybody knew. Now he's thirty, he can't talk, but he paints the most amazing pictures. So I'm trying to get them to see if they can find some artists or galleries or something who will just include him in whatever it is that people like that do. I brought along one of his paintings in my suitcase. I want to know what you think about it, Helen, and maybe get some advice."

Helen feels herself flush with pleasure, and again feels annoyed at herself. *I am an artist, after all,* she thinks. *Why shouldn't Judy expect me to know something?* Carefully, she spells out WHETHER on the board. Tom whistles admiringly, but it's only 15 points. Helen hears Deborah suck in her breath as if she is about to speak, but then she says nothing. Helen decides to pursue it. "What do bridges mean to you, little sister?"

"I wasn't going to say. It's just stupid. Well, it was a mistake, actually. I went to a Quaker wedding a few months ago. Somebody in my class that I'd got to know. I was curious how they do it. They don't have a minister."

Tom grins as he adds an ED to some word and writes down his score. "We know you're interested in weddings, Desperate Deb."

"Shut up, kid brother. Well, anyways, you expect everybody to be saying things about eternal faithfulness and all that crap, and instead somebody read a thing about how some people are faithful by nature but other people keep falling in love over and over again and they are supposed to make bridges of their affections." The tone is of irony, but her eyes are a bit too bright. "And I liked that, do you like it?" *Go easy on her,* thinks Helen. "Anyways, it was a mistake. It turned out they'd said 'riches': 'make riches of your affections.' But I liked the bridges. Pass the fudge."

"This is so neat," beams Tom, brown curls waving like antennae as he gives Deborah the plate of fudge and nods toward his sisters around the table. "All four of us. Everybody else gone to bed."

"They lack the constitution." Deborah refills glasses.

"How long has it been since we were all here in the house together?" Helen is earnest, figuring it out.

"This is the first Christmas we've been here in eight years." Judith sounds as if she's blaming someone. She slaps down FEZ. Thirty-five points. "First time since the twins were born. For sure nobody's ever come to spend Christmas with us. You guys always come to Mum's and so she never thinks how nice it would be for our kids to have a grandmother some Christmas."

"You don't have snow." Deb's little-girl voice. She frowns at the board. "Jude, you're so far ahead."

"Hey, I think we need to mark this occasion somehow, what do you think? We need a ceremony." Tom is still beaming.

Helen shakes her head, meaning to be funny. "Isn't getting drunk together good enough?"

"God, Helen, is this what you call drunk?" Judith sits back abruptly in her chair. "You should see some of the down and outs that come wandering into my office, you want to recognize drunk. And excuse me, but you don't have to be our mother anymore."

Helen is dismayed to discover that her eyes have filled with tears. It must be the damned whisky.

Deborah is gazing earnestly at her older sisters, her eyes blue and moist, innocent. "Look, Judy, you're making Helen feel bad. Mom brought us up, not Helen, the way I remember it."

Helen feels grateful, but foolish too. As she dabs at her eyes, she notices that Deborah is getting a double chin. She used to be so cute. . . .

"I meant it as permission," says Judith crisply, "but it's getting late. I think we've finished the game." She tilts the board and the tiles clatter back into the box.

Tom and Deborah toss their own tiles in after the others, but Helen stares a moment at the word she was putting together before she realizes that Judith is right, it is late, and anyway the game is over. She tips hers in as well.

Deborah picks up the empty bottle and stands. "How about Snapdragon? Remember? We did it last year."

"Snapdragon!" agrees Tom, jumping to his feet. "Right on! You two bring over the coffee table. Helen and I will get the fixin's."

Judith smiles and seems to relax. "Is this a game? What is it?"

Tom and Helen leave Deborah burbling: "Oh, Jude, it's so dramatic. You'll love it. Didn't anybody tell you? It's some kind of ancient solstice custom. . . . "

In the kitchen, Tom loses his smile and quirks an eyebrow.

"Where did all this tension come from? Is it all of us or is something bugging her?"

"Oh, she's just getting used to us again. I think she's been lonely out there, don't you? Judy's always had this kind of fire inside. Even when we were kids. She's the dragon with a heart of gold."

"Snapdragon." Tom reverts to his high good humour.

"Yes." Helen finds her mother's raisins and scatters some in a frying pan. Tom pours brandy into a saucepan and sets it on the stove to warm while he looks around for the matches.

"This was a good idea, Tom. I'll go back in with these and see if they've sorted it out."

The living room looks like a Christmas card as Helen returns: the tree, the stockings all hung in a row and stretched into interesting shapes, two youngish women in long gowns, one in red and one in green, dragging a square deal table to the corner near the tree. The thought crosses her mind (she remembers this later on) that it might be dangerous, they ought to set the table further out, but in the next moment the danger of the conversation takes precedence. She can hardly believe her ears. Deb, the cute one, the baby of the family, is hissing:

"You left this family years ago, Judy — it was your goddamned choice, so you can't come down on us now if we left you out of some of this. Anyways, I didn't even tell Helen. Don't be such a bitch. You're not the one who has had to see her every day no matter what was going on in your own life, and worry that she was going to burn the house down around her . . . "

"Hey, you two." Helen sets the pan on the table. "Are you fighting about Mum? Is that sensible?"

It is as if she hadn't spoken.

Judith has pulled herself up, her eyes narrowing, in her high-necked gown looking like the successful executive about to censure an errant office girl. Helen becomes aware of the shabbiness of her own clothes. And Deb, she sees again, is fat, in scuffed slippers, and that old robe of their dad's pulled round her swelling hips.

"I wonder if Mother realizes, Deb, that you're turning into a lush."

Deborah's response is low, loving, and full of surprise.

"Jude — are you jealous of me?"

"Gangway!" Tom strides in, then slows as the blue flame on the burning brandy flows back over his hairy arm. "Whoa there! Get out of the way but get ready to grab your share!" He pours liquid fire over the raisins. Flames leap high. A few dribbles escape the pan and for a moment fire races dramatically out of control, flaring across the tabletop. Tom's hand plunges into the pan, comes out triumphantly with hot brandy-soaked raisins. He stands gobbling them down.

Helen can't remember any real quarrel among them since they were young and one or other of them tried to skip a turn doing the dishes. Trembling with fatigue and distress, but deciding to be a good role model and fake excitement, she sticks her arm into the flames and scoops up raisins for herself. If she ignores it, perhaps it will come out all right. Tom is rambunctiously pushing in for seconds.

Deborah squeals and pulls back the sleeve of her robe as she reaches in for hers.

In a flash Judith's hand is there too, striking the raisins away. For one surrealistic moment the frying pan hangs in midair. Bright shooting stars arc into the tree, blue eyes of flame light along needles, the floor, edges of tissue-wrapped gifts. There is a lick of orange fire, the smell of paper scorching.

In Helen's startled memory, there is the whoosh of a Christmas tree their father fired in the backyard one January, the way the dark snow-clad world in an instant turned blood-red. She grabs her mother's fire extinguisher from where it has always hung, behind the piano. She presses and presses and presses. A scream fills her ears, a terrible sound, seeming to come from every part of the house.

"Helen, you can stop now." Tom starts to laugh, flapping a tea towel at the smoke alarm. The scream cuts off. There is a gasp of relief.

Helen looks about. Her mother is there in a white nightgown, looking as if now she has seen everything, but worried, not mad, and Judith's husband, sleepy-eyed, and one of her own two grown sons.

"Where's Patrick? Where's Gary?"

"I guess they'd sleep through a fire alarm: I guess we just proved it."

Babble of voices, laughter, kisses, hugs, loud sighs, exclamations of dismay over the maybe-ruined gifts, over how all the ruckus still hasn't wakened the others. The practical shuffle of their mother, out to the kitchen to put on the kettle —

what catches all of them off guard are the tears.

There they are, sitting in the middle of the living room floor at 1 AM on Christmas morning, in the house where they were young, faces and arms flecked with white foam, Helen's son slipping back to bed, their mother in the kitchen with the kettle and the cat. Helen holds onto Judy against the hard shell of her back, their little sister Deb who is only thirty holds onto her from one side and little brother Tom who is only thirty-six hangs onto her from the other side and Judith's man strides about in the background pointing out to the ceiling that nothing can be untangled tonight, and Judith . . . cries and cries and cries and cannot stop. Her long body shakes, sobs catch and return, the weeping of a very small girl. All of them have tears on their cheeks, scared silly at what might be coming undone, hugging, reaching for comfort — but Judith the tough one, Judith the wise kid, the one who has always known all the answers and always heard all their news, Judith their tall and beautiful and sophisticated senior executive sister, is crumpled on the floor without recourse, and it seems her heart has broken

and nobody understands why.

Mother comes in with tea. Judith, still in spasms of sobs, shrugs off their hands, shakes her head, stumbles up the stairs with her husband.

Soberly they sip tea, feeling some guilt. Upstairs, Judith's weeping goes on and on. Tom hides the whisky bottle behind a chair. Their mother sees him do it, sits up straight and says, "If your father were still alive...." They coax her and kiss her soft white hair: "Oh, Mom, don't say that." She resists and then, as if she feels her power truly on the wane, relents. Mother and grown children make plans for pulling a Christmas Day out of this mess.

Which helps next morning. Mother is up before anyone except Judith and Michael, who speak to her quietly and go off on their own. The message they leave is that they have gone skiing, and they are sorry to miss the kids' stockings but to go ahead without them and they will be back tonight, and to tell the twins that they will bring back something special. Everybody makes sure that the twins get lots of attention, and Helen's boys take them tobogganing (first having to sandpaper off the bumps of white foam). The family plots to be playing guitars and the violin and singing Christmas carols when they return, with turkey smell and everybody tired and happy from tobogganing and skating, and killer games of Scrabble and Clue. Could it have hurt that much, they think and sometimes discuss in low tones among themselves all day, glancing uneasily at the children. Can life hurt that much? Deb drinks less. Helen notices the fine lines forming at the corners of her little brother's eyes. She kisses her husband on his receding hairline. Of course it can. It does. What made them think they could come home for Christmas and not remember loss?

In the lull after the stockings, Helen unpacks something special she's brought, the painting of the lost girl, and props it near the tree. She feels shy about it, but determined. She wants a chance to explain to Deborah and to her brother and then later to Judith about the way the figure changed. They don't have to talk about it: she just wants them to know.

One of her boys gets a rabbit in the afternoon, not the sweetest thing to do on Christmas Day, but he's very proud of himself, and so there are blood and guts and a furry hide on the kitchen floor along with the aroma of dinner cooking and a bright line of song, when the missing ones stomp snow at the door and take off their boots and come on in. Bridges have been made of affection this long day. There is singing and foolishness and playing of games they can't believe they all still want to play: Grunt Piggy Grunt, Poor Pussy, Ring on a String. Judith and her husband open their stockings and find copies of *The New Internationalist* for Judith and *MacUser* for her husband, and black and white film for Judy's camera that her mother had put in her stocking when she wasn't looking. Deborah gets the quarter in the Christmas pudding. Their mother says it means a husband, ten thousand a year, and a park.

Storm Of Life

A sharp bend in the river. Above it bright beds of marigolds, a stucco bungalow, and the memory of tragedy. Housewives running out for groceries in the morning, or perhaps called to the school to ferry home a sick child in mid-afternoon, would sometimes glimpse a small blond boy pedalling furiously on a red tricycle near the house. On the porch or kneeling at a flower bed they would always also see the mother, and some knew her name, which was Lois Thompson. No one remembered the name of the boy, who had been just a baby when the older child drowned. The two disappeared inside when traffic increased in the late afternoon, so most people saw no other sign of life than the tricycle parked neatly near the fence that separated the front yard from the dropoff to the river.

Before her son Robbie died, Lois Thompson had been active in the Smithville Women's Institute. They were working on a Lady Tweedsmuir scrapbook, and she became interested in local history. She was the only woman who had dared to tackle Bernie Hutchinson, the community's oldest inhabitant, who lived in a bachelor's shack down Catfish Lane. Bernie served Lois tea and store-bought cookies, and willingly told her numerous facts and tales about the village that he would never have told to anyone whom he felt really belonged. Lois was still a newcomer in the village when her older boy drowned, and after the first time of sympathy for her loss, no one knew her well enough to continue visiting her. She seemed all right. In the summer months her marigolds glowed inside straight borders. A red, white and navy-blue For Sale sign began appearing outside the house every spring as soon as the river went down, and stayed there until the first cold days of September, when once more it came in.

It stood propped in a corner of her spotless kitchen. Over the real estate company's name brooded a navy-blue block with abnormally long eaves — a signpainter's symbol of security. Lois glanced at it irritably in the course of her morning's cleaning. She wished Jack had taken it all the way out to where it belonged in the shed when he had brought it in. She was tired of looking at it. She was going to have to stay in this house between the highway and the river, with the basement that flooded in the spring. She would never be able to leave. She would have to stay with the backyard, gouged at its end by angry spring runoff.

If they had been able to move, perhaps then she could have left behind with the house the way her body still clenched with the memory of the terror that threw her desperately across that yard, calling, straining her eyes across neighbour's land both ways, and finally brought her the sight, the evidence she did not wish to see and tried to make herself believe when she saw it that it was something — else where the yard sloped steeply to the muddy beach, a pile of stones and clamshells, and the padding busy footprints of her son Robbie's three-year-old feet, trotting back and forth collecting them, at one point turning and leading to the water's edge.

She had told him not to go near the river. That excuse was so weak when everybody knew he was still only three. But it was like a voice in her head, repeating, endlessly justifying herself before some invisible tribunal. The women from the village, perhaps. Her husband. I told him. I promised him that as soon as the water went down we would go to the Flat Rock near old Bernie's and he could paddle and try to swim. We did do that the summer he was two. We went often. I was going to keep my promise: I wasn't just putting him off. If only he had waited.

But irony caught her, the spasm of helpless guilt. I expected too much. The river called. He couldn't wait. Too young. Probably didn't even remember that Mommy said no. I thought he understood. He was big. He seemed to understand. But then something happens, doesn't it: she was learning that now from all her reading. Children go through stages. One of the magazines said that a four-year-old wants to break out of his boundaries, find out where the limits really are. That it's part of growing up. Maybe if I'd known that then.... I never had a child almost four before. And it was like Robbie to be ahead of schedule for any part of growth which needed independence and strength. His shoulders. His smooth, brown, defenceless little-boy shoulders. He had the build of a boxer, Jack used to say. Jack used to love to pretend to box with him, show him off for visitors.

The dark bubble of guilt rises and bursts. Despair invades her, like poison released in her blood. Her arms and legs feel weak. She sits down. I was too long in the house. I was playing with the baby. No, I was changing him, changing Philip. I watched television while I did it. I watched "Storm of Life." I was watching TV and staying too long in the house, caught up in the lives of imaginary people, and real life took away my son. I was changing Philip, that is my excuse. But Robbie had time to pick up those stones and those shells. I lingered, I must have, maybe waiting for the commercial. I don't remember.

Between ten and eleven in the morning, precisely, if the day were bright, and lately, since Philip had given up his afternoon naps, from two to three, Lois allowed the boy to play outside. She went with him, making time from her busy day of cleaning and scouring and preparing food. He could ride his tricycle, on the path, near the house. He must never, never go into the backyard. Lois watched him, sometimes taking her sewing with her, sometimes tending the marigolds, but mostly just keeping him before her eyes. At three o'clock the yellow schoolbuses would start to lumber by, on their way to pick up the children at school.

"Come inside, Philip. I don't want you to get run over by a bus!"

He would follow her, obedient as his brother had never been. Inside she always had work. At moments when she could find nothing else to clean, she would pick up magazines and read and reread everything she could find on childcare, on what to expect.

"I want to go to school."

"Soon, Honey. When you're five. Don't put your fingers on the window. Why don't you play with your schoolhouse?"

She searches out the box of wooden people. Philip flicks repeatedly at the schoolhouse bell and after a while its incessant chime annoys her. She is ironing, and trying at the same time to watch the latest episode of "Storm of Life." At first the set had stood silent and blank as she passed and repassed it, keeping busy. Lately, however, she has begun to watch again, this one show. For some reason she has become intensely interested in the lives of these characters. In spite of herself, she thinks about them as she is working, wonders how things are turning out. She is ashamed of herself. She had watched it only casually before; she never used to be this involved. But, she thinks defensively, I had someone to talk to then.

Jack has no idea she has begun to watch the show again. On weekends he will sometimes invite her to join him in front of the set. But she recognizes this as a trap and moves off. Always there is something else to do. And someone has to keep an eye on Philip.

"Well, maybe it's just as well," he will agree, and she knows that he still blames her. They have only really discussed Robbie's death once, although sometimes before that they had remembered him a little together. That one time, Jack had turned from the TV, and a rather dull boxing match, to remark, "D'you remember how young Rob used to put on his bathing trunks and his mittens and come out pretending to be the big fighter?"

She had been unable to reply, finding herself gazing once again in horror at the limp body of her son in the arms of a policeman. It wasn't his bathing trunks he had on when it happened. That day he was wearing the denim overalls her sister had made for him and the red striped shirt. He hadn't meant to go swimming. Perhaps he had just wanted one more clamshell and had hardly waded in when the current surprised him. If she had been there it would have been so easy to grab him, set him on his feet again, scared but still alive. She saw herself doing it. She heard her voice: "Now listen, fella. Don't you ever do that again, you hear? See how it grabs you?"

The need to scold, to have him there safely to scold, filled her lungs and throat like smoke.

Jack's voice had come at the end of this long silence, choked, angry.

"Lois... all you had to do was to take care of him. Christ Almighty, I do the work, I bring in the cash, all you have to do while I'm away is take care of the house and mind the kids.... It isn't as if it's that hard."

That was the moment she had chosen, the worst possible one, she saw later, to admit she had been watching TV. When it was over and he had not killed her — perhaps because of Philip, she didn't know — she knew that she would never tell him the other things: that it had been his choice, his own stubborn choice, to buy this house between the river and the highway, and surely it had been his doing more than hers that Robbie had grown so self-willed and so certain of himself. Instead she worked out her penance in immaculate floors and punctual mealtimes and flawless vigilance over their second son. And the end of tenderness between herself and her husband. What she had not expected was the way he cut out Philip too.

The boy had a way of managing to get onto his father's knee in the evening, sliding across the sofa without coming in the way of the television screen, or creeping up from underneath the opened newspaper.

"Run along and play now, son." Jack would shrug him off absent-mindedly, returning to absorption in the paper or TV.

At bedtime, it somehow always fell to Lois to tuck him in.

"Can Daddy come?"

"I'll see, darling, but I think he's too busy. Good-night."

Even when the red tricycle was left in the driveway and Jack arrived with an angry curse, he always addressed it to her, as if it were she who had been careless, not his son. It was never: "Philip, go move that goddamned trike and don't leave it there again!"

Instead it was: "Jesus Christ, Lois, can't you keep the kid's trike out of the drive?"

They got along, the days passed. Philip grew. Soon he was as old as Robbie had been when he died. Then he was older. Now he would soon be old enough to go to school. He had passed the dangerous fours and he had fretted, but she had brought him through alive. She began to understand that she could do it after all. It was about then that she sometimes let herself start watching television again. First she would go around and lock the doors.

One fall day Jack arrived home with a white rabbit in a cardboard box. It was a present, he said, for Philip. She stuttered as she attempted to take in this surprise.

"But how...? You... is this...." She stopped and smiled.

"Philip will love it. But where did it come from?"

"Oh, I was just going through the market on my way to the Post Office and I happened to spot these rabbits in a cage and a gang of kids looking at them and I thought: why not get one for Phil? He hasn't got a dog or a cat or even a fish, does he? And rabbits are supposed to be good pets."

He set to work at once with the boy's excited help, sawing and hammering boards and taking a trip to the feed store to buy wire mesh and a bag of alfalfa pellets. By suppertime they had finished the cage and they let the rabbit into it. Philip picked grass and stuck it through the wire. The cage was behind the house, and the boy kept running in and out of the back door, full of questions and news about his rabbit, whom he had decided to call "Peter." She could see that much of his delight was really because suddenly he was in forbidden territory, the backyard. He was nearly five and a half, and the back of the house had been off limits to him ever since he had sat on the grass as a baby while his mother ran from one side of the yard to the other, calling and screaming for someone he probably cannot even remember, someone who hadn't come.

Peter seemed to enjoy his new home. Philip brought him greens and kept his dish filled with pellets. Helen went out now and then to look at him, and saw that there was usually water in his other dish and that he could get back in the shade of a nearby shrub when the sun was too hot. On the fifth day, however, something went wrong. The rabbit began shedding his fur all over the floor of the cage. He looked bedraggled, and whole tufts of fur had come out, as if they'd been pulled.

Lois and Philip checked on him every little while, and she allowed the boy to go out by himself from time to time and bring her reports. Peter was eating his pellets as usual, and nibbled at the extra greens Philip brought him. Philip gave him fresh water. Jack took a look at him when he got home and again, with a flashlight, before going to bed.

"He can't be moulting. It's fall, not spring. In fact, it's going to be a cold night."

"I heard that too. Do you suppose it could be a vitamin deficiency?"

"I don't know. We'll keep an eye on him for a few days and if it doesn't clear up I guess I'll have to take him to a vet."

"Could you check with the people you bought him from, do

you suppose? Who was it anyway?"

"Just some people in the market. A couple with two young boys."

It was a clue. Lois took a moment to gather courage, and then suggested, tentatively, "Robbie always wanted to have a rabbit."

Jack's voice went gruff. "I was always going to get him one."

"I think Philip needed a pet, too, but he didn't even know it."

"Or didn't say. Rob would have been bugging the life out of us. Phil's quiet."

Lois let a pool of happiness seep into her. He had identified his son. It was the first time since the death.

That night when she fell asleep, she dreamed as she so often did that Robbie was calling her from the river. For the first time she did not feel anxious. Instead in the dream she walked tranquilly to the water's edge. She saw that her son was not in the water, but standing on the opposite bank. He had grown. He was a big boy now, still with those broad shoulders and the determined set to his chin.

"Come over, Mom. It's okay. The water's low."

She saw that the water which moments before had seemed swirling in flood was now calm and shallow. Trees from the farther shore spread flat green reflections across its surface. She stepped in. The current sucked at her ankles as harmlessly as a breeze in grass. She picked her way across to her son. He stood apart from her, not wanting to be hugged.

"Mom," he said to her, and she saw he looked vaguely irritated. "Mom, have you seen Phil? Do you know where he is?"

She woke, still not feeling anxious. She had seen Robbie. Everything was all right. She tried to hold onto the feeling as she drifted further into wakefulness. Philip was safely in bed. The early morning light was beginning to show at their window. Suddenly her scalp prickled. She held her breath. The side door had clicked. There was a hesitation, then she heard it again. Someone had just come in — or gone out. She lay motionless, straining to hear. Behind the house there was a muffled bump. She laid her hand on Jack, and he stirred.

"Jack — someone just went out, I think. There's a noise behind the house. Maybe Philip is checking the rabbit, do you think so? It's only five o'clock."

"I'd better check." Sleepily he reached for his dressing gown, laced on his shoes over bare feet. She found herself getting up too, the memory of her son calling from across the river still strong.

When they opened the door, there was hoarfrost on the grass. They could see Philip's dark tracks leading around the corner of the house. They found him kneeling at the door of the pen. As they came nearer, Lois could see odd-shaped black lumps lying strewn about the floor of the cage, too solid to be lumps of fur. A moment later she knew what they were. "Peter" was a female. The fur-pulling had been her distracted effort to make a nest.

The babies were dead. They were bleeding as well. One was torn open at its side. Evidently the mother had attacked them. Two were caught by their thin arms and legs in the wire mesh and must have struggled there helplessly before they grew cold. One had worked his blind way to the front of the cage and had died with his pointed pink muzzle through the wire. She realized suddenly, with a start, that there was one more. Philip had it in the palm of his hand. She squatted beside him and looked silently at the tiny body. It was unblemished: a grey, mouse-like creature with ears like petals, closed eyes and a bubble of moisture at its mouth. She glanced at her son's face. He appeared stricken, but she was impressed by his composure.

"It had crawled into the grass, Mom. It got out between the wires. Do you think it might be still alive?"

She held out her hand. Philip placed in it the creature's infinitesimal weight. A soft ear brushed her middle finger and the rump with its truncated tail finished at the base of her thumb. She had thought that newborn rabbits were pink and hairless, but this one was covered with grey down. Feeling as if her fingers were suddenly large and clumsy, she attempted to move its tiny limbs. They seemed stiff and the body felt cold. She sighed.

"I'm afraid it's dead."

She laid it on top of the cage but Philip took it up again, warming it in his hands.

All this time Jack said nothing. He now went back into the house and Lois realized that Philip was shivering in his thin pyjamas. She hugged him and he let himself be warmed by her, but still shielded the rabbit close to his chest, making a cup of his hands. The spring on the side door clicked and Jack reappeared, carrying a cardboard box. He began reaching into the cage and piling the tiny carcasses in one end.

"This is what she needed in the first place. A box, filled with grass. Should be wood, with a cover, actually. She would have burrowed in out of the cold and made a proper nest."

"How do you know about rabbits?"

"My dad kept some for a while when I was a kid. It used to be my job to feed them. I even know how to tell a boy from a girl, but I just took that woman's word." He stopped suddenly, as if remembering something. The yard was growing lighter and Lois could see the thoughtful look on his face. When he spoke again, his tone had changed. "I did know. Damn it, she told me. I had chosen a black one. She had told me it was a male. She'd told me earlier on that this white one was a doe and there was a chance it might be pregnant. I didn't listen because I was only interested in getting the male, and I was getting it on a whim anyway. Then at the last minute I changed my mind." He paused. "There were six or seven rabbits in there," he added, lamely.

The last body was removed. Jack shut the cage door. The hoarfrost was changing to dew and all of them were becoming cold, aware of wet feet. The mother rabbit watched them from a corner of the cage, her pink eyes expressionless. Nothing of the horror of the night showed in her behaviour, not even so much as a speck of her offspring's blood on her smooth white fur. If anything, Lois fancied that she looked relieved. When the cage door was firmly closed, the mother hopped over to her feed dish and began eating. Lois and Jack glanced at one another, caught by surprise sharing a moment of scandalized amusement.

"Philip had better come in."

"Well, how about you get him a sweater, and some boots. He and I have a job to do, haven't we, son? D'you think you could get the spade, Phil?"

Don't question it, Lois. Don't spoil it. Something of the tranquillity of her dream came back. She stepped into the warm kitchen and took Philip's heavy blue pullover from its peg. When she turned, she found that her son had come in behind her and stood, still holding the baby rabbit. He looked as if he had just seen something he was afraid to believe.

"Mom, I think it moved."

"Bring it under the light."

Silently they watched the little thing, waiting on it. Jack came to the door.

"Phil, where —"

"Just a second, Jack. He thinks he saw this one move."

Her husband came in and joined the intent circle under the light. A minute passed. The creature remained still.

"I'm afraid we've lost this one too, son." Jack's voice was gentle. "We'll have to put it in with the others. You see?" Jack laid his finger against the small body. A hind leg drew up slightly. "It's just a muscle, Phil. Even that is getting stiff. It's dead."

A tear slid down the boy's cheek. He set the little rabbit on the kitchen counter and began to struggle into the blue pullover.

"D'you want to come along, son? You don't have to: it's not a nice job."

Philip's voice was muffled but determined. "I'm coming, Dad. Let's get it over with."

His head popped through the top, the blond hair pulled straight and smooth as if he had been swimming. He moved toward the door. For the second time that morning, Jack and Lois's eyes met. Jack followed his son. The door clicked shut.

Alone in the kitchen, Lois soaped her hands at the sink, washing off the feeling of dead babies. Through the kitchen window, she could see white mist rising from the river. Near the muddy bank where Robbie had gathered his stones and shells, she could see her husband and her son speaking together as they went about their task.

Siren On The Shore

There had been a time when Kathleen's day did not stand or fall by that shadow at her window. Jamey, her son, would clamber down from the back of the couch in the living room, where he loved to stand to watch people go by, and toddle in delight to the kitchen door. Trevor would say, "Hey, fellow," swinging him into the air and down again, and then he would grin at her from Jamey's height, glad to be there, letting her know. She would close the door softly behind him, and plug in the kettle. She kept him for at least an hour, sitting with her at the table in a shaft of sunlight, laughing, arguing, until suddenly it was time for his next class and he would go. She rode out the wake of the silence. Her day hesitated, grew pale before it again opened out. Kathleen remembers sun as if there were no grey days that whole fall, and winter, and spring.

All of the hassles — deadlines, exhausting staff meetings, bright ideas, disagreements — all of the reasons for being together in the first place, have blurred now into a memory of the flash of his blue eyes, the determination of his mouth and chin — latterly (this would be after the move, when he and his girlfriend came to visit) with the softness of blond beard. He had always about him the air of an English schoolboy: red lips and cheeks, books strapped to his back before knapsacks became fashionable. Or a Swiss schoolboy, perhaps. Hadn't he mentioned spending part of his childhood in Switzerland? So much has faded. It is a short list of memories on which to hang the whole of a friendship.

In four of them she is objectified. She finds that curious, thinking about it now. She has the idea that other women pay attention to clothes, remember colour and style, whereas she believes she doesn't: her memories are of faces, feelings. Yet in four of the memories in this short list she knows what she wore, how she must have appeared to his eyes. In three of them she waited for that lifting of his brows, that appreciative smile. In the fourth she was naked, and hoped he did not see. She remembers the whiteness of her breasts as she reached across the bed for her clothes, the softness of her belly, the bluntness of her thighs. She hoped he hadn't come to the door of the bedroom when she called.

The first time that she wore the blue dress (with the matching band in her fair hair), she'd been sitting under a lamp in the lounge above the newspaper offices, and when he saw her there, when he came in for the meeting, he stopped short. "Well," he said, and there was that smile. What she remembers now is the feeling it gave her, that's all.

And the day before she moved, when she was wearing the faded orange Chinesey dress and he was helping her sweep up the office, what he said was something about her intelligence. "A person as intelligent as you." What was the context? She remembers his eyes. He had topped the dean's list himself each of his three years in university, his newspaper was winning prizes, and yet he admired her. She remembers his eyes; she remembers his smile.

"You live along this street like the sirens on the shore," he announced one fall day, shaking his head at her protesting jokes. He reached for a sheet of paper and drew a map, the newspaper offices at one corner, the residences at the end of the street, the classroom buildings two streets behind. All the lines ran through her. He labelled it: "*For the Record*: Communications Structure," and tacked it to the bulletin board over her kitchen table. Then he became interested in the other things on the board: lists of German verbs, groceries needed, a doctor's appointment for Jamey, an announcement of a wine and cheese party at the university that her husband Mike had suggested they might attend.

"Hey, look at all the connections! You could put a frame around it and call it 'Fragments of Kathleen.'"

"Why not 'Kathleen Integrated'?" she had asked, a little uneasily, looking over this collage of herself and glancing back and finding him watching her, eyes very blue, very bright. That moment she remembers, and the feeling again — that she was being admired, or recognized. She reacted by covering it with chatter. As usual he listened well.

On many visits he would remain silent a long time (while she ran on, rising in his presence to outrageous ideas, daring schemes), until suddenly he would laugh happily, reach for another piece of paper, and start to talk, drawing plans and diagrams, making decisions... the community editions of the newspaper, the anti-calendar, the columnists he chose to encourage or drop: *For the Record* had never been so good as it was the years Trevor was editor. Professors liked him, fellow students trusted him — and Kathleen found that she waited for him to begin her day, and that when he didn't come, which was most days, and she had her mid-morning cup of coffee alone, her day limped on from there. When he did come — sometimes, miraculously, three or four mornings in a row — her days lightened and flew. There were always important things to talk about: *For the Record* was in chronic financial and ethical crisis, not to mention the shortage of volunteers, or stories that hadn't come in, or tensions among the collective putting it out. Kathleen retains a memory of sunshine flooding through the ground-floor windows of her basement apartment, the shadow across the kitchen window, crunch of gravel and his rap at the door.

Sometimes, while they were still talking, George arrived, too, and a blizzard of messages would be interchanged. Other days George came later (Kathleen would make another cup of coffee), or Gillian dashed in, or Rosemary. Or Amos, from Nigeria, or Jane. And Mike, dear husband, arriving home for lunch or after work would find them in the midst of some prolonged and heated discussion, and would put down his briefcase and join in.

Sometimes it was almost too much, getting meals ready, keeping dates and deadlines straight, changing Jamey for the umpteenth time, and trying to finish the next chapter of her thesis in time for her weekly meeting with her thesis director. Because that was the year, in addition to her part-time job as resource-person-cum-general-factotum for the newspaper, that she finished her postgraduate studies in German, tried to keep the apartment clean, and got her son into training pants. She was not exactly a bored housewife with nothing to do but project escapist fantasies onto one of her friends.

Yet it happened. One morning Trevor was no longer like George, or Amos or Rosemary or John. She waited for him. She put off taking Jamey to the park until she saw whether he came. She rearranged her day so the professor she was to interview would be seen in the afternoon, after Jamey's nap. When the milkman made a shadow across her kitchen window, she jumped — and proceeded to notice that her day had gone into orbit around Trevor's going and coming. Kathleen felt foolish. I have a crush, she thought, an adolescent crush. She wondered why this was happening, how it could happen at all to a happily married woman. Something must be wrong, she thought, chalking it up to an aberrant hormone, and keeping it deadly secret, from Mike, from Trevor, from any friend. Even, partly, from herself.

So that she wonders now whether it was really the force of her thesis that held her at the kitchen table in her dressing gown one morning, writing until the shadow fell and Trevor appeared, unexpectedly, it seemed, catching her in this state of undress, causing her to feel uncomfortable as she let him in. She wasn't going to let him go now he was here. "Come in, come in," she said, and he did, but with a quizzical look to which she had to reply. "I'm going to get dressed," she said, confusedly, holding the top of her gown closed with one hand. "Will you make the coffee?" He knew where things were.

Then, a few moments later, when Jamey toddled into the bedroom, leaving the door wide open, she panicked (she thought) and called, "Trevor! Don't come in!" backing ass-end into the dresser and reaching across the bed for underwear. "Pardon," he asked, and sounded very near. "Don't come in!" Never looking up as she hurried into her clothes. So she never knew, for sure, what happened at this moment in her life. Considering the noise of the kettle and the fact of the wide-open door, why hadn't she called, "Stay out!" instead of "Come in!" — even a "Don't!"? Why had she felt a need to call out anything at all? And why on earth, in retrospect, was it that the whole idea of his seeing her naked seemed so momentous, so irrevocably compromising? She forgot the incident, of course, as soon as it was over. She had to. They drank coffee, they talked. After awhile he came less often.

One day he mentioned he was nineteen. "How old did you think I was?" he asked. She tried to meet his eyes without letting him see her shock. He had seemed older, so competent, so quick. Kathleen was twenty-six. I have been in love with a teenager, she thought. For a moment shame made it difficult to continue the conversation.

Later, she attempted to recall some of the secret excitement which had formed the background to her days. She fantasized a bit about being an older woman to him, teaching him, then shook that off. She thought about Mike, and about their marriage and little son and even, with a giggle, about the sirens along the shore who (she had looked them up), if they failed to charm a man, turned into rocks. And if they just let a few sail by? she asked herself. Ships in the night? Or gave up sirening altogether and did some other thing, voyaging inland, testing other powers? She imagined those sirens getting into safari suits and pith helmets and hacking their way through the bush. Where would they come out, if they once dared leave the shore? She would make up her own myths as she went along. She was trying commitment, she thought, staying with it, finding out what's on the other side of the rainforest. There were unconfirmed rumours of a different kind of love, not the teenage excitement she had rediscovered in her conversations with Trevor. A love that grows slowly through the years.

She was wearing her antique crimson silk dressing gown with the golden dragon down the back, she had bothered to brush out her hair, which had grown long, and she knew perfectly well the effect of the silk over her bottom and her fair hair loose on the red. She and Mike were living in a house by this time and she was older: it was after the move. Jamey was four; Betty was an infant; Trevor had grown the beard. He and the girlfriend had laid out their zip-together sleeping bag in the guest room in the basement and he was on his way downstairs to go to bed. Kathleen had turned busily away, mixing orange juice for the morning. Trevor paused. He ran his hand over her hair.

"It's very nice."

Kathleen headed for the fridge with the juice, returning his look with the warm smile of innocent friendship. It really was so good to see him again.

The summer after Trevor and his girlfriend finally got married and moved to the Maritimes, she and Mike received a letter from him, several pages of tight script. It seemed as if he wanted to fill them in on everything that was happening to them, on everything they were thinking and doing. Kathleen never did answer that letter properly, partly because she had felt puzzled. He'd told too much — more, in a way, than they wanted to know, although most of it was interesting. Also, she was still very busy.

Lately she has thought about it again, turning over the short list of memories. She suspects that now she almost understands. It was easy to stop feeling the way that she did, once she knew he was so young. And she has not grown into a rock. Perhaps they could have been friends. But they were friends. Yet what sort of friendship is it that disappears so completely with the passing of time? Something more had begun. That was what could not be, had no place, turned itself into a siren's enchantment, broken with laughter and chatter and cups of coffee and juice. It could not be, there was no spot for it, not there, not then, there was no shore.

Heinlein's Death

Mr. and Mrs. Bentham like to step out for breakfast. It breaks the domestic monotony, the conservative flow of their early mornings — although George makes delectable pancakes at home, and Sarah rarely breaks the yolk of a good fried egg. Breakfast out gives them a sense of naughtiness, a rendezvous after who knows what interesting night. It doesn't occur to them that of course they are unmistakably long-married; the companionable silences give them away. In this instance, George has lost himself in contemplation of a grainy blown-up photograph of Marilyn Monroe at the back of the restaurant: saucy, mischievous, young, leaning toward the camera, all bosom, black lace and long bare legs. Sarah, facing the other way, has her ear cocked to the news.

"Heinlein is dead," Sarah reports.

George looks pleased. "Are you sure?"

"Yes, I think so. They said 'heart attack' and 'author of *Stranger in a Strange Land.*'"

"Well, I'll mention it then to the grade twelves. Do you remember the book at all?"

"Grokking."

"Did you say something? It sounded like 'grokking.'"

"Some kind of ESP communication, I think it was."

"Sarah, what are we talking about?"

"*Stranger in a Strange Land*!"

"Oh. I lost you. You didn't introduce it clearly or something. You left out the verb."

"It was when I said 'grokking.'"

"I'm sorry, it sounded as if you said 'grokking.'"

"Yes some kind of ESP communication, I think. Sort of the opposite of what we're doing right now."

Sarah stirs her coffee, smiling, vaguely frustrated, scolding herself: It's just the way men think; it's silly to be mad.

"If only you wouldn't keep handing me a non sequitur," George complains, "and would put your verbs in. What I was wondering was whether it's safe for me to recommend it to grade twelve."

"I think so. But there may have been a lot of sex in that book. I forget. I get it confused in my memory with *The Harrad Experiment*. They must have come out around the same time. A completely different kind of book. You said at the time that *The Harrad Experiment* was 'just a skin book.' I can still hear you saying it. I remember I was hurt; I thought you just didn't understand."

"But now you know I was right." He smiles. She admires the nice wrinkles he is getting beside his eyes.

She can see he doesn't remember the incident, or the book in question, at all.

"You probably *were* right. My dear, that was nearly twenty years ago. Anyhow, I think we have at least one of Heinlein's books still kicking around the house. If we get back in time this morning, maybe I can find it and use a piece from it with grade ten. We're doing science fiction right now."

"Well, if it's got sex in it, watch it. You know what your principal and mine did to that poor bugger who tried to teach *The Diviners*. I figure I'm safe with the twelves."

"I do like the way you draw the kids' attention to authors who have died. Didn't you bring Morley Callaghan's books in last month?"

"Sarah, the good ones are all going. But it marks the passing of time. I like to drag their names into the classroom, pay some small tribute."

"Well it happens to be good educational theory too, sweetie. Remember when we taught in Labrador when we were first married and Robert Frost died? I brought his poem 'Birches' into class: 'I'd like to go by climbing a birch tree.' There's a dramatic quality: somebody who was alive a few hours ago suddenly goes to join the dead authors in books. It shows they were all alive once too. I still remember that Robert Frost lesson, and I bet some of the kids do too."

"Don't count on it. But I admit I remember when I was a student and the professor came in almost in a state of shock and told us that Camus had been killed in a car crash." He opens the package of orange marmalade and takes some out on his knife. "If I died, would you work me into your lesson plan?"

It is one of those questions. Like "Do you still love me?" Mrs. Bentham hesitates a heartbeat, then finds she can improvise.

"Why, certainly, George, my love. 'Former head of this very English Department,' I'd say. The day after your death I'd come in early and get Jenny in the office to run off copies of your love poems so we could compare them with Michael Jackson's songs and Madonna in grade ten. I'd show the students that you had a superior grasp of diction."

"Love poems? To Jenny?"

Sarah chuckles. "No, no, no, to me! But I'll get the ones you wrote to Jenny, too, later, when we put together your collected works. I didn't actually realize you had written love poems to anyone but me. I'll send out a memorandum: 'For a Collected Works: all staff members with love poems from George Bentham please send in copies to his widow. Prize offered for best poem.'"

"What will the prize be?"

"Your Mazda."

"WHAT?!"

"Oh hello George, I see you're back! They said you were dead!"

The Benthams burst out laughing.

"Sarah," says George, his attention veering off again into Marilyn's cleavage, "are these love poems from when I was courting you that you're planning to share with your slowest class?"

"Only when you're gone, sweetheart. No. I don't remember that you wrote me any then. I was thinking of that time in Burnaby."

"Burnaby?"

He doesn't remember, Sarah thinks. Well, it's too bright a morning to remind him.

"Never mind. You write a mean department memo, too: we could collect those. The grade tens hate poetry anyhow, but they might appreciate a nice useful memo. Right now none of them believe they may actually have to read and write to hold down jobs."

"So when I'm gone you'll encourage your remedial grade

tens to apply for my job?"

"My dear. You know you are irreplaceable. We will bronze your job and mount it on the wall of the English office, we'll light candles in front of it, and then run the department as a collective with, yes, input from my grade tens."

She follows his gaze.

"And Marilyn's dead too. Isn't it weird that her body when she was young, not to mention alive, is still being used to sell breakfasts?"

"She doesn't look dead to me."

"Neither do you, sweet — I won't give away your Mazda yet."

The waitress brings their bill.

"I think I invited you this morning," observes Sarah, pulling out her change purse. It doesn't really matter who pays the bill; this is just one of the little ways the Benthams have of pretending they are still dating, that their love is new, they have not been married for twenty-seven years, with grown children, and ambiguities and old pain behind every word they exchange.

Out on the street, heading for the Mazda, George picks up the fantasy once more.

"And this collective: you'd name it after me, of course?"

"Of course. The Bentham Memorial Collective. They'd all have to wear little Colour-Your-World caps."

"Colour Your World?"

"Like yours, dear: grunge and paint stains and those little threads hanging down? I'll have replicas made."

George smiles fondly.

"Sarah, you're such a romantic."

He stops her for a kiss in front of a vintage clothing store. Their lips brush, almost meet. George holds open the Mazda door. Sarah flips her skirt as she slides in.

"I feel remarkably fresh for having been up all night."

"Just so long as your husband doesn't find out."

"Oh? Not him! He writes science fiction and lives in a dream world. To him I'm just a maiden from another planet who drifts in and out."

"I wonder if it's really like that," says George. "For a writer, I mean."

"Why not? Everyone else does."

George looks puzzled.

"You did it again, Sarah. I think it was a preposition this time. Could you say it again and put in the preposition?"

Erotica

Agnes sees Danny step out from behind the stacks the moment she locks the bookstore door, but she pretends she doesn't and goes on totalling the cash and putting things away. It's better like this, going slowly, thinking about what is going to happen in a few minutes when she goes down to the basement.

"Hey, Aggie."

"Danny — were you there all the time?"

"Yeah, you know, I hung around. Okay if I look around some more while you finish up? I'm going your way."

Danny lives in the Glebe like she does, she thinks, checking this offer against facts. Only down by the canal, so it makes sense that he might walk over there with her after they are both finished work. But she thinks he gets off before she does. He's never offered to walk home with her before.

So here she is down in the basement and she's hiding the money and entering her hours and subtracting the cost of two books she's going to take from the running account of her wages and she hears Danny coming down the stairs. He gives her a grin from over there by the steps but then goes serious and tender and keeps on coming to her; she steps toward him too. He is laughing as they meet and his arms slide around her and their bodies pull tight and warm against each other. His curly hair brushes her face — she is startled and moved at how soft it is. His whiskery chin rubs rough against her cheek and then that's Danny's soft mouth on hers, and his tongue is in her mouth. She tears herself away from him and goes and turns off the blazing light. The switch is at the bottom of the stairs.

"I like to have it dark down here, Danny," she whispers boldly into the black cellar. "I like to turn off the light when I dream about you."

She hears his voice, not very far away, a little tremble in it. "This ain't no dream, Aggie."

Then they are back together and he's got the front of her slacks unzipped and he's sliding his hand in there and she's doing the same to him, ripping at those stud fasteners on his jeans and —

Agnes comes, knees gone unsteady, body collapsing across a table whose sharp corner is wedged into her crotch. Suddenly a sob shakes through her. She moves into the padded office chair near the table and, gasping, she holds herself and rocks as the waves of the orgasm return, clench, diminish. Why do I weep when I come, she wonders, otherwise reasonably satisfied with the way she is handling her sex life. If anything is going to really happen between her and Danny — and she feels a lovely wave of weakness again thinking maybe, maybe something *will* — maybe it's *started* already — then it won't be because she couldn't stand it anymore, it won't be because she has turned into a repressed old maid, she won't be driven into it. She is just fine. And if Danny gets driven, well, anyhow, she'd like that.

Agnes sits in the dark laughing at herself. This is either awful or it's wonderful, but it seems to her that it works. She doesn't know how other people handle it.

She remembers the moment when he brought over a book to show her today in the store, and the way his front curl fell into his eyes as he teased her about carrying a book that had illustrations to the *Kama Sutra*. He had it open to some sexy drawing — sexy in Hindu terms anyhow — a line drawing of a couple coupling in an odd position. The penis looked thin and snakelike and the vagina was carefully and unrealistically drawn, looking like a sort of pitcher plant seeking whom it might devour. She had already told him — they sure get into talking sex a lot if nothing is really happening — another day, the hilarious story about the time when she had a serious literary window display during National Book Week of books which at one time or place or another had been banned, and a policeman came into the store. He spent ages looking at the pictures in the Time-Life *Encyclopedia of Sex*, which she just happened to have displayed on the centre table. She explained to Danny, since he had started to smirk and, she thought, miss the point, that a secondhand bookstore is often going to have a few books on sex, but is not necessarily always going to have the whole damned *Encyclopedia of Sex*, with coloured pictures yet. It had just been a coincidence. But anyway, it was Time-Life, right? Very, very clean. And then, after her nerves had been put thoroughly on edge by this lengthy perusal of these very clean pictures of clean naked people, which were getting to seem more and more risqué to her the longer he spent over it, the policeman had come up to the desk and asked her whether those really were banned books in the window. She started to explain, and when she got to the thing about Homer's Odyssey, which Plato didn't want in his ideal republic, he suddenly interrupted her and said, "Oh, so it's a joke!" It wasn't at all, but she had blushed and agreed that yes, of course, it was a joke.

Danny hadn't seemed to understand. Probably she had explained it all wrong. When she is talking with Danny, she tends to chatter. At any moment he might drift away. She always wants to make it last as long as she can. Probably she's really obvious. Certainly he seems to enjoy teasing her, leading her on. Maybe he's just flirting; maybe he has a girlfriend who likes bicycles. All the time Agnes is talking to him, she watches him, noting details: the wayward way his eyebrows grow, the particular curlicues of his particular ears, the exact twitch of his lips when he smiles. She looks as much as she can, too, at his hands. Later, at night, in the basement, she runs her tongue into his particular ears, smooths his eyebrows with her fingertips and kisses, creeps up a thousand different ways on that moment of the meeting of their lips.

She had been engaged in this business of taking notes on him today when he suddenly came over with that rare leatherbound *Kama Sutra* in his hands, kidding her about it and threatening to call in the cops. She almost missed the part where he ran his broad fingers over the leather and said what he did about skin. Now it comes back to her and she sits shivering, uncertain whether in pleasure or pain.

"A good thing to have around," he said mischievously, his fingers caressing its spine, running back and forth across the covers. "Keeps a guy from wanting to touch the wrong thing, eh? Can't have that. And hey, Aggie, did they know what they were doing in those days or what? Covering the — cof, cof — *Kama Sutra* with ni-ice smoo-o-oth skin."

She had laughed too merrily, some part of herself — the primitive part, she thinks — mesmerized by his fingers, memorizing them as they moved on the smooth leather and returned to move across it again.

There is a faint blue light from a front basement window which lets onto the street through cobwebs and years of grime. The desks and filing cabinets are heavy presences, felt rather than seen. Under the stairs is opaque with piled boxes filled with used books. Agnes likes to have a backlog of about a month under the stairs, and she has it now. In the morning she will pick out one box to carry upstairs with her, while she balances the money drawer from the cash register on top. She likes to choose at random: it is like Christmas, opening the box and not remembering which one it is, what is inside. She doesn't own this store, but she runs it, and on evenings like this, when outside it may be still light but down here it is dark, she feels her spirit flow out into all the hidden crannies of the basement. This is her space. She spends more waking hours in this store than in her bachelor apartment in the Glebe.

It's time to switch the light back on, collect her sweater and her carryall bag, and go back up into the store. When she came down she had been pretending that Danny was there; now she gives a proprietorial glance down the aisles, to be certain that in reality no one is lingering in the shadows. But she's alone. She dims the lights and starts to leave, then pauses beside the desk. That *Kama Sutra*. She goes back to the erotica section above "scarce and rare" and takes the smooth leatherbound volume off the shelf. It feels warm in her hands. Her fingers move on the spine. She slips it into her carryall bag, along with the two other books she has paid for. This one is much too expensive to own, but she wants to keep it near her, just for a few hours. Agnes goes out into the warm summer night.

The owners, Jim and Nancy Bright, are expected soon. Nancy called today. Agnes had been in a funny space when she had found it was Nancy on the phone. It was right after Danny had left the store. That's partly why the incident with him fondling — that really was the right word for it — him fondling the leather book in front of her like that — it *has* to mean something; he's being so *blatant*, isn't he? Or is she just overreacting? — Anyway, that's why she forgot it for awhile. She had started right away to dash around getting the store tidied, phoning people who had books on hold, and getting the books she had just priced out on display. She always does these things, she's very conscientious, but she speeds up when she knows that Jim and Nancy are coming to town. They are nice people. She's not sure about her relationship to them: more like a kind of substitute daughter, she thinks, than a manager. They had been so quick to hire her that day she had banged on the papered-over window of the empty store and found them inside, painting and putting up shelves. They live in Toronto and run another bookstore near the university. They have a manager there as well, since they like to spend their time travelling in search of books. They have been down to New England recently, to a book fair, and then they flew to San Francisco and did some buying there. So it is always Christmas Plus when their van pulls up outside. They will have new stock for the rare section, always exciting new titles and bindings that none of them has ever seen before. Agnes has learned the official definition of "rare" in the rare book business: it is a book which a person active in the trade doesn't see in ten years. As Agnes has been active in the trade now for only two years, she supposes she's not yet qualified to identify a truly rare book. But she is certainly getting the idea.

Persons, now, persons she feels better qualified to pronounce upon. Persons parade past her all day in this business: housewives, students, collectors with their odd fixations and often odder appearance, ordinary bookbuyers in search of a good read, scholars in search of anything in their area, the more abstruse the better. Some of these people are rare. In the context of the customers who choose to shop in her store, Danny is not only rare: he's exotic. He has worked at the Bike Shop only since the spring. He's a roamer, a traveller: he has ridden a bicycle, by his account, through the Sudan. He has backpacked in the Himalayas. He has bicycled from the tip of Italy's boot to the north of France. He knows bikes better than she knows books. But he reads books, too: that combination she has found irresistible. And he's good-looking, with an Irish grin and those unruly curls. Danny, Danny, Danny. *Take me with you, Danny.*

He would turn up like this, walking by her side. He would just happen to bump into her a bit as he turned her corner with her, walking her way and not toward his own digs. "Invite a guy in for a cup of coffee? Eh? Eh? How about it?" Teasing her, making it easy, and then when they were inside. . . .

Agnes had lucked into this job. It had actually started at the Bike Shop, a long time before Danny showed up. She had taken her bicycle in for its spring checkup and overheard the guys saying that a used bookstore was about to open down the street. She didn't know yet then that she was a bookseller, just that she had a brand-new useless degree in English Literature, a longstanding interest in old books, and no enthusiasm for becoming a librarian, no excitement in the idea of going back to university and finding a specialty. She thought that she liked being a generalist. What she really wanted was for somebody to pay her to read all day. But it turned out that what she was was a bookseller. Everything she knows turns out to be useful in the store in some way or another. And as part of the job she gets to read bits of every interesting book that comes past. She reads publisher's blurbs on dust jackets. She reads chapter one or whatever chapter the book falls open to as she tries to figure out what it is. She reads enough of it to ascertain a price. Then she is to close it and move on — but if she simply can't, then it has to go on the pile of books she hopes to read in the store in her breaks, or might indeed have to own. An occupational hazard, that, the acquisition of books. Jim and Nancy give her a generous discount, and nearly every day Agnes deducts the price of a book or two from her small salary. She is busy and happy from day's beginning to day's end. When Danny came into the store and her life she just added a layer of erotic fantasy to everything else. She seems to have room for it. Everything is under control.

Except what is this very expensive rare leatherbound book doing under her pillow, and will she remember in the morning to take it back to work?

It's raining in the morning and maybe because of the greyness she sleeps in a bit, so she has to rush. She remembers the book when she's halfway to the store, and if she goes back for it now she'll have to open late. It won't be missed for one day; she keeps on going. Then from down the street she sees that the sandwich board is out, and the truck of reduced books. The owners' van is parked in front and they have already opened the store. It's a surprise that upsets her a little: she feels as if it's a criticism. But it can't be. She's right on time, and everything (except for one wandering book) is in place and under control.

Except her day goes sort of downhill from there.

Nancy has her long skirt on and her brown hair with thick strands of gray loose around her chubby face. She is in her elegant, or academic, mode, rather than the old-hippie laid-back mode that seems to come with the braid and the oversized jeans. Nancy asks Agnes about the *Kama Sutra* the moment she walks in. There is a nice welcoming smell of coffee in the air as Agnes wipes her wet feet on the mat and thinks what to say.

"I know where it is," she says to her boss, and heads for the basement as if she is going for it, but really to get off her raincoat and think about what to say next. It's embarrassing. Why did she take it home? It's only the world's most famous sexy book and it's only worth three hundred and fifty dollars and she has only slept with it under her pillow all night. She decides that the story is that she had an overwhelming urge to take it home with her last night, that this has never happened to her before, and hope that her employers' own irrational love for a fine binding will see her through.

"Yo! Agnes!" Jim Bright, a big red-bearded bear of a man, is downstairs tenderly pulling books out of the boxes he has unloaded and arranging them for pricing on the basement shelves. He wraps her in a big hug, then steps back and looks at her. "You're even more beautiful! This business is good for you!" He gives her a big wink and goes back to work. She feels self-conscious as she takes off her coat and combs her hair and slips into her shoes. These visits are always exciting, but for awhile she loses her sense of being in charge. It is sort of like Mommy and Daddy coming home. And now this time she has something to feel guilty about, dammit.

Jim is unpacking some leather bindings, and with a considerable feeling of subterfuge she begins exclaiming over them from across the room and hurries over to them, lifting them and stroking them sensuously as Danny did yesterday. She even throws in a mention of skin.

Jim is smiling at her affectionately. "Speaking of skin," he says, "did you sell that full-leather *Kama Sutra*? We've got a customer for it."

"Yeah... no... Nancy was asking me about it upstairs." Here it comes. For a moment she has a wild story about some customer of her own, someone who wanted to see it in their own home . . . no, she's deep enough in as it is.

"I'm sorry, Jim, and I'm feeling stupid, but I took it home last night and I forgot to bring it back this morning. I never do this. It's just such a nice binding, I couldn't let it go last night. We can just get it from my place whenever you want."

Jim is looking at her very oddly. "I didn't remember that the pictures are that good," he says finally.

Agnes feels herself flush. "They aren't! I mean . . . . "

Her employer roars with laughter and she escapes upstairs. It's still embarrassing, but it looks as if she's going to get away with it.

Nancy takes it a little more seriously. "Well, it can't sell if it's not on the shelf," she says first, reprovingly. And then: "My God, Agnes, what if you'd got rain on it? Those leather bindings are fragile!" She waves her beringed hands and stands with them posed in the air dramatically. "You can bring it in tomorrow, I guess. We'll still be in town." Suddenly she drops her hands onto Agnes's shoulders and a dimple shows in her cheek: "So anyway, Aggie, did you look at it? Did you learn anything you didn't know? Huh?"

She is rescued by a brisk step at the entrance. Danny strides in. Agnes nods to him and begins shelving books. To Nancy she gives a wry look intended as a response. With a customer in the store, she is let off the hook: the usual rituals begin. Nancy disappears down the stairs to work with her husband and Agnes prices and sorts and shelves and takes care of the till.

"Hey, Aggie."

She jumps. Somehow in her abstraction he has come right in behind the desk.

"Danny. You made me jump."

He grins and shakes his head at her. She notes that there is a place on his crown where his hair stands straight up. And one of his teeth is a little crooked. And he's standing too close.

He takes a step back. In an exaggerated whisper, he asks, "Are those your bosses down there? The fat lady and the bearded man?"

She nods in delight, opening her eyes wide at him and pointing at the floor. It's easy to hear through there. He leans on her counter with an air of conspiracy. Still speaking in a low voice, Danny says, "Do you ever go dancing, then, Aggie?" It might be an invitation; it might just be a question.

"I'm — I'm not very good at it."

"Ah, well, then, my little chickadee — I'd better be getting to work."

He opens the door. She smells the rain. He closes it behind him. He is gone. She stares after him. Wait. She grabs her sweater from the back of the chair, puts it over her head and walks out onto the sidewalk in front of the store. She looks down the street toward the Bike Shop. Already he has disappeared. Agitatedly, she starts after him, but the rain is coming down hard, and then she thinks he must have gone the other way, and starts back. In a moment she comes to her senses and goes back into the store. The telephone is ringing, and Nancy is answering it.

But I never do this, Agnes thinks of saying to her, for the second time already that day. I never do. I don't think that I do. But Nancy says mildly, "Were you checking the reduced table? I was afraid it might be getting wet!" And goes back downstairs.

For the rest of the day, Agnes tries to be sensible. It is hard. The layer of erotic fantasy has been replaced by a searing pain in her gut. Danny asked her out and she didn't say yes. Her love is down the street and she doesn't know how to get to him. But maybe he didn't ask her out. Maybe it was just a conversation about dancing. In the abstract. Maybe something happened. Maybe it didn't.

The owners finish their sorting in the afternoon and go off to check the other bookstores in town. They say that they'll be back in the morning to pick up the book. They say not to worry: she's doing fine. The store returns to being hers, but she still feels as if she is a stranger suddenly. About five o'clock, as the rush-hour traffic is pouring down the street, she looks out and she sees Danny bicycling by on the other side of the street, heading home. She still has another hour. And anyway, maybe nothing happened.

Maybe her whole life is nothing happening.

She gets to six o'clock. She brings in the book truck and the sandwich board and locks the door and does the till and goes down to the basement and turns off the light.

Look Danny. Just once more. Just once more let me believe that you've stayed behind in the store. But I don't believe. I saw you going home an hour ago. But maybe he came back. She never has done this before, but she slips upstairs and unlocks the door. Just for a few minutes. Just so that, if Danny happened to come back to look for her, he could get in. Just so she can believe.

"Hey, Aggie."

At first she still can't quite believe that it's him. But his hands going so familiarly to her breasts convinces her. She stands against the corner of the table, starting to believe. After awhile she just reaches up under her skirt and pulls her panties down partway. She pretends that Danny has done this. Grief hits her like a flash flood and a sound like a sob bursts from her as she comes. The basement light blazes on. There had not, of course, been any sound of a key.

Agnes collapses rumpled into the padded office chair. She wipes at her tears with her hands while one more spasm shakes her body, beyond her control. She stares into the face of Nancy, who is approaching her with surprise and concern.

"I thought you were gone... But the door was unlocked... Is something wrong, kid?"

Nancy's arms are around her. Sweaty, feeling as if she stinks of sex, Agnes stands up weakly into the embrace. With one hand she scrabbles at her panties through her skirt. Nancy kisses her cheek and then Nancy's lips are soft and then hard on her mouth. Nancy's tongue is in her mouth. Nancy's hand is under her skirt, has found the panties still at half-mast. Agnes does sort of know what is happening, but it seems too late to protest.

"God," Nancy is saying, "I... I'm sorry, Aggie. I didn't mean... I mean, I had these fantasies, I admit it, but I'd never, I never intended... Aggie, did I take advantage of you? Oh God, I'm sorry. I think I did."

Agnes always maintained afterwards that she didn't quit her job just because of that incident. She claimed it had been the best job that she was ever going to have, although time proved this not to be the case. She said there was a personal reason why she just didn't want to be seen in the store anymore. And neither Jim nor Nancy could budge her.

It was awkward for them, her quitting like that. Jim had to stay on in Ottawa for a couple of weeks to run the store while he interviewed and then trained somebody from the long line of overqualified people who always are longing to work in a bookstore. The way some of them think of it is: to be in a bookstore after it's locked for the night!

The only really odd thing was that they never could get that book back. Agnes kept saying that she'd bring it by, but she never did. Jim finally threatened to take her to court, but Nancy persuaded him to just drop it. She said that it was just one of those things, that Agnes probably couldn't have explained it herself.

The Personals

In the course of their move, Rick Harvey became very involved with his post office box. It had a key, his only remaining key. Even his car key was gone, along with the old Pontiac itself, to a used car lot. Their last night in Vancouver, he and Pam stayed with friends. Their house in Kitsilano was in the possession of its new owners. The furniture and dishes and even the files from Rick's desk were in storage in containers under the moving company's own locks and seals. All Rick had for his possessions was one tiny piece of paper, a receipt. And the post box key. At the back of his leather writing case there was a pocket with a zipper. He stuck the key and the receipt in there, and carried the case everywhere he went. At good-bye parties in Vancouver before they left, Rick waved the key at his friends and joked about the new address:

"Hey, it'll be small quarters and kind of cramped at first, but we'll get used to it. They say there's zero point one percent vacancy rate in Ottawa, so we might be in there for quite a while. Meanwhile, we're saving money, right? The rent's only eighty bucks a year."

But then he had a dream about that, about living inside of the post office box. He and Pam kept slipping on the shiny metal floor. When they stepped out on the balcony this box had in the dream, he could see that it was a sheer drop of many storeys to the ground.

Rick paid attention to his dreams. It was something he had learned from his friend Ann, whereas Pamela never could remember hers. He wished he could just drive on over to Ann's and tell her about this dream, but the reason he was reduced to the post box in the first place was that Ann had moved. She had crossed the country to Ottawa and he was following her. In two weeks he would hold her in his arms again. Only for a moment, only as a greeting. But even after all these years Rick liked to imagine things going on from there, one thing leading to another, Pam conveniently busy someplace else. Ann would be settled in by now; she could make tea; he was already planning to bring brandy in the flask she had given him the first Christmas after they met. Brandy in hot lemon tea was a ritual: he remembered sneaking it to her even in the hospital when she had her last attack, the one that finished off her eyesight and left her blind. This dream about living in the tiny box with Pam was troubling him. The more he thought about it, the dicier it seemed. At any moment they would be in danger of being crushed by the incoming mail, and the key was not going to work from inside.

Of course it was just an anxiety dream. He was feeling insecure because they didn't have a house. At least when Ann had arrived she had gone straight to a definite place, a co-op building with some disabled people in it; she had lucked into a semi-private room with wheelchair accessibility and with help from her family had moved in her stuff. Family had been her main reason for leaving British Columbia: she had a married brother in Ottawa and a sister in Kingston. The decision had not come easily, but when it did, she had been very clear. She had a disease of her neurological system; it was progressive; she needed help. She wrote letters on the voice output computer that she had bought two years before with her severance pay; she made long-distance calls; when she decided that it was the right thing, she packed up and went.

In their last time together she showed Rick some of her poems. This was for them a role reversal. Ann had listened to many of Rick's poems over the years, and had always asked to hear more. She had encouraged him and made suggestions. The fact that his poetry often referred to a sense of disappointment in his marriage had never been discussed directly between them. But Ann let her hand linger in his at greetings and partings, and she never let him leave without mentioning when they might get together again. Rick was her main remaining connection to the world of editing and publicity releases where they had first met, where they had worked together on a campaign for United Way. He could remember her as a woman who could walk and who, although she wore glasses with thick lenses, could still see. She had always had a quick, shy smile and long, curling dark hair. As well, she had a knack for getting him to talk about himself. But he had not mentioned his secret life until one particular day when, at coffee break, Ann had unsnapped her briefcase and slapped on the table a year-end report from one of the banks downtown. Inside it, hidden like a subversive document — which for Rick it was — there was a literary magazine with one of Rick's poems.

"Guy in here with the same name as you," said Ann. "He's good."

It turned out that she was an avid reader of literary magazines. She went to readings whenever she could. She had a collection of books signed by Canadian authors she admired.

"I'm the original literary groupie."

"But do you write anything yourself?"

"Maybe. I play around a bit at poetry. But seriously, this is a nice piece." She told him what she liked about it. By the end of the coffee break, they were deep into a discussion of metaphor, rhythm, whether anything serious could be said about deconstruction, and the ideas in an article Ann had just read about natural stresses inside of sentences.

A world opened. In this world Rick Harvey was not a crass guy who wrote advertising copy, never mind that it was usually for benign social service agencies, but a sensitive type, a poet. He began attending readings, with Ann as his critic, cheering section and friend. He invited her for dinner, and she and Pam got along really well.

Pam had never been much good at appreciating literature: she was too practical. She was a social worker and in some ways Rick felt he was one of her projects. It wasn't a bad feeling. At least he knew where he was. He was loved by Pamela with a steady, slightly maternal love that never seemed to falter, even when he fell in love with other women, which had happened now on several occasions. He never acted on these infatuations: he just mooned about and wrote more poems. This was the first time he had actually made friends with the object of his obsession. Pamela remained unthreatened. After dinner, on the evenings that Ann came over, Pam would go off to their bedroom, where she had a desk, and happily lose herself in her own paperwork, leaving her husband and his good friend to their intense conversations.

When Ann was hospitalized, both of them went round to see her, at different times. Pamela never saw the poems that Rick was writing at this time, and although Ann did, she confined her comments to the shape of a metaphor or a question about the number of beats in a line. She had brought a tape recorder with her and Rick knew she was struggling with some work of her own, but she would never show it to him.

So on the last night, when she drew out the folder and handed it over, he felt admitted to a new intimacy. He sat reading silently, feeling that he had to get this right, but increasingly uncertain what to say. They were all about her body, about the breakdown of the reflexes she had come to count on. He had hoped for maybe something about himself, some reference to love or even friendship, or the grief of saying good-bye. Instead these were about stumbling and falling down, about having to ask strangers for help. There were poems about wetting the bed and poems about the mess and futility of her menstrual periods. There was no hope in them: they were all statements of loss. She made a sound; he looked up to find her smiling.

"It's a metaphor," she said. "Come on, Rick. 'Illness as Metaphor'; we've talked about it enough. Anyway, what do you think? Did you get to the one yet on wheelchair maintenance? Is it too shrill? I feel a hell of a lot better every time I finish one of these. Maybe it's just therapy. . . . "

He set out to reassure her. The poems made him uneasy and he didn't understand some of them, but he had no trouble giving her praise. Together they made some changes. He offered to send them out for her, and in the ensuing weeks, he did. It was hard to fit it in with all the rest he was doing, applying for jobs in Ontario, persuading Pam that it was time that they shook up their lives and made a fresh start somewhere else. They needed to play around a bit with insecurity, he argued. He made no secret of the fact that it was the absence of Ann that was suddenly making Vancouver seem to him like such a dumb place to live. Pamela humoured him, but at first she wouldn't budge. Mid-life crisis, she said. Then he got an offer of a job editing government reports, and the salary was almost twice what they had been making together. It meant that Pam could cut back on her caseload and do some work that she really wanted to do. She would have preferred to do it where she was, but she began to make her own inquiries. Almost right away she was hired for a women's shelter, which suddenly made her dissatisfied with her own work and anxious to get into this thing that she felt might make a real difference.

Ann's poems went out in batches and during the six months that she and Rick lived at different ends of the country five were accepted. One magazine actually sent payment. Rick had never had this kind of response. He told Ann excitedly about it on the cassette tapes he was sending her, keeping her up to date on his news. In the same period of time she sent two letters to him. She said that she was very pleased that he and Pam were coming, and had a friend, some fellow in the house where she was living, draw a map for them of where she lived. She also got her brother to recommend a good real estate agent.

The night after Rick sent his last cassette to her, he had the post box dream. He couldn't tell her about it, even on tape, because the tape recorder, along with the air mattresses and a few last pots and pans and plates, had just been packed into one last cardboard box and shipped to the new address. When they got to Ottawa, the real estate woman that Ann's brother had lined up had appointments for them the very same afternoon. The woman actually met their plane. He joked with the agent about his silly dream. He discovered that he had entered a very strange space: all his known world was left behind.

It was almost a week before he finally saw Ann again. He had phoned, of course, the minute he got to the hotel — he kept the real estate agent waiting while he did that — but he just got her machine. Eventually they connected and he felt his universe start to steady again. Ann's voice was as warm and bright as ever, and she invited them to have a cup of tea with her on Friday, say about two. As this was Tuesday and Rick and Pam had a full schedule of appointments, plus having to locate a lawyer and make contacts about their jobs, there was nothing to do but to thank her and say yes. He really wanted to see her alone. Her two letters were tucked at the back of the leather writing case, next to the receipt and the key. The front pockets bulged with real estate ads and brochures, along with quantities of coupons for discounts on meals and concerts and golf lessons that he and Pam had picked up at the hotel. In spite of the fact that life had simplified to a few phone calls a day and the uncertainty of where they were going to live, Rick felt hemmed in and tied down. It was partly that Pam was constantly there, although she was making telephone connections with people about her job. He felt responsible for being with her in a sense that was not for them normal. Somehow he just couldn't find the excuse to walk out the door of the hotel room, take the elevator down to the parking level and drive the rented Maverick to Ann's front door. He wanted to ask Ann something like: are you still there?

But she was. That was immediately obvious. On Friday they arrived at her place promptly at two. It was an older house in Ottawa South, with a front door ramp that went onto the verandah from one side and was cleverly hidden behind a low wall. She had said that the door would be unlocked and so they rang the bell and went in. They heard her exclaim in the next room, and in a moment there she was rolling toward them, her strong hands manipulating the wheels, her face radiant, eyes meeting his as if she had full sight. He took a stride, closed the gap and the wheelchair ran up against his leg, so that they were laughing as he held her in a big hug. Then Pam hugged her too and they went into the living room. Ann had set out tea. He realized with chagrin that the flask of brandy was back in his suitcase at the hotel.

For about an hour they all compared notes on the differences between Vancouver and Ottawa, everything from house prices to the look of the sky. Then Pam checked her watch. It turned out she had an appointment that he hadn't known about, something to do with her job. She had mentioned it to him, she said, but he didn't remember. They decided that Rick would stay a little and talk poetry with Ann while Pam took the car. He would walk back downtown. Everybody was happy with this. He didn't think that Pam had planned it as a nice thing for him: that wasn't her style. She had just planned her afternoon without understanding how much catching up there would be to do. Hell, as far as he was concerned, they hadn't even begun.

Ann put the kettle on a second time and warmed up the tea. He stretched out his legs. He felt more like himself than he had in weeks, maybe months. Silence spread between them, and he watched her as she went about making tea. Then he took the teapot from her hands and poured the two cups. She smiled at him.

"So, Rick... how are you really?"

"Discombobulated, I think is the word. No place to hang my hat." He thought fleetingly about the dream, but suddenly decided not to tell her about it after all. Instead he returned her smile, admitting, "I'm not even sure if the hats I have along are mine in the first place, now that I'm here."

"Oh, your soul is still back in Vancouver?"

"Yeah, kind of. I guess so. I feel like I'm one dimension: nobody knows me here. Everybody I meet, it's for the first time. It's great to be with you right now: it makes me think I might have some other dimensions after all. You do remember having met me before?"

Ann spilled a little tea. Rick reached over with a napkin and wiped it up, touching her hand as if by mistake.

"I hope it's going to be a good move for both of you," said Ann.

"How has it been for you? How do you feel about it? I couldn't tell from your letters. Good God, two letters in six months!" He stopped. The next sentence would have been, "I nearly went nuts."

She cocked her head sharply. "Was it only two? I asked my brother to call you about the agent and send you all that real estate stuff — did you get it?"

"Yeah, yes, sure we did. Thanks very much. We're using his agent right now. And of course you've had a lot on your mind. I didn't mean to sound critical. My God, getting moved in here and finding your way around — you've done miracles! Are you making any friends?"

"Well yes." Uncharacteristically, she stopped. Rick felt the hair rise on the back of his neck. "It's — a new life opens up a lot of new doors, do you feel that yet? Doors we thought were closed. I ran into a guy I knew in university."

"You hit it off?" He spoke, perhaps, a little too heartily.

"Well, yes. I — I haven't had a lover for a long time, you know, Rick. I don't know if we are going to want to get married, but right now I'm feeling like a silly schoolgirl."

Rick felt as if he were being incredibly stupid. What had she just said? Had he got it right? "Hey, good for you, Ann. That's really news. I'm happy for you. A lover. Well."

This was where she could still say — Oh, I didn't mean that it has happened *yet*! And laugh. Instead she said that they'd all have to get together very soon again — she would invite Kyle, they could meet him. Then she chattered charmingly about all the reading series there were in Ottawa, and what nights they were, and how she was trying to gear up to read some of her poems in public. She reached until she found his hand and held it as she thanked him for having sent out her poems.

He began to offer to go with her to one of the readings and then broke off in confusion, remembering the other guy and not knowing what she wanted him to do. Throughout the rest of the encounter he stood outside his own head and admired himself, how seamlessly he carried on from one remark to another, and how anyway, because she was blind, she couldn't see him shaking. Probably in any case it wouldn't show.

It was a long walk back to the hotel. Some of his tension dissipated by the time he got into the room. Pamela hadn't returned, but she had left the paper open on the table at the personals.

Except of course neither of them ever read that stuff, and so she wouldn't have done that. She must have been reading the real estate ads and just happened to leave the paper opened to the next section, which happened to be the personals.

He sat down and read them.

Ottawa, it appeared, was full of kinky sex. Behind those bland bureaucratic faces seethed every sexual quirk you'd ever want to think of, and lots more he couldn't figure out and might not want to anyway, hidden behind letters like NS and WFW and SD. NS meant Non-Smoking, he decided. Funny that smoking had that much to do with sex. His attention was drawn to one ad that in contrast to the others seemed rather sweet. What he deciphered was: Woman, writer, forties, wants to meet male companion for cups of coffee, walks and talks.

He tore it out along with the real estate ads above it, folded it so that the house ads were at the front, and tucked it in with Ann's letters. Ann had every right to live her own life: he had no claims on her. On the contrary. And Pamela, living her own life, was an angel. He did not want to think about the fact that he had done something so sleazy as to save that ad. It was just that nothing else was happening right now. It was a bit of spurious reality. He hustled about, straightening the suite. They had a kitchenette, and he opened up a can of soup.

That night he dreamed again. When he woke it was still vivid. He dreamed that he lived in an apartment above a laundromat, and that he and Ann were about to leave on a journey in her car. He was all packed when Pamela, who in the dream had a separate house, phoned to ask him to look into a problem she was having, something about a leaky tap. He went over and quickly became absorbed in plumbing problems. He was in a hurry to get it fixed before Ann came. He was half-expecting at any moment to hear her friendly toot. Suddenly it hit him that Ann could not possibly know where he was. They were all in a new city, and he had failed to leave a note. It was already past the time when they had been supposed to leave. He woke in a spasm of angst.

Pam was already up, and taking a shower. They had appointments all morning to look at houses. The real estate woman was coming in an hour. This time they went out to Nepean. After lunch they signed a bid. It was a place they both liked, near the Sportsplex, with a view of trees. It was further out than they had planned, but there was a quicker getaway into the countryside. Rick's job was nearby at Tunney's Pasture, and Pamela's hours were odd ones, later most days than the rush hour traffic. It would work.

In the afternoon, Pam had someone else to see again for a little while, and Rick was left alone. The dream about the note was still strong in his head. He tore a page out of the notebook where he had been calculating mortgage rates and hastily, but in limpid sentences that he admired as he set them down, he wrote a note to the unknown woman who had placed the ad. He described his dream and told her that he was a writer and that he was married, mentioning for how many years. He wrote, "I don't see why a person whom I met this way could possibly turn out to be a friend, but just so that you will know where I am I'm sending this note." He gave the address of his post office box, hesitated, and then signed his full name. What went through his mind was that if Pam cleared out the box it would look funny if a letter came addressed just to "Rick." He hadn't decided not to tell Pam he'd done this but he hadn't decided to tell her either. God, he hadn't decided to do this thing at all. He watched himself as he searched out an envelope and the last stamp from the cache he kept in his case, and then walked out with himself to the elevator, watched his finger push the button and felt himself travel down. Somehow he had to get Ann out from under his skin. There was a mailbox right in front of the hotel. He dropped the note in. It thunked on the bottom of the box.

Immediately he knew he had made a mistake. Why hadn't he researched it better? How could he be such a fool? But wait. Maybe it was all right. It had to be all right. "M" stands for Male:

what else could it stand for? "Wants to meet Male companion," it said. He walked around the block in an erratic state of mind, inventing M-words. He grew more calm. It couldn't mean Menstruating, Macho, Mixed-up. It could mean Masochistic, he supposed, but didn't that always come with an S for Sado in the same ad? If it meant Man or even Married, that was okay. He was both those things, and he intended to stay married: that's why he'd mentioned it in the letter. So — and here was the crunch, the horrible possibility that his head must have known but didn't let out until the letter hit the box — if M meant Male didn't WM have to mean Woman? That was what he had assumed. WM, writer, forties (he saw her as much like Ann, dark-haired, thoughtful, mischievous, but walking and sighted) wants to meet M companion for cups of coffee, walks and talks.... The opposite of Male is Female, but not one ad had said F or FM: he had checked that far. WM had to be Woman. Of course it was. It was all right. Beginning to breathe again, and to feel foolish about feeling foolish, Rick walked over to the canal to look at the boats. Witch Male, he thought. Naw, not even in Ottawa. Whispering Male: there'd be a different wrinkle. Wrinkled Male. WM, Walking Male, seeks to meet WW, Walking Woman. No, if M meant Male, then he could imagine no adjective in the world (Wordly Male) that would make sense applied to Male, not right inside the same ad. No. He'd written to a woman, all right. But God, what kind of space was he in to take this kind of chance? What if he *had* gone and written to a guy? But he hadn't.

So all he had to worry about, or the main thing, was whether Pam would be really hurt if she knew. She had come to accept Ann over the years as some sort of almost religious relationship in Rick's life. This other thing might be hard to explain. Maybe he should have just written a poem.

When he got back to the hotel, Pam was reading the personals.

"What are you looking at those for?" Ironic, detached.

She grinned. "You left them open here on the table — bet you didn't realize they come right after the real estate ads. But hey, Rick, what kind of a place have you dragged me to? It's crawling with racism. Look here."

"Racism?" He stood behind her and followed where her finger pointed.

"White Male," said Pam. "Look. Here it is again. And WF: White Female. It's enough to make you sick."

"How do you know that's what it means?"

"Oh, Rick, what else could it mean?"

She was right.

At the risk of having his wife wonder what he was doing in there, he took his leather case into the bathroom and locked the door. He wrote another note.

"Dear White Male. Sorry about my stupidity. I'm new in town and I was in a weird space. Ignore the note you will have received by now addressed to Woman." It had been so beautifully mysterious a salutation, that one word: "Woman." He put the note into an envelope but had run out of stamps. It was not going to be easy to find a moment to mail it, with Pam almost always by his side. He slipped it into the back of his case. Then he took the ad out and shredded it and flushed it down the toilet. The next day, late in the day, he finally managed to get the letter mailed.

They entered a period of forty-eight hours when Pam had no one else to see and there was nothing to do but wait to hear about the house. Rick kept looking at house ads but his heart wasn't in it. He thought that they'd likely get the one they'd bid on. Anyway, his stomach was upset. They prepared their own lunches in their room, but both evenings they went out to nearby restaurants. It ought to have been fun, but he was under stress. Ann phoned once to see how they were doing. As soon as he heard her voice his world went ridiculously light. This annoyed him so much that he was almost rude. The highlight of each day was going for the mail. Rick proposed that either he go for it or else they go together. A friend from Vancouver sent them a card. Pam's mother wrote.

Otherwise they were in a state of suspended animation. There were men hanging around in the postal box area, opening their mail. Pam said it made her feel creepy: who were these guys?

Rick said a lot of them were small businessmen and not to worry. They were trying to make a go of some business in rented quarters and wanted a definite address in case they had to move around. Perfectly legit, he said, but added that maybe they'd both feel better if she didn't come here by herself.

Very slowly, like a glacier receding, the tension went off. They did get the house, and after only two more weeks of living in the hotel and signing papers with lawyers, they moved in. They drove Ann out once in the Maverick to look at it, and she was delighted for both of them but disappointed it was so far. She had them come to dinner the night after they moved, and they met her man. Kyle was one of the nondisabled men who lived in her house. He helped her pour the tea.

Rick realized that now he could send new change of address cards, and eventually cancel the box. That came as a relief. At the same time he could cancel the feeling that every man hanging around in there was WM, waiting to identify him by his mailbox and to attempt blackmail. Well, if that happened, he told himself, he'd definitely just tell Pam. In any case, he was going to tell her sometime. He wanted to wait until the whole thing had turned into a joke.

When he had met Ann's lover, he discovered that of course he had this problem that any man he met in Ottawa, even apparently straight men, could be WM. But he had something on WM too: he knew this guy was looking for a man. "So you're WM!" he imagined himself saying in a ringing voice, at the party or wherever it was this WM had sleazed over to him.

No, he was safe. Somewhere out there somebody had something on him, but it gave the city, which was otherwise blank to him, a little edge. Ann was still his friend. Pam was happy, and she still loved him.

He began to check the car ads. In his pants pocket, with a copy tucked away for safety in the leather writing case, was the key to his new house.

What Really Goes On Between Men And Women

Sarah is in the front parlour mixing dyes. Matthew is in the kitchen separating eggs. Nearly every morning begins this way, now that the children have flown the nest and the married couple has made his and her accommodations. Years of useless anger over housework she wanted done but not by her have come down to this minor matinal rebellion: to go first thing to her studio and to open her paints and slowly, like a meditation, to swirl bright colours into the hues of this particular day. Here is how and when she plans, ochre swirling into carmine, cadmium enlivening tangerine. Today it's a dress for a regular customer who likes colours of the earth (and don't forget to choose among the greens) and a young pianist choosing a vivid silk top for performing for her first concert audience. Peacock shine and earth's steadiness: set out stone, set out soil, set out tint of autumn hill.

In the kitchen, before he even checks with his answering service, Matthew cracks eggs, holding them as his mother taught him to do, the white falling off in sheets like cum, the yolk intact and winking in its broken cup. This is his penance and his joy: penance for being a man and somehow seldom being in the house, joy in this early morning creative act, whipping and coaxing and seducing until the foam lies thick and fluffy and then he too stirs, stirs fantastic shapes into the yellow viscous pool. Life, the yolk. All that the growing embryo needs. Matthew is a physician, so perforce he thinks cholesterol: one of these mornings in their separate rooms he must begin the experiment with continental breakfasts or fancy tofu. Not yet, please Lord.

He applies heat. His soufflé, his omelette extraordinaire, begins to rise. He sets their places, halves the grapefruit, slips his knife cleverly in between the chunks. Time to rap on Sarah's door.

This morning, though, is sadly different. Somehow Sarah and Matthew have acquired a puppy. Each thinks it was the other one's idea. All last night it whined and carried on in the basement, and Sarah took it out the back before she disappeared into her room. Walked it, let it up into the house, where now it's eating Matthew's polished shoes, jumping against his immaculate pant leg, yapping and begging and whining a piteous high-pitched moaning whine so that this morning he cannot escape down into the vortex swirl of the beaters and observe the usual genie of his own soul-for-the-day smoke from the centre. Instead this yapping, this importuning dog. This impossible spaniel.

Down, stupid pup! He kicks. At the squirming bit of tan puppy flesh. Well, he shoves the dog roughly with the side of a polished shoe, hard enough that the animal skids across the tiles, scrabbling frantically, bounces off a wall and wriggles right back again. Yap. Yap. It squats. Acrid warm aroma of bedpan assails the pristine air around the now-despondent soufflé. Matthew wipes his hands on the towel at his waist and leans to his task. Shove the nose in. Hold it. Whack. Whack. There. Do you get it? Not here. Where in hell is Sarah?

Vague memories of sweet early mornings when the children were small and Sarah more docile, intern days over, doctor not expected in the office before nine; 7 AM kitchen sounds, water running, sizzling noises, oh, they ate bacon and drank black coffee made with real Brazilian coffee beans then, their carefree youth (salad days are where they are now: a misnomer, that), Billy and Sue rattling, shoving at each other — "Stop it, Billy!" Three syllables: "Mu-hu-um!" The damnable racket of that damnable plastic toy lawnmower he'd given his son, had to take it away later and put it on a high shelf, but all blessedly, blessedly, out there in the kitchen, and he the father, the provider, calls received late at night, hush, children, let Daddy have a few more minutes' sleep. Those were the days.

Too much. The pup has got hold of his suit jacket where he left it draped elegantly on the end of the couch and has pulled it onto the floor. Worrying it — *I'll worry you!* Splat. Dog careens again; he shakes the jacket out. No great harm done. Moving slowly because of the puppy licking at his feet, he looks around for a better place, folds it, there, I dare you to get it down from there, you nuisance. The soufflé has flopped, omelette ordinaire browning at the edges of the pan. Holy fucking hell.

Sarah!

Today he can't respect privacy, raps and opens in one movement. Sarah naked in a way he has seen before; he's uncomfortable she weeps alone here, though, by herself. One glimpse only, her face ugly with grief, and then she has turned away, from him and from the painting beside him by the door. In the back of his mind somewhere he knows which one. She painted that last summer at the cottage, a geranium spilled from a broken pot, the empty bright red chair. Good likeness of that chair. He painted the real chair himself. She even got the bit he missed on one of the rungs. Sadness there for her, why now?

"Breakfast is ready."

She stands sideways, face turned away.

"Thank-you. I'll be right there."

Her hand shields her face.

He closes the door. Damned pup at his heels. Go see Sarah. But the pup likes him, follows him, whines, bumps against his legs.

"I know what you want. You want your breakfast. Go get Sarah then. She'll feed you."

She takes a moment changing out of her painting tunic. She comes in fresh and rosy-cheeked and bright-eyed, laughing at the pup. "Oh, you're cute. I know. Yes. I'll get you your breakfast." She starts washing its dish out at the tap.

He feels severe. It has been a hard morning over here on this side of the gender divisions. He feels put upon. "Everywhere I go I trip over him. He spoiled my morning. My omelette's a mess."

She giggles, watching him out of the corner of her eyes with some question there he has no time for now. He's a man with a mission: a man with a grievance. Something that has to be fixed.

"He wouldn't take no for an answer. He wanted to be fed. I had to hit him twice and he made a puddle on the floor."

She measures kibbles into the pan, moistens them with the

puppy's morning ration of meat. Thoughts with no great substance, from before last summer, from before they made these successful accommodations, got this marriage back on the road. She used to think that something in him looked for excuses to be cruel. Took delight. Wriggling babyflesh, wanting only to be fed. Six weeks old. What does baby know of this wide world. Well, baby is learning that sometimes we get fed. Sometimes other stuff comes down. From within her own flesh, she considers the things she knows that the man does not seem to know, hasn't guessed over here, separating eggs and needs. She guessed it right away this morning but then she left her bed, went to colours, the slow mixing of her bright-dark day.

She puts the puppy's dish down on the floor, laughs as his eager tongue swipes her hands and wrists. Wriggle, wriggle, delight in every muscle, every pore. A simple creature, baby dog. And fresh water. Here. Don't spill it now. She holds the pan. Aloud, looking up, no condemnation, at least she hopes he hears none because she intends it straight: "It's all right with me if you ever want to feed him. There's no rule."

He shifts uncomfortably, cuts the spoiled omelette into servings, sparks of satisfaction firing behind the movements of his hands: hey, it still looks edible. He's got a point to make, though, sure now of his ground; he'd better get this clear: "I thought of that, but I thought it was unfair. Here I am every morning, holding the fort, while you're in there enjoying yourself."

Something in her eyes.

But then he sees she's fine, maybe even for some queer reason relieved. She says that she'll be glad to feed the dog before she goes into her room. Every day. No prob. She'll do it. Puppy pushes at his empty bowl, waddles over and flops beside the woman's chair, falls asleep. Tail: thump.

Breakfast not so bad, he's added Worcestershire sauce to the tomato juice. Always a little extra style. She smiles at him. She checks her watch.

"You don't have to phone in quite yet?"

"Not quite yet."

"You wouldn't have had all this trouble this morning if I'd just lured you back to bed."

He looks at her unbelievingly, but liking the idea. "I think it was the dog." Inside he melts. What? What? Sarah. Somehow you come in here. She does the thing they do in movies: stockinged toe under the breakfast table, exploring his groin.

He checks the clock. Looks back into her eyes. A woman is not so hard to figure out.

He takes her hand. Pretends it all was his idea. They sneak past the sleeping pup. She lets herself be pulled until they shut the bedroom door with the dog safely on the other side.

It's a naughty encounter; they're both fully dressed, their professional day has started. There is a swift removal of essentials.

A zipless fuck, she murmurs, quoting, he thinks, some women's book. The edges of his day rise to a perfect soufflé. Hastily she thumbs her pack of worn fantasies: the one she wants is the high school girl in the pleated skirt who trusts her boy — the exact right mix of trust and betrayal, innocence and ignorance, earth and slut red is incendiary.

The Ideal Place

I mean, if I lived in a village anywhere, even with some dictator in charge like Saddam Hussein, where probably they wouldn't even let me out on the street without a black cloth over my face, I bet I still could keep my dog. A dog would be useful in a village. A dog could help herd sheep or cows or just guard the village from harm. Rusty is a good guard dog: he growls all the time at other dogs, when we're walking down the street. He's protecting me. Never until today did he ever growl at me. And he won't do that again, because he doesn't know it yet, but I've finally found the ideal place.

I thought I had it last week. That smart-ass social worker who lives upstairs here, she figures Rust's dead or else anyway that I've forgotten him. She probably thinks they knocked him out of me in the electroshock, but no way. Rust is my dog. I keep my eyes open, and I find some neat spots. Like last week out back of the hairdresser's on the corner, between them and the apartment building, hid half behind a tree, I saw what looked like a doghouse. I couldn't believe my eyes. There was this little green roof and I could see the top of a door. In winter it probably is usually covered right over with snow, but it thawed last week and this was before it froze over again. I walked across the mushy yard as if I owned the place. Really I felt as if everybody was watching us from the windows in the apartment building, but Rusty was with me and anyway how do they know I'm not somebody else's guest? So I got down and cleared the snow away from the door with my hands. Sure enough — it actually was a wooden garbage bin, the snow was piled up in front of it and there was just one old garbage bag at the very back, frozen hard. It wasn't stuck and I hauled it out and put it at the curb with some other garbage. That left a perfect doghouse. It locks with a piece of wood that turns and holds it nice and snug. There's room for Rust to move around, and room to put in his blanket and his food and water dishes. If he gets caught short he won't have to poop in his food dish, which he did one time in the last place. I've never been so disgusted, cleaning that mess up. Then he got away, and he wouldn't come back, and I was awake all night worrying about him. When I went over that morning, I knew right away that he wasn't far off, because there was a blue teddy bear lying in front of the place, which was basically a lean-to I'd made with scrap lumber over an old coal chute at the back of a warehouse. It was only fall then, the weather was still warm. I tied him up in there, but he had chewed through the rope.

I don't know how Rusty got this thing about stuffed animals, but he's had it since he was a pup. When I and the other girls lived in the apartment where we first got him, whenever he got away he'd bring us back a doll or a bear or some poor kid's stuffed dog. Talk about embarrassing. One time I borrowed a wagon from the kid next door and I went all the way around the block with a humungous pile of toys, knocking at every door, but I couldn't find the owner of a single one. He must have stolen them from further off. I gave up. In the end we gave them away to a rummage sale, except for that one teddy bear that I decided to keep for myself. It doesn't take the place of Rusty, though.

He sure was an armful when we first got him from the so-called Humane Society. Us girls went in together to pay for the shots that you had to have done before you could take him home. He used to jump all over us and lick our faces and run around like he was crazy. He was full of energy in those days. We used to take it in turns to walk him, and he'd pull us all over the street. But then he grew up and stopped being cute and the other two girls lost interest. Anyway there was this bad scene and I was left holding the poop-bag, so to speak. Just because they were jerkheads and I couldn't pay my rent because I really had lost my job, they wouldn't give me a break and I got kicked out. So there we were, Rusty and I, in a jam. Ms. Know-it-All Social Worker told me like months ago I absolutely had to get rid of him if I was going to get any help at all: "That's just the way it is." I let on a little while after that that one of the other girls had taken him. So if she sees me with him on the street, it's supposed to be that I've just borrowed him. But if I get caught with him in the room I have now, in the halfway house, it's the end of the road for me, or so she informed me when she let me move in. We had one of those heart-to-heart talks. I guess I'd be on the street.

One day last week when I knew she was out of town I got Rust in here through the window and boy, we had a time. He was so damned happy to be let off that leash! We rough and tumbled just like old days, him wagging his tail and smiling, you know how dogs do. But when I went to put the leash back on, he was off like a streak through the window, and next morning, wouldn't you know, there was a flannelette duck. In the middle of winter. He must have taken it right out of some baby's hand. Anyhow, I caught him, and now he's in the garbage bin behind the hairdresser's. He's been there for, I think, a week. As long as nobody lets him out, he should be just fine. This is the best place yet. Sometime, though, somebody's got to notice that path in the snow and then maybe they'll go take a look. The trouble is every time he hears people on the street he starts barking, and that's no good. If somebody lets him out and the Humane Society gets him, we're in deep shit. I've got no money to bail him out. The last time, anyway, they almost didn't let me have him, they said he was skin and bones. I convinced them that he'd been gone longer than he had and anyway it was so obvious that he was really glad to see me, they knew it had to be my dog. There's a lot of killing goes on in that place. If they get him this time I think I won't see him again. They say they give you so many hours to pick them up but really it's an animal concentration camp. That's the first place I'd knock off if I had a machine gun. Just kidding: I'm not violent. I'm in the peace movement even. Rusty and me marched in the last peace walk. I made signs for him to wear: KILL THE WAR MACHINE and MAKE WAR ON WAR. I brushed him and combed him and he carried his tail up that day like a flag, like he used to. I was so proud. Dogs like him carried messages in the last war — I saw a TV program about it. Rusty could do that perfectly, I bet. He'd be great in a war.

I wish to hell he wouldn't bark, though, in back of other people's houses.

Here I am wide awake again in the middle of the night. I think I hear him barking. I can't help it: I've got to get up and go over there and check. It's not like the warehouse: it's just three blocks away. It's against rules to go out after eleven, according to Ms. Mother Superior, but she can't stop me. She'd have to put bars on the window, and before she did that I'd blow the place up. Just kidding. But I know where I could get some dynamite. Seriously.

There is a time when this city finally gets quiet, just going on 4 AM. You wouldn't think so two hours earlier, listening to the drunks still yelling in the street, but they're on their way home, and Mrs. Cassidy, the old nutcase in the fur coat who screams all over the neighbourhood during the day, they've had her under lock and key by then for a long time — they've got a special hostel now, I hear, for the noisy ones — and the party boys, the university types, they quiet down too. The construction workers aren't up yet, the cleaning women who work at night are still cleaning — I know about this, I had one of those jobs once, it was from 11 to 6 AM. In fact that's the one I got laid off from when I was living with those two bitches who turfed Rusty and me onto the street.

So there's nobody out right now but me and maybe the break and enter artists. I listen. I hear it again: a noise like a cough. It probably is Rusty, maybe wanting to take a 4 AM crap and complaining that he doesn't want to do it in his bed. He's a clean dog by nature. He's a beautiful dog. He's the best thing I've got.

It's him all right. I'm freezing cold by the time I get there: I should have put on mitts. I guess he's cold too. I creep across the yard. It sounds like I'm an army on the move as I break through ice and snow at every step. But there's no lights on at any of the windows except for the stairs. It doesn't seem possible no one's heard him. But then it's not their dog and they don't know how close he is. He's just this muffled bark in their dreams. He's background noise.

"Rusty!" I shout in a whisper at him from outside the bin. He hears me all right: he makes a kind of moan. "Shut up!" I say. "You're going to get us both in trouble!" He rattles his leather leash around in there, but he doesn't bark. Good dog. My hands are frozen. I stand there shivering, trying to think. I should have brought him some food. He's bumping with his nose at the door. Then he does this other sound, this awful sound. This gut-stopping snarl. What the *hell*. Suddenly I'm *afraid* to open the door. They took me to therapy yesterday and I felt fuzzy afterwards: I think I forgot to come over here. I think it's been two days. Maybe Rusty's mad at me. Maybe if I open the door he'll tear off my face.

I mean, that other time, he bit my hand, real deep. I still have the scar. It was when I left him tied on his leash behind the Dominion Store parking lot for a few days while I had to go away. It wasn't the best place. But that time I did leave him lots of food. It was summer, and I'd been scrounging in the supermarket dumpster for bones and anything meat I could find. Maybe some other dogs got it away from him. He was tangled up in his leash like an idiot.

I'm doing the best that I can. When I act mad he always whines and starts in to licking at me and making up. He'll try to bring me another teddy bear, I know it. I know that we're trying to be friends, Rusty and me.

It's just that I'm sorry, but I'm really afraid to open the door. I'm afraid what I'll find. And I'm still like half asleep. Like maybe it's been more than two days.

I crunch away out of the yard. The barking doesn't start again until I'm nearly back home. By then I can hardly make it out.

It's okay. Really it is. We'll make war on this one too. I've got a bag of cheezies left that's supposed to be for when I'm really low. I'll take him that in the morning, or the afternoon, whenever I can make it out of here. When I can see him and he can see me, it will be all right. If the people there see me doing it, that's just fine too, because we'll be moving out.

Because on my way to therapy today I found a new place. A super place. Down a lane between two side streets, where nobody but garbage trucks ever goes; no windows to spy on us. There's an old toolshed, I think it must have been an outhouse, it looks like one anyhow. Definitely they aren't using it for anything now: I looked inside. There's nothing there. It has a hook on the door. Rusty can stay in there like forever. I'll move him tomorrow, right after whatever it is they've planned for me here. I think I'm to go onto a new drug.

It's not as if Rusty can herd any sheep over there, but as long as he and I are stuck living in a city, I figure this is it: I've found it at last — the ideal place.

Owl Girl

My name is Cynthia, which means "goddess of the moon."

"Why choose that name?" I asked my mother.

There are no Cynthias, as far as I know, among any of our known Loyalist forbears.

"Well, you were first," Mother would say, as if that explained anything.

All my other brothers and sisters have names which appear again and again on family charts our mother used to work over in spare moments: Andrew, Edward, Susan, Elizabeth, John. Six of us in all.

I decided as I grew older that it had to do with some story of my conception: a full moon, a country lane — my parents were always going to be too shy to tell. At any rate, there I was, Cynthia, Cindy, growing up in the country four miles west of Guelph, eldest daughter of a carpenter and of a lady who collected antique washstands, local history and, as the years passed, kids. I don't think she resented her growing family: there was a feeling that she had married our father for love, had not regretted her choice, and that we were the offspring of that love. But there was also a feeling that she had chosen to marry below herself, that she remembered a finer and rarer life she could indicate to us only in the form of a tapestry from our grandfather's house, or a miniature china tea set she had been given as a child.

Some of this I am understanding in retrospect, after the long talks she and Alexander had during her last year. Alexander is the curator of our local museum, and the man I live with. Also, in the last year of her life, my mother's friend. He would arrive to visit armed with his notebook, and my mother would tell him all the stories she knew about the antiques in our home, some from her Loyalist background, many gleaned from friends and sales and shops — and flea markets — whenever she had had a chance. Alexander and my mother shared more than a love of the past, I think: there was a world view they shared too, a kind of vigorous despair, that this life is all we get and that it's to be cherished, but that somehow it's never nearly enough. In the early days of our acquaintanceship with Alexander, the three of us talked together several times of my mother's death. She was able to joke about it then. She had been ill, but I think we all took for granted that it was something that would rapidly be fixed. She had always been so full of life. I remember her trying to give us some ideas about her funeral, or maybe it was just about how she hoped we would react to her death.

"The peonies need strengthening," she'd said. "I'd like to be buried alongside the fence. I'll be gone and I might as well be of use. I'd rather make my last act the saving of peonies than the growing of carrots and peas. But maybe that's selfish of me! I don't mind if you decide to bury me in the garden."

I was a little scandalized, passing the oatmeal cookies and tea. I had met Alexander only a short time before, and we had not yet reached the afternoon when he bore me off to his room back of the museum and we became lovers. I was afraid that my mother would scare him off. But instead he was delighted by her, and after that began bringing his notebook. Mother's illness did not go away; gradually we all stopped talking about death. I thought that I didn't want her to think about it, that I was afraid she would give up; I know now that it was myself I was attempting to deceive. At any rate, I fell silent as she told Alexander the stories I had heard before, about the red chair that had lived in the vicarage and about the blue jug that had been a wedding gift to Aunt May. I sat and listened to their voices weaving back and forth, loving them both, revisiting my childhood, and refused to consider that the light voice telling the stories could ever stop.

I am a scientist, an ornithologist; I study birds and specialize in owls. I came back to my home town after university to work in the owlery at the Farm outside Guelph. I keep good records. I go from what I touch and see. My life is a matter of receiving clear perceptions and of quantifying them if possible and writing them down. Yet at the same time the owls are part of another story, a secret journey that leads back through a man named William and a woman named Marie, to a day in the year I turned twelve, when I was chosen by owls.

In those days a box of books used to be sent out to our school from the public library, and on one occasion there was a book entitled, simply, *Owls*, with a drawing of a solemn snowy on the dust jacket. I read it through and then turned to the back of my workbook and took notes. This would be the first time in my life, I think, that I felt this urge to catch facts as they came by, to pin them down. I was excited and wanted to keep the book to myself: it was as if it had my name on it. When after awhile my conscience bothered me, I returned it quietly to the box and buried it at the bottom, hoping no one else would dig it out. I had known instantly that I wanted to be the girl who knew about owls.

And owls came my way. The service station at the turn of our road acquired a hawk owl, in a tall wire cage rigged up near the pumps. I had to go by as I walked to and from school, and I noticed that people went there for gas especially to take a look at the owl, then lingered to curse it out. Farmers spoke to one another bitterly of chickens lost, even young lambs; they would stare up angrily toward the bird on its perch near the top of the cage. I thought they must be exaggerating: a hawk owl isn't a hawk. But the question made me ask to be let off at the library on our family's next trip to town, and I looked it up. Chickens weren't mentioned, but rabbits were, and so after that I wasn't sure. Then the service station manager told me it was no good bringing pocketsful of seeds as I had been doing, pulled off weeds from the side of the road. An owl will eat only live things, he told me — not quite right, but that's what he said — but added that he could use the seeds for the box of field mice he had in the back room to feed to the owl. I emptied my pockets into the box he showed me, and peered at a nest of squeaking pink baby mice without emotion. Somehow I accepted it all at once: this was the adult world, the real world, where things were harsher and yet more important, and for that reason more attractive, than stories I read in school.

Then my father's sister bought a plaster owl for the wall of her kitchen, but all she could tell me about it was that it was supposed to be wise. The plaster owl served another purpose, however: I realized I could make owl shapes myself out of various things, and learn about the birds as they took form under my hands. Now I pestered my busy mother to teach me skills which I had never been interested in before. In spite of all the calls on her time, she gave my request serious importance, and set aside time on Saturdays to teach me what she knew. We grew close in a new way as my hands followed hers, a long, intricate initiation rite into the world of grown women. She taught me first to crochet, and I chose to crochet little beige owls, flat ones as doilies and as wall decorations, then plump ones good only as themselves. Then she showed me how to tat, and I was amazed at how easy it was. I tatted great lacy owls, trying for the pattern of their soft feathers and the spiky ruff around their eyes. She showed me some tablecloths she rarely used, with homemade lace, and from her bedroom wall took down a sampler which had been made by my great-grandmama when she was a little girl. My mother pointed out each variety of stitch, and taught them to me. Together we embroidered owls on a pair of pillow slips, but on that project I lost interest, so that Mother finished off the hard parts to bring the job to an end.

There was a wedding down our road, and we took the pillow slips there as a gift. Leslie Thom, the grown son of widow Thom, had married a Dutch girl, Marie, dark-haired with laughing blue eyes. Leslie was away all day at work in town; Mrs. Thom Senior still ruled the kitchen, and Marie was new in the community, and lonely. We invited her to visit. Soon she would often come down the road when I got home from school, to see us, and to help me with the owls. From the beginning Marie never questioned my obsession: it was as if she had always known me, and understood what I certainly did not understand myself. It was Marie who showed me how to make baker's clay with flour and salt, a skill my mother hadn't known. Referring to books I always had on loan from the library, together we turned out trayfuls of saw-whets, burrowing owls, barred owls, long-eared, short-eared, barn owls and hawk owls. I bought paints with my allowance and painted them in all their proper colours, being meticulous. Again Marie seemed to understand. The Dutch have a knack, it seems to me, for persistence and for getting things right. But they also know how to laugh. Soon my days turned around the sight of Marie coming down the road. We would joke and giggle as we worked, and inside I felt myself coming into myself, like a gift. In the background Mother came and went, always busy, always glad to see my friend, making sure we had enough provisions for whatever it was we were doing that day, sitting near us from time to time, often bringing in a figurine or a little carving from among her treasures, showing us the skill of those early craftspeople, encouraging us to try to do as well.

That fall, Leslie Thom suddenly announced that his company had promoted him to a job in Niagara Falls. The farm was sold and the family moved away. Marie's English was not good enough to let her write to me, and to a country child like myself, Niagara Falls, only eighty miles away, might as well have been Timbuctoo. I missed her painfully.

Through all this you have to understand that my parents were working desperately hard. There was always another child on the way, and there was scarcely enough money to go around. My father, the carpenter, had his workshop in the old summer kitchen of our house. They kept a cow, too, and some chickens, from time to time fattened one or two pigs, and my small mother turned brown and freckled every summer, working an enormous garden, with excess to sell or give away to neighbours in late summer and fall. I was needed around the house and had regular chores — feeding chickens, weeding a certain patch of peas, watching the baby. Yet somehow space was always made for "Cynthia's owls." My worktable was set up in a corner of the kitchen and Mother kept the smaller kids away from it. As for my father, for my fourteenth birthday he presented me with a block of soft wood, some knives and an expensive chisel.

"Try carving an owl," he suggested. After that I was often in his shop, labouring to create the illusion of fluffy plumage in the harder contours of wood. There was some comfort, too, in this work. When at last I finished one I liked, Mother helped me package it and mail it to the address Marie had left. In time a thank-you note arrived, a few words, a sketch of a smiling face and of a little smiling owl.

I was now in grade eleven, and falling in love with our handsome young science teacher, William Routledge. He taught us grade eleven Physics, but his thesis had been in ornithology. One day near Christmas he happened to come upon a scene in the corridor which had often occurred before but to which I had never become accustomed: several of the girls crowded against me, bugging their eyes and chanting in low voices, "Owl girl. Owl girl. Cindy eats mice." Then, sweetly, cocking their prettily coiffured heads, "Don't you eat mice, Cindy?" Mother had long since told me to ignore them and they'd leave me alone, but I had never figured out how to do that. Instead I laughed, pretending casual amusement, and said, "No, of course I don't eat mice," which made them fall over each other with delight. We were all reenacting old roles: some of these girls had been at school with me since grade seven, when once I had found a dead mouse in my lunch. There had been a rather clever chant then based on something the kindergartens learned about the stork:

> *Cindy's such a funny bird*
> *All night she's on one leg*
> *And in the morning when she wakes*
> *What an icky egg!!*

They would shout with laughter. I had never known what to do. I was not ashamed of being the owl girl. I knew it was simply true that I was. What I didn't understand was why this was so threatening to people I would have liked to have had as friends.

Most of all this I explained to William Routledge when he had me come into his classroom after the girls scattered under his glare. He was being very kind, very interested, and I told him more than I had ever explained to anyone else. He offered to lend me some books he had about birds, and to arrange for me to come in to the grade thirteen class when, later in the term, they would be dissecting a pigeon and discussing the anatomy of birds.

That night I ran most of the way home, clutching William's bird book to my budding breasts and recalling over and over again his understanding face, his gentle rumbling voice, over and over, a second repetitive thrilling reality between me and the noisy, busy household at home. I invented scenes where somehow (over and over) his red TR3 went off the road into the ditch just down from our house, and I the first one there: oh William, needing sweet help to get him out of his shirt. He was conscious, he was unconscious — I ran it both ways. I fantasized tending the bruises on his white male skin, I dared, (he was very brave) (so was I.) I read his bird book. The birds came alive in colours on the page; I could hear their songs.

At the end of that school year, abruptly, William, too, moved away, to another school, far away in Kingston. He married the woman we had caught him writing love notes to in class, and I have heard they have several children. He still teaches Biology in some school there. And I did, of course, go on to become a biologist, with a master's in his specialty: birds. The Audubon book he awkwardly handed me as a gift at the end of that year still sits on my office shelf.

By then I was fifteen, and had begun selling the owls I made, at flea markets and bazaars. I would phone on my own to arrange the table, but needed help with transportation and with carrying in and setting up. Somehow when the day came, my mother would always manage to make time, putting off her canning or mending or the overwhelming weeding, asking Dad to watch the baby, or if he couldn't then leaving it with a neighbour, and driving me to wherever I had my booth. She helped me set up, chatting shyly to people nearby, and would go the rounds of the other displays, coming back to encourage me and to whisper that perhaps my prices might be too low even if I wasn't selling, because my workmanship, according to her, was so good. I would get into a happy glow just from having this time with my mother to myself, and feeling her approval. Sometimes sales were poor, and sometimes she had a suggestion, humbly offered, of what might help. She took a very active interest, in other words, but left it clearly my own thing. I would sit there tatting or carving and waiting on customers. My mum would work away at some project of her own, her needles flashing in and out of knitting or a hoop of embroidery. Sometimes at flea markets she would come across a treasure, a cream jug or crock or fancy spoon, and secrete it in its paper bag under our chairs. I sensed vaguely that my special time was also hers, her day away. Often she was working at gifts for other members of the family that she didn't want them to see. Those days were like secrets we two shared, and I came to take it almost for granted that when it was time for me to go out and be the local "owl girl," Mother would always make space.

Later in her life, ambushed by ill health into premature old age, she remembered those times we had had and talked of becoming the "owl lady" herself. She had picked up some new skills by then: crewel work and macramé, and she thought she could stock a table and earn a little money. She did make a number of owl shapes for church bazaars, but never launched her own business. Nevertheless, planning for it and laughing about old times helped her over the hump of coming to terms with her suddenly reduced energies.

She died two years ago, in May. My birthday is four months later, in September, September 24. Birthdays have always been important in our family, perhaps because of Mother's concern about dates. I knew that I had been close to her, but I had also been aware of our differences. I was totally unprepared for the abyss of grief into which I tumbled with the shock of her dying. Four months later, as I came into the days preceding my birthday, still in an emotionally skinned state, it had come to seem to me that I was being inundated by odd happenings, striking coincidences, people coming into my life whom I didn't expect to see. I had begun to believe that something was going on, that there was a message I was intended to receive, but I didn't know what it was, and felt angry that any of this was happening at all.

On September 20, then, of the year my mother died, we received a phone call at the owlery where I work. A pleasant male voice:

"I know I'm not supposed to be trapping one of those arctic owls — what are they called?"

"Is it white? How big is it?"

"This one's almost pure white, and big: twice as big as the owls you usually see around here. A couple of feet high, I guess."

"It must be a snowy."

"That's it. That's what it is. There's something wrong with him, with his left wing. I found him flopping around beside the fence in the field, trying to fly but falling on his face. I've made him a cage you can borrow if you need to, and we're feeding him bugs for the moment, but obviously he needs more help than we can give him. Could you folks come out and take a look?"

I drew a long breath. A snowy owl is always an event: they are rarely spotted this far south. I had never had a chance to observe one up close over any length of time. The man gave me directions and I promised to come right out. I tried to locate a carrying cage but they all seemed to be missing and anyway he had said I could borrow his, so without proper preparations, really, I let people know where I'd be and signed out the Farm jeep.

As I turned into the driveway leading to these people's house and a large shed which seemed to have been turned into a barn, I suddenly was having trouble with my feelings. There was an almost uncanny resemblance to the yard and house and drive where I had lived as a child. There were the two pigs rooting in a specially made pen beside the shed. Chickens scratched in the yard. In the field behind, the Holstein cow munched and watched my arrival with mild eyes. There were even the two tall poles set into the side yard, with two swings. In my childhood it had been a swing and a trapeze.

The man came out at once, short, rosy-cheeked, looking as harmless and friendly as he had sounded on the phone, and behind him two young boys.

"You the lady from the Farm? Pleased to meet you. These are my sons." He introduced them, I introduced myself, and he led me to an area behind the shed, where he'd built an extension to the roof to shelter some rabbit pens and, in a large pen made by removing partitions from a number of the rabbit cages, an enormous snowy owl. The owl and I stared at each other, each as unblinking, I guess, as the other. I know owls and so knew in advance a fair amount about the habits of this one. It stared back as if it knew as much about me. I was seized with an irrational, unscientific desire to sit there and talk with it a bit, but of course the man and his boys were with me and so I stayed professional and cool. I had had enough foresight to bring a couple of live mice in the usual container, and with the farmer's permission, and to the boys' very active interest, shoved them in. The owl, which had been motionless, darted upon them at once. I watched the clumsy way it handled itself and realized that whatever damage there was might extend to the left leg. We opened the door; it let me touch it. I wired on a temporary splint and covered it with a sock to keep the bird from pulling it off, not a great job, but it would do until we got it to the Farm. The man invited me into the house for a cup of tea, and I was glad to accept.

Inside the house, it was again as if I had been there before. There was even the shop at the back, although this man had something to do with computers rather than carpentry. Times do change. But there was his slight, dark-haired wife, starting up from some crocheting, bustling about the kitchen in a cotton apron, laying out oatmeal cookies and a pot of good tea, just as my mother would have done. I put my purse and sweater down on an antique washstand near the door, kept my eyes on the man and the boys and appreciated the fact that we were all talking steadily about owls.

What I had not reckoned on was the size of their cage. It was a humane size to have made, but it would not fit into the back of the owlery jeep. We could have made do temporarily with an upended rabbit cage, but as it happened this was not easy to arrange, all of the cages being sturdily wired together and all occupied. It seemed better to accept the farmer's suggestion that he bring the owl in himself the next day, when he would be coming into Guelph anyway with his pickup truck. It was the kind of offer my father still makes. I accepted, thanked his wife for the snack, still hardly able to look at her straight on, and headed back for the Farm to make ready for our new guest. As I turned out of their driveway onto the main road, I was overtaken by a storm of grief so heavy that suddenly I could not see through my tears, and very nearly sideswiped an oncoming car. But didn't, the storm subsided, everyone on the road got back safely, and I cleared and set up Cage 3.

The next day, September 21, the farmer phoned to say he was having trouble with the starter on his truck. Not to worry, he said, the boys had found a nest of mice and so the owl was being fed for a day or so. He'd have it in as soon as possible. I thanked him and said the sooner the better, as we'd have to stabilize that wing.

Also on that same day, I fell victim in a very simple-minded way to a con man, having by this time drifted into such a vulnerable state that every event and gesture seemed to have Meaning. There is a certain amount of ambivalence towards our operation from some of the people in the countryside, because they know we breed owls here and actually release them at designated spots. Far from believing that this is a measure to keep down pests, they believe that the owls themselves are pests. They know it is against the law to shoot them, but somehow the owl population keeps being depleted. On September 21, then, someone phoned, saying he represented the aviary at Granby and that they were desperate for a saw-whet, a common owl in Nova Scotia and Quebec, but harder to find in our part of Ontario. They had budget left over from the season, the person said, and wouldn't mind paying extra if we could supply one fast. I was surprised at the whole message, actually, but said we didn't have one at the moment and I'd certainly let them know when we did.

Three hours later, in came a shifty-eyed fellow with his beaten-down-looking wife and a bedraggled little saw-whet in a cage hardly big enough to hold it. It had been at his chickens, he said — an impossible story — and he'd trapped it, but would let it go in the woods unless we were prepared to pay what he asked, a quite outrageous price. Ordinarily I wouldn't have given him the time of day — the whole thing was ludicrous — but with the first message still ringing in my ears I couldn't quite let him go. The owlery is in perpetual need of money. I had wit enough to know that likely the telephone caller and this man were one and the same, but not enough to be sure. I felt as if my capacity to believe were being tested; I was in a mood to believe that the angels of God were walking into the owlery in varied disguise. I did dicker; he did reduce his price a little; I bought the bird. It is still in a corner of the owlery. I feed it every day, and it certainly looks a lot more chipper than it did the day it was brought in. No one, and in particular not the Granby Zoo in Quebec, which has two, wants a saw-whet. By now we ought to have let it go. But I have made a bit of a pet of it, and it has probably come to believe that dinner comes regularly in a box. In the day it sleeps there on its perch, a reminder to me of the fine line between daring to believe and taking leave of one's common sense!

On September 23, I phoned my farmer to see if he'd be in. I wanted to go out for a few hours and didn't want to miss the arrival of the Bird. There was no answer. I hung around. Nothing happened.

On September 24, my birthday, the pickup truck pulled up just as I arrived at work. I was surprised to see the farmer's wife jump out. Her husband had had to spend the whole preceding day at the garage, she said, and had got behind in his work, and so she'd volunteered to take care of his errands in town. I went in and found a carrying cage — easy to find now, three of them piled up in the holding room — and manoeuvred our owl into it. They tend to be a bit dopey during the day, so for this or for whatever reason again it gave me no trouble despite its size. We lugged it in and released it into its new quarters. It waddled out almost comically, and turned to look at me with its great eyes, as big as the eyes of a human being. Above all else, an owl has dignity. If it was in pain, it did not show it. It shook its feathers a little, gazing and gazing straight at me. It is not true, you know, that an owl cannot see in the light. It sees perfectly well. It also hears even better than it sees.

The woman beside me laughed with relief to see it safely in care. "It was quite a responsibility while we had it. They look so smart and they have this great reputation for being wise, but they're just like chickens really, aren't they: stupid and maybe even kind of mean. That bird needed us or else by now he'd have had it. Of course, judging by the look in his eye, he may not have a much higher opinion of us."

"Well," I said tamely, "I'm glad you thought of it as a chicken instead of a chicken-killer. It's a beautiful bird." We smiled at each other.

In that moment, I was utterly convinced that my mother, through the person of this woman as a special sign, had just presented me with a snowy owl. As a gift for my birthday. And as a gift of faith: the faith she hadn't had herself. She was sending me a message: from beyond death she had stage-managed this whole event. With her characteristic thoroughness she had started in on it a day or two too soon, and it had taken no end of business with lost cages and wired cages and starter problems to make it come out right so that I couldn't miss it: that this particular woman should present me, on my birthday, with a rare and beautiful owl.

Now, I am not in the least interested in joining the nut fringe. I am merely being forced, really by my scientist's training, which tries not to control or ignore data, into ideas which sit most uncomfortably in my mind alongside plans for our expansion here at the Farm, the applications I have written for government grants, and even the conversations I have with Alexander. Of course I have long since told him the story of the birthday owl. I have told him about William, too, and about Marie, but obliquely, as if they were part of the normal world to me and not part of the other story, the strange one. Alex listens sweetly, seems interested, even makes suggestions. Yet I know that somehow it doesn't come together in his head the same way it does in mine. How can I expect him to understand when I do not myself?

Some days I find myself fighting the urge to drive again to that little farm, if I could find it, and tell the whole story to that woman who so much resembled my mother. I won't do it, of course. I can't. Surely that is just another way of wanting to have my mother back, but she is dead. Somehow the message must be that I already know all these answers myself. But it seems I need a key.

Thinking about all this, I find the next paper under my hand (I have gone into my office to catch up on my record-keeping) is about a meeting that has been called by the Agricultural Association to discuss pests. And there in front of me is the man's name, the man who called us about the snowy owl. He is one of the organizers. I could contact them if I wanted to. It seems a funny coincidence, except that I have the impression that these coincidences have been happening all along, and I am ignoring them. I am determined to ignore them. This morning, for instance, as Alex and I were waking, there was something. I remember now, I am right, there was something on the radio about names. I woke up because they said the name Cynthia, explained it was the same name as Artemis, protector of small animals and birds. Well, I knew that. It means nothing. She was a huntress too. These things do not add up, they do not compute.

Tears. I pretend to be very interested in the notice of the meeting, and in the sheet under it, the records of Cage 3, formerly the abode of our snowy owl. Once it was fully recovered, I drove the snowy myself as far north as I could manage in one day off, and released it at dusk.

Oh, that enormous slow spreading of its silent wings, first white then black against the darkening sky. It knew exactly where it wanted to go; my eye could follow it only a short way before it disappeared into the night. I was left alone in the coarse stubble of a frozen cornfield with an empty cage. Snow swirled along the hard black furrows. Then the wind that caught me up was no night breeze, but a sweeping, intense exhilaration in which I felt whirled into the sky in the path of the owl and set down again, laughing, shouting, shaking, quite outside myself. When I bent to pick up the cage, I was lightheaded, unsure of distances, of when objects about me would reach my hands. I walked back toward the dark shape of the jeep parked beside the country road. Incredibly, I walked away from my grief: it slid from me like a scarf dropped behind in the snow. The relief was as strange and as sudden as the sharp upwellings of tears I had stumbled into so many times since my mother's death. The tears would return, as they have just now, but that evening what had seemed too great to bear began to heal.

I am in control again. A party of tourists led by our door by our summer student found me so engaged in intricate analysis of these reports that I couldn't even manage to say hello as they passed. No more tears.

I think that what one must say is that one must begin with the Mystery. The strange story, the inner one. All the rest — the owlery, my research, friendships, even dear Alex — is (deadly serious) charade.

I loved Marie.

I loved William Routledge.

My mother, who should have lived forever, instead died young.

My entire being summed up in three meaningless statements, meaningless unless you are me, the owl girl, Cynthia.

Mrs. O'Hara

Her weight had dropped alarmingly, said Mr. O'Hara. Finally they had packed her off to the hospital.

"It's not the least bit like her." He turned from the shelves to look at me, his movements heavy. "She won't eat. She's very down. She's never been this bad before, even when Sharon died. You remember, Colleen."

Outside, November rain pounded on the plate-glass window. It was the day of Alma Townsend's funeral. Just for once there was no one sitting on the registers below the window, warming their behinds and passing the time of day. Usually Thomas Townsend is there, but that day his wife was dead and he was at the cemetery, along with most of the rest of the village. I had been at the funeral, but then I had to return home because my children were coming home from school. And Mr. O'Hara had to run the store. Mrs. O'Hara had been home ailing for several weeks — ever since, in fact, the news had gone out about how seriously Alma Townsend was ill, although I didn't think of that at the time. Mr. O'Hara sorted change with his normal dexterity, separating the coins with the broad fingers of his one hand.

I was told the story of how Mr. O'Hara lost his left arm so

long ago that it seems part of my own memories. He was attempting to break in a horse on his father's farm, as a lad of only fourteen, when it crushed him against the wall of an outbuilding and mangled the arm so badly that the doctor judged it had to come off. He wears the loose arm of his business suit pinned into his pocket, and works as fast with his one good arm as most whole people do with two. When I was a child and used to come into the O'Hara kitchen with their daughter Sharon, we delighted in watching him do up knots. He could tie a child's shoelace in a moment, and had a warm one-armed hug for his little daughter all at the same time.

In those days he was a dairy farmer. My first paying job, when I was thirteen, was helping Sharon on a Saturday morning, while her parents were at market selling vegetables and Mrs. O'Hara's preserves. There was a lot of work and also I think her parents must have decided they felt better knowing there were two of us in the house. There is just a chance that they thought I might be a good influence on Sharon, who was always up to mischief of one sort of another. But the influence went the other way. We played silly games and dared one another as we scoured out the milk pails and set them in the sun to dry. We had beds to make, bedrooms to dust out, the long dark dining room table to rub hard with lemon oil. Somehow we managed to get through our list, but in between we would be running out to the barn to climb the rafters, stealing strawberries from the boxes that were set out to sell to the neighbours, and deciding to mix up some cupcakes to surprise her parents when they came home. Mrs. O'Hara kept a meticulously clean house. It didn't occur to me then to wonder how on earth she managed it all: the house, the pails, preserves, chickens, still finding time to teach music all through our district, from S.S.17 all the way up north to S.S. 25. I took it for granted that a grown woman must be able to handle all that.

It was Tuesdays that she taught at our school. I remember the chalkboards covered with words of the song we were learning, and our music teacher, no longer the overalled figure of the strawberry patch but in the kind of demure dress that schoolteachers wore in those days. The one I recall was a mauve print, with a self-belt and covered buttons up the front. Her brown hair was longer then than she wears it now, but permed as now into small tight waves. Everything about her person was under control, and so were we in her presence. Repeatedly, Tuesday after Tuesday, we were caught up into the intensity of her passion, repeatedly pressed by her towards an ideal sound we almost could hear. But best of all I remember her smile: we could not help responding. The joy we gave Mrs. O'Hara by singing it right was like a miracle taking place right there in our class.

Sometimes we sang sitting at our desks. Then she bobbed up and down our rows, listening to everyone in turn. The moment came when it would be your turn and she would bend close, listening with her head cocked like a bird: you would sing your sweetest and best; she would nod and smile and her eyes would dance with delight. Ordinarily, though, she had us stand; she knew we sang better that way. Her hand would sweep upward, bringing us to our feet as one (except for the grade ones, who would be a moment stumbling and falling off their seats), and then the ritual would begin: a brisk pitchpipe note, our hum, her smile; we would be off. "There's a Bluebird on My Windowsill," "Sweet Coral Bells," for Christmas "Up On the Housetops Reindeer Pause" (reindeer don't have paws, I used to think, singing it enthusiastically all the same). In spring for the Easter Festival there would be an anthem: "Rejoice, rejoice in glorious hope." For every song we learned all the words, every verse. Even now I astonish my friends and dismay my family with my recall of all those words. Mrs. O'Hara has never been the kind of person who cuts out stanzas for personal convenience. She is the kind of person who gets things right, and then can be happy.

"She's too particular, you see, Colleen." Mr. O'Hara glanced up from the box he was filling with my groceries. "She even complains sometimes after I brush my hair in the morning. She gets out the brush and does it over again."

Why did he tell me that? His loneliness looks out of his eyes: his fear. I looked at his balding pate and got ready to joke with him that he'd have a real tidy hairdo any time now.

But Mr. O'Hara said suddenly: "They might have to force-feed her."

We both fell silent. "She's down to eighty-two pounds. She won't eat." He sounded vaguely irritated, paused, then picked up the box of groceries to carry it out to my car. "It's just not like her at all."

That's what I heard them saying about Alma, I realized. It's not like her at all. She's changed. You wouldn't believe how much she's changed. She's just not herself. You know how cheerful she's always been? We remembered readily: a big, raw-boned woman with a laugh you could hear a mile away, or at least on the other side of any room; a joiner, an organizer, an open, friendly woman who always made you feel welcome and did more than her share of any work without complaint. Proud of her grown children: "There's no flies on my kid," she said to me one day, speaking of her son, and her laugh rang out. Then she changed. She became cross and depressed and wanted no one near her, not even her old friend, Ruth O'Hara.

Well, she was allowed. She had held off as long as she could. One week she couldn't take her Sunday School class, and said as her excuse that she had a pain in her stomach. She made it sound as if it must have been something she ate. Next Sunday she was in the hospital and it took only a month and a bit after that for the cancer to finish its work. Alma gone; an emptiness left at the centre of the village.

Now Ruth O'Hara was changing, too, another sudden change that no one understood. It occurred to me that she might not come out of that hospital. There might be going to be two deaths in the village, two women gone whose presence was needed, whose stability, too, in a time of too much change.

Alma Townsend and Ruth O'Hara went to High School and to Normal School together. I knew this as everyone in the village knew it, a small fact. What a pair they must have made, big, cheerful, generous Alma and tiny, chirrupy, meticulous Ruth! In later life they both kept busy, and as neither was the sort to take coffee in the morning at each other's house or talk on the telephone much, perhaps the friendship lapsed somewhat. I remembered, however, thinking it over, that when Sharon died it had been Alma who, more than anyone else, had been able to reach out to Ruth, bring her through. I didn't want to remember Sharon's death, not at all, but thinking of Sharon's mother, and trying to understand the change in her, thinking about what I knew of death and the way it is mixed in with life, I got to thinking about Sharon too.

I was working up north that summer, in Muskoka, when the letter came from my mother with the news that Sharon had been killed. I spent a long time walking back in the bush, the letter crumpled in my pocket, beating my way over rocks and through underbrush, crying, thinking, remembering. I tried to live through her death in my mind. I thought of the nice feeling moments before it happened, the hay smell of the barn where we had often played at touch tag, shafts of dusty sunlight from the high windows and the stencilled cutout at one end reading "1895," with a piece broken out of the "5." There was the ladder of slats nailed to the wall, which Sharon used to scale in our games as if it were flat ground, to balance on the rafter overhead, whooping in victory. Never had I seen her fall. It seems curious even today when I think of the hay giving way and sending her over the edge into the silo.

She was raising a heifer calf that summer and perhaps she had decided to check the level of feed in the silo, casually, with winter in mind and helping her father later with the corn. We all knew that the little door to the silo must be kept shut, but Sharon was seventeen and coming into adult roles then. One moment she must have felt so strong, and calm in a way that the barn loft does to you, and then there was the mistake, something giving way, the almost comic reflex — hey, hold on here! What can I grab? Here I go! — Maybe never feeling fear at all, landing and thinking: Ow! My foot! — Reaching to hold it, and then perhaps never even thinking about the deadly silo gas that sometimes builds up, or ever thinking — I'm going to die. . . . My mother said it was a quick death. I think it was. It was hours before they found her, but in the few minutes Mr. O'Hara was down there they nearly lost him too. At seventeen my faith in life after death was very strong. Straining to understand how it had been for Sharon, suddenly I could hear her cracking jokes with Jesus, moments after her death. I could hear her voice, wry and funny and bold and brave, the way she had always been. I got back to the lodge in time to take my place with the other waitresses and serve dinner. No one noticed I had been crying.

"It's hard to know what to do," my mother had written. "I'm making a casserole. Alma Townsend stayed there all day yesterday. Probably she can do as much as anybody."

Sharon's parents closed off from the world for awhile. People learned to stay away, leave time to heal. Mrs. O'Hara took leave of absence from teaching and never went back. Mr. O'Hara got the corn in that fall and by next spring the farm was sold. They bought the general store in our village and made it a warm and friendly place. After awhile, Mrs. O'Hara took over the junior choir at the church, and it began to win prizes every year at the Festival. Things got back to normal. When I speak of the death of Alma Townsend, I am talking about something that happened twenty, twenty-five years later. I have grown up, gone to university and married, had three children and moved back.

I have grown accustomed to the sight of Mrs. O'Hara at the front of the church at Christmas and Easter, leading the congregation in song. The deep-blue choir gown swirls around her slim frame, the elegant, imperious hand of the music teacher sweeps upward once more, and we rise as one, except for the little kids slipping and bumping off the pews, and a few old codgers who take a little longer than they used to. The organ sounds the note; we are off. My mother fusses with her hymn book, finding the right music. The scent of evergreen or of Easter lilies drifts back from the front of the church. You can hear Alma Townsend's voice over everyone else from the choir. Rejoice, Mrs. O'Hara bids us. Rejoice in glorious hope! Briefly she is no longer the sparrow-like woman behind the counter in the general store. She is small, but her smile is like a miracle that fills the whole room.

We are having more than our share of deaths in the village at the moment. The old folk I remember from my childhood have nearly all gone, and now it is the generation of our mothers and fathers who are starting to go. Nearly every week last winter there were flowers in the church from somebody's funeral, mostly people I didn't know. But Alma's death hit me hard, because she was relatively so young and vigorous — in a word, a lot like my own mother, and I have not yet given any thought at all to the idea of my mother's death. I went to the funeral and thought about my mum and tried to work it out. It didn't help much. There was an open casket and Alma's beaky nose rose above its edge, her glasses perched on her nose as usual. It seemed incredible that her laugh would not ring out again in a minute and she would sit up and begin organizing us all. Instead they closed the coffin and took her off to the cemetery, and I went home, stopping at the store to pick up groceries, because life goes on.

"Well, I hope Mrs. O'Hara's well again soon," I said, getting wet in the rain as her husband slid the box of groceries into the back seat of my car with his one good arm.

"Yes, well, without hope all is vain," said Mr. O'Hara.

Somehow I felt comforted. I went home and was nice to my children, and the rain went on all that evening and into the night.

Lucy Gray

I'm undersexed, and my husband, Roy, is quite sexed, but that's all right, it really is, because what counts is love, and that's what I want to teach our children. It bothers Ray terribly to have to stay out of the war, but I'm grateful he hasn't had to go overseas. I love being his wife. There may be some small physical reason down there, too, that makes it difficult for me, but he's very clever and very gentle and certainly thanks to him I do know what it is to be — satisfied. Not every time. In fact, not often at all. But I like the cuddling part. And nearly every time he asks me, "Would you like to try?" Or sometimes he says, "Your turn now, Lou." I expect I shouldn't be this way but I feel pushed, even though he's so nice about it. I say, "It's all right," and sound a bit more sleepy than maybe I really am. By then it's usually late and I am tired, and so is he, especially after . . . and so when I say it's all right, it is. I fall asleep in no time: insomnia's not one of my problems!

Sometimes when I wake in the morning I've been having a sexy dream, but you're not responsible for your dreams, are you. Once I'm awake it fades. I never have been able to remember my dreams. There's something to that old idea about the Devil tempting you in your sleep. I don't mean that the Devil is doing this to me: I think it's just a physical thing. When it fades so fast it feels as if it wasn't meant for me in the first place. I pay no attention to it.

I don't know why I'm thinking about all this right now. The children will be back any moment and I will have spoiled my little time to myself. I really don't think about this much, ordinarily, one way or another.

Shirley, our first, is growing up: she'll be five next month. She's the same age as the war, and it looks as if that might be over just about the time she starts school. She can take good care of Bobby now. I trust her to take him for a walk down the street for half a block and bring him back to me in one piece, even though he's such a scallywag and won't always let her hold onto his hand. He just started walking but already he's fast. I worry that he'll think he's funny and get away from her and scoot out in front of a car. The first few times I never let them out of my sight, but I saw that she keeps a good eye on him. It takes a load off my mind, even if it's only for a few minutes, to have both of them outside.

I'm tired a lot of the time. We're expecting again at the end of the year — November, likely. Roy and I meant to wait a little longer, but something happened. I've lost two babies, one before Shirley that I carried all the way to term and then lost in the birth, and one only five months along in between those two. So I'd like to keep this one. I know I need to take it easy, and I do — as much as I can with two little ones.

But I just can't keep up. The darning hasn't been done for months, except for the odd emergency, and I'm ashamed to say that I'm always behind on the ironing. We're saving for a roller iron that will do the flat things, like sheets and pillowcases, and the pyjamas and underwear. Roy says he'll help out with the garden this summer and that would make a difference. He'll have to fit it in, though, around his job at the engine factory, and they're working long hours as it is because of the war. The government classified his job as essential to the war effort, which means he can't quit and pretty well has to work whatever hours they need him, but it also means that he stays here.

It's been hard on him. He's forever turning on the radio or reaching for the newspaper, searching for news from the Front. Three summers ago one of his high-school chums from back home was listed as killed in action at Dieppe. If Roy had gone, I think I would have taken Shirley and gone back to live with Mother and Dad until it was over. Of course then we didn't know it was going to last this long. But otherwise I don't see how we could have managed. I would have been back on the coast, back under Mother's thumb, with Roy in danger on the other side of the world. I have a lot to be thankful for.

Mother and Dad are coming to visit just after Shirley's birthday. I'm trying to get things in order here before they come. I'd dearly love to have Mother arrive and find no darning to do but, as I say, I can't do everything, not with this fatigue and two little ones and another on the way. Some days, as Dr. Marion Hilliard says in *Chatelaine*, all you can get done is to make it to the end of the day. Most days I get more done than that, thank goodness! Today so far I've cleaned the bathroom and the kitchen, changed Bobby three times and put him on the potty six times: he's due to be toilet-trained.

And I answered Shirley's question. This was her day for philosophy. She was playing under the grape arbour with her friend Carol from two doors down (that's another thing I did, made sugar water with red colouring in it so she could have a tea party) and goodness knows what those two mites were talking about, but Shirley came in with that sense of urgency she gets sometimes, her brown curls bouncing:

"Mummy — " her eyes got big — "It's im-por-nant." She drew a breath, being really dramatic: "Can God make a stick that has — *no ends*?"

I told her yes.

She went out with this news, and I think those two girls had been discussing it over tea!

A stick with no ends.

Yesterday it was fairies. She came back from her walk with Bobby and announced that they had both seen a fairy. She told me all about it: blue see-through dress, standing on a toadstool, yellow hair. It was the exact same fairy from her Peter Pan book that Roy and I gave her last birthday, but she seemed to believe that it had been out there on Traill Street and that she and Bobby had seen it.

What should I have said? If it had been Mother, she probably would have told her that fairies are only in your imagination, even accused her of lying, but I don't think Shirley lies. I think she thought she saw that fairy. How do I know? Maybe children do see things that we don't see. Mother says that I'm a romantic.

So I listened to Shirley's story. I said yes. I didn't try to make her take it back. She went off to her little place under the grape arbour, and I heard her talking to herself. She's a good child, awkward in some ways and not much help, but she tries to be responsible.

She's back out there again. Carol went home for her lunch and I got Shirley to clean away their little china tea set. After that she dragged her blue rocking chair into the sunshine and I think she's been practising reading. She does it with the form letters that come in for Roy as Sunday School superintendent, advertising material from Ryerson Press. I wish we could afford to buy those colouring books about children in foreign lands for me to use in the junior class, but there's a limit to what the church can afford. I enjoy teaching those classes. I find it very interesting to learn about foreign countries. We're doing a study packet on Africa this year in the Women's Missionary Society, and I'm the leader. Anyhow, Shirley puts circles around all the words that she can sound out. It's getting to be most of them, although she still doesn't know what half of them mean. She's really ready for school.

I should stop ironing and go out there with her. Bobby went down for a nap after their walk, and I'm sleepy myself, but I can't drop off when Shirley's up. Sometimes she goes to Carol's house and I get a catnap. But Carol's dad is in France and her mum has her own problems, so when I can I like to encourage them to play here. I'll just finish these few hankies and then I'll take a break and go out and sit with my daughter in the sun.

This is more like it. I ought to rest more. The sun feels good. I ought to put my feet up, or I'll have varicose veins again. The little blue rocking chair is going lickety-split.

"What are you doing, sweetheart?"

"I'm riding-my-horse-to-Brambley-Cross!"

"*Bambury* Cross. That's nice. But why don't you practise your reading? I want you to read nicely for Grandma when she comes."

She shows me the letter: she has put a circle around every last word.

"I got done." The chair slows down a bit. "Where's Bobby?"

"He's having his nap."

"Maybe he's hassing dreams."

"Having, you mean ... do you have dreams, honey?"

"I ... dreamed ... there was a whole lot of big men with nossing on ... " She giggles; obviously she thinks this is very funny, and the chair speeds up again: " ... and they standed in a circle with their big tinks pointing up, and they *peed* like a fountain!"

She laughs merrily as if there's nothing shameful about it at all! Lord! What if she told this story down at Carol's? What would they think?

I tell her no — don't ever tell me again about men with nothing on. I tell her it's not polite. She seems to understand, and looks crushed and worried, thank goodness. I don't think she'll tell this story around the neighbourhood now. I ask her where she learned that word "tink." I'm not surprised to hear that it's from those Campbell kids across the street. I've noticed before that that boy especially has a dirty mouth. I tell her that there's a right word for it, but it's a very private word and we don't say it. If she had asked me, I would have told her, but she didn't ask.

I was brought up ignorant of everything to do with sex, and I'm determined to bring my daughter up differently. I try to answer all of her questions, just like Parents' Magazine advises. So she already knows where babies come from, because she asked. I always explain to her that it's part of love and is too precious and private to talk about in public. It's for grown-ups, I tell her. I think she doesn't consider Carol or the Campbell children to be "public," because I've overheard her busily educating them. I hope it's all right with their parents, that's all I can say.

I send her off to fetch the Boy Jesus book that Mother gave her last Christmas. This is the one I'd really like her to be reading well when they come. I think from Mother's last letter that she didn't believe me when I told her that Shirley has just about got this book down pat. In one of her letters she said that she thinks we're spoiling her.

Shirley comes running with the book, and turns to her favourite picture, the boy Jesus in a long white robe with his arms raised and doves — Shirley always calls them pigeons — flying all around him. It is pretty.

She sounds out the verse under the picture:

We'll bring the little duties
We have to do each day;
We'll try our best to please him
At home, at school, at play.

Mother should like that. Shirley gets it all correct, except for "duties," which she reads, perfectly seriously, as "dollies." "We'll bring the little dollies." It makes sense to her! I do hope that

Mother enjoys her half as much as I do.

Well, my time in the sun can't last forever. The ironing calls, and then Bobby is waking up and it's potty time again. I push his little thing down into the pot and touch it with a bit of cold water, and he goes in the pot! This is the second success today. Shirley and I both give him a lot of praise, and he looks very pleased with himself. Of course with the number of times that I've put him on the pot, I don't know whether it's the baby or me who is being trained!

By the time Roy comes home tired from his long day, I have a good meat and potatoes supper ready — well, hamburger, really: shepherd's pie. But with creamed corn it's one of his favourites, right after scalloped potatoes and meatballs.

We put the children to bed. Roy sits on the step between the kitchen and their bedroom and sings the lullaby they like, "Lucy Gray." I listen as I finish the ironing. I see the tenderness in his eyes as he watches me and hear it in his voice as he sings. The song is that sad one, about a little girl who loses her way, and when they set out to find her they follow her footsteps in the snow until they come to the middle of a bridge and then they just stop. The song doesn't say what happened to her.

He's been doing some motor repairs on the side and we both work late. It's eleven before we come to bed. It's been several days since we last made love and I check to make sure that there is a roll of toilet paper in the nightstand just in case. Now that Bobby sleeps all night, I do hate to get out of bed again once I'm in. Roy gives me a cuddle. I tell him about the stick with no ends and about bringing the boy Jesus her dollies and we have a chuckle together. There is a long silence. His arm across me grows slack and heavy and I hear from his breathing that he's sound asleep.

I am deep under myself when I hear Shirley's voice. I pull myself awake. She is right beside our bed. I can partly see the white nightgown that I made for her, glimmering in the dark. She says she has had a bad dream. Fumbling, I switch on the bedside lamp.

Roy has a habit, when he has had a long day and is disturbed in the night, of not quite waking up but starting to talk in his sleep. I think he sort of knew that it was Shirley who was there, and that she was upset about something or other, but somehow in his sleep he got the idea that she had a motor that had broken down. If there is anything that Roy knows how to fix, it's a motor.

So he heaves himself up to a sitting position and looks at her with his eyes open, but I know that he's really still asleep.

"Here," he says in a helpful tone of voice, reaching across to her as if he has something in his hand. "Here's a bolt that should do the trick."

"Lie down, Roy," I say, pushing at him. Tired as I am, I start to laugh. But then I see the look on her face. Tears are rolling down her cheeks. She hasn't seen him like this before and all she knows is that her daddy acted as if he is handing her something and she can see there's nothing there. That scared her even more. I try to explain to her, but I'm not sure she understands. "What was it, dear?" I ask. "Tell Mummy your dream." I'm afraid she's going to catch cold, standing there on the linoleum in her bare feet.

It was down at Carol's house, comes her voice, very shaky. It was in the backyard. The Boy Jesus was there and pigeons were coming down and and suddenly she was one of the pigeons! She was flying! It felt very nice! "I flied and flied so high! And I could see Carol's playhouse and the boy Jesus and then I flied right down to his hand." She is beginning to move her arms about and her curls are bobbing — I become caught up myself in all this skilful flying my daughter has just experienced as a dove.

"And then Jesus . . . Jesus . . . . "

"What is it, honey? Maybe you shouldn't tell me if it's so awful." Maybe I should just get up and tuck her back into bed, sing her a lullaby.

Jesus grabbed her, she says. "He teared me up! I bleeded!"

I put my hand on her. I'm shocked to feel how violently she's trembling.

Children just take for granted that you can fix their bad dreams.

And I know the magazines say you shouldn't bring children into your bed, it starts a bad habit. But I'm too tired to tuck her in again. I lift the covers and, just this one time, I let her snuggle in between Roy and me. She is still shivering, and clings to my nightdress the way she did when she was little. I hold her tight to me and remember her as an infant at the breast. Already that seems a long time ago: she's becoming so grown up. Gradually she settles down. I keep my arm around her, to protect her from whatever she imagines is there. Roy turns over toward us and gives us both an awkward hug, maybe in his sleep trying to protect both of us — but what could he have done if he had had to go to war like so many of the other men on this street? I know the point is that they are supposed to be protecting us over there. It's hard to think about, this war.

What a terrible dream. The poor little mite. Jesus — the blood — why would she dream a thing like that? What did we have for supper? Did I put too much sugar in their tea? Surely that wasn't it. Oh, my pillow is tempting. The baby turns over inside; I think it's healthy. I think I'm better on my side. In one more minute . . . I'll be back . . . asleep.

Violet

The three plump Baird girls all had their diamonds. The oldest, Doris, was already married, and living with her husband in the house beside the church. Thelma Baird planned a December ceremony. Joyce Baird would be married more hastily, but still with due decorum, a mere month from her engagement. The husbands were all in construction and would find jobs building the new subdivision. Highway 401 was going through and was really changing the neighbourhood. Right where Shirley still went to school there was going to be a new thing called a cloverleaf.

These changes were the last of Shirley's worries, however. She'd be moving on to high school in the fall. The changes which fascinated her had to do with the whole mysterious business of getting engaged and married. It was time to sort out what love was before it started to happen to her. Besides the flurry of interest around the Baird sisters, she knew that Eleanor, the choir director, was seeing somebody, but Eleanor kept her business private and nobody knew just what was going on. A few of the women in the choir were established matrons, already with children at home.

It was typical of Shirley that at thirteen she was a member of the church choir. She took her religion seriously. Her parents had allowed her to join the church when she was only eleven. Actually, her mother had wanted her to wait, but her father took her side and said he felt she was ready. Eleven had been a big year: her periods started; also she had to get her appendix out. Unlike the others in the confirmation class, she actually read the pamphlets the minister handed out: "United Church Membership," "I Believe." And while she convalesced from her appendix operation, she whiled away the hours by rereading them and by memorizing the books of the Bible. At the time she joined the choir, it was clear to her that there was a commandment to love everybody. It was her own idea to begin making lists. In her diary she inscribed the names of people towards whom she had succeeded in feeling love. All three of the Baird sisters had made it, the moment of success usually coming when one of them was singing a solo. Thelma, for instance, with her big chest and full voice, wearing her yellow sateen Sunday dress, building one Sunday to a thrilling climax: "And I knew I could love him fore-e-ver, that Stranger of Galilee!" Shirley drew a glowing circle around Thelma, and held her within it; as the music swelled, she felt a movement somewhere in her solar plexus and, sure enough, love flowed in.

    She was still working on Eleanor.

    Another hard one was Violet Hiram.

    Violet was older than the other women; Shirley thought of her as an old maid. Nobody teased Violet about boyfriends: there was about her none of the richness and fullness of the Baird sisters; she was thin, angled; something about her body or the way she walked was off-kilter. She had a long face, wider in the jaw than in the forehead. Her features were small, the pointed nose red on the end in cold weather. Her hair was brownish-blond, tightly permed. A wispy smile seemed stuck on top of knowledge that really things were sad. Yet, Shirley sensed the community's dependence on women like this. Violet asked nothing for herself. She was no drain on anyone's resources. She was totally dependable.

    And she played the piano. Before anyone else showed up for choir practice, Violet was already there, going over not only the pieces they would need for Sunday, but also exploring the complicated variations from the back of the hymn book, pieces she liked to play for the introit and the extroit. Few paid attention to these: in the United Church it was the norm for the

VIOLET

piano to play over a loud buzz of conversation. People stopped when the minister walked in, started again when he walked out. Nevertheless she laboured over this music, never playing anything flashy or beyond her capacity, but from time to time surprising those who did listen with a nice passage from Handel or Bach.

Violet lived with her mother, in a small house set back from the road, with no trees. Her father had died in a backhoe accident many years before, and she supported both her mother and herself, working in a bank in Brinton as a teller. She was one of those careful, mature women who, in Shirley's short experience, could not be imagined making mistakes when they counted out one's cash. They did not ask the next teller which form to use. They approached the question of one's money with seriousness and restraint. Violet was exactly right for this job. Although she looked as if she were easily flustered, she was not. When the choir floundered in rehearsal, Eleanor would cut them off and make them go over and over the same bit. Over and over again Violet found the right spot. She never lost her place.

When a man named Herbert began turning up after choir practice to drive Violet the half-mile home, Shirley hardly noticed he was there. To her mind, Violet was a woman to be respected: she was reserved, on time, correct, and she had admirable skills. The man lounging at the back of the church was youngish, baby-faced, with a truly enormous belly and a coarse, joking manner. People said he was big because he had been a bus-driver and didn't get any exercise. Shirley noticed that they didn't seem clear whether Herbert were still driving a bus, or, indeed, just what he did. Some of the women teased Violet when he arrived: "Violet! Herbie's here!" and she flushed. She had very nice skin, pale and soft, velvety-looking. When she flushed she went a raw red colour, blotchy, embarrassing in and of itself.

One Thursday when Shirley got home from school, her mother said that Eleanor had called and asked her to get to choir practice half an hour early. She hurried, and when she walked in, Violet wasn't yet there, but there was a great deal of giggling and whispering and scurrying going on in the choir loft. Eleanor sat at the piano, complaining that she wasn't sure she could do it. She kept stretching her fingers over the keys, silently practising chords.

When Violet appeared, Eleanor banged down the chords. "Here Comes The Bride!" The choir broke out in loud laughter and cheers. "Congratulations!" The woman started and turned. For a moment it looked as if she might run away. Then her thin lips pursed into what passed with her for a smile, and she moved quickly up the aisle with her lopsided stride, heading for her place on the piano bench. The choir director was slow giving it up, still leaning over the piano, picking out final chords and ending with a crash. Violet lifted her left hand close to her angular body and spread her fingers, not a generous gesture but a minimal display. Choir members jumped up and craned over the railing to view the spark of light on her third finger. It wasn't big like Thelma's florid cluster that she had to take off every time she wanted to do something useful. But it was there. Violet had her diamond.

Meanwhile, Shirley had been experiencing attention herself, unpleasant attention, during recess and noonhour at school. Next door to her family, a quarter-mile down the road, there lived a boy named John Wilson. Both families were large, and the children often got together outside of school and chores, to play hide-and-seek in the Wilsons' big barn, visit the new calves or pigs or, in the case of the girls, play school or sew dolls' clothes. She admired John's older sister, Meg, and was willing to tolerate his younger sister, Jane, who was really more friends with her own younger sister, Beth. Meg Wilson was on the list of people she loved, and she was working on Jane. Beth got on the list because of being a sister, but quite often had to be scratched off. (Shirley was troubled about this: she had written to David C. Cook, the publisher of their Sunday School paper, about this problem she had about hating her sister, and he had sent her back a comforting letter, with a number of Bible passages to look up.)

So she and John knew each other but it hadn't occurred, probably to either of them at this point in their lives, that a girl and a boy could be friends.

On a certain day after school, though, after they had passed the hill between them and the school, and the Farber kids had stopped at their house and the smaller kids dropped back, she and John found themselves walking along together, and it turned out to be nice. His sister Meg had started high school that year: this might be why they suddenly discovered each other on the opposite sides of the road.

Suddenly she stumbled upon a new feeling, a sense of connection over sharing conversation about school and the new calves in the Wilsons' barn, news about a fire in a haystack down their concession road, their rotten brothers and sisters, and how did Meg like high school: she had to ask him about that. The realization dawned on her that she was actually talking to a boy. She became terribly excited. It had nothing to do with him as a person at all.

The night that the choir celebrated Violet's engagement, it was very hard to concentrate on the anthems they rehearsed. Violet played some wrong notes, greatly increasing the general merriment. Eleanor had to become professional and severe and act like she did at work at the telephone company when somebody had an overdue bill. Finally they sobered up enough to sing through all the hymns, and the anthem for Sunday, and practise a new way of doing the final "Amen."

That night Herbert didn't come, but Shirley thought a lot about the new couple, trying to make sense of what seemed to her all wrong. The way she said it to herself was, Violet and Herbert are in love. This changed her perception of both of them. Violet began to look more romantic. If Herbert could be in love with her, she must in some way be beautiful. Shirley noted Violet's nice skin, and reconsidered what her little eyes and pointed nose and tight undersized mouth might look like through the eyes of love. Violet, she decided, was kind of fragile-looking, really, and upright with a sorrowful dignity. She began to love her.

But to imagine Violet loving Herbert was too much. Presumably she must, or else she wouldn't be engaged. Shirley began to see that love might be an incomprehensible state that just falls on one without sense or warning. From this view she had to feel a little sorry for Violet, caught up in this ridiculous emotion with a great crass man, but she was certain also that being in love must be an intensely pleasant sensation. And it would, after all, carry Violet forward into a woman's fulfilment: marriage, sex, probably even children. The church pianist had lost her peripheral old-maid status in her community, had instead become a centre of interest, a bride-to-be. Shirley worried that nobody seemed quite certain whether or not Herbert actually worked. A man who didn't work was an unthinkable category, like getting married without being in love.

Another thing worried her, too dark to actually pull out of her consciousness and look at straight on. She didn't understand how they were going to make love. Violet was going to get squashed. One day she opened this topic indirectly, over dishes, with her mother, and gathered from the ensuing conversation that there are, well, a number of different positions. Shirley couldn't quite imagine one that would do the trick. It might be, she thought, moving uncomfortably away from the graphics that kept forming in her mind, that perhaps a man's thing (she imagined it hairy) gets a lot longer than she had formerly thought likely.

Violet seemed happy. Shirley thought she could detect a quiet romantic glow in her small eyes, and when Herbert came for her after choir practice and grabbed her crookedly toward him, with his fat arm weighing down her narrow shoulders, she kept on smiling her wispy smile. Shirley got knots in her stomach at this point, feeling that somehow he seemed unaware of the one thing she had always definitely valued about Violet: her dignity. But Violet smiled, and the diamond on her finger flashed under the church lights.

Her own feelings, Shirley was learning, were a slippery and untrustworthy way of sorting out her world. Without putting it clearly to herself, she knew she needed to learn to apply exterior explanations to what she saw around her. What was shameful and what was precious often seemed completely reversed, and there was nothing to do but to learn the proper way of experiencing things, and later on bring her feelings into line. She had made some gains focusing on love; her feelings of disgust were, she was quite certain, similarly immature.

For instance, she had got it all wrong with John Wilson. She had noted, from her side of the road, what a handsome fellow he was: he had heavy dark eyebrows and lashes as long as a girl's. She remembered overhearing his mother admitting to her mother that she worried sometimes that he might be too good-looking, might be, you know, a Pretty Boy. She was unsure about this distinction and tried to check him out: how could you tell the difference? None of this had anything to do with the words they shared back and forth, or the warm feeling inside of her that perhaps they were becoming friends. She had not been very good at friendships so far.

This idyll did not last long, perhaps less than a week.

Inevitably, the other children noticed that Shirley and John were walking home together after school.

Inside and outside the outdoor privies, on the board fence

and even in a few places on the concrete foundations of the school itself, chalk hearts were scribbled, with J.W. Loves S.M. in every conceivable colour and script. They were the great new event of the schoolyard, and she hadn't enough sense or experience to realize that their enemies couldn't keep it up: the taunts seemed only to increase, in volume and persistence and in cruelty. "John likes Shirley!" "Shirley li-ikes Jo-ohn!" "Don't you think you want to come over *here*, John? Shirrr-ly's over here!" "Don't you want to give her a *kiss*?" The sensible thing to do on the schoolyard was to pretend loathing of one another and say the most cutting things they could think of: "I wouldn't look at him if he were the last boy on earth." "Her? Give me a break!"

Shirley had only a sketchy notion of what was usual in the society outside the classroom. Her preference had always been to stay in if she could and help the teacher prepare art projects or number charts for the primary grades. There were sixty children in eight grades that year in a one-room school, and the teacher was grateful for any help she could get. So Shirley was unaware of what a juicy target she made of herself when, drawn in spite of the ridicule by her new feelings about John, she ventured day after day into the schoolyard. The older girls tended to clump together, and she looked about anxiously for them, feeling awkward and exposed with no one about except the older boys and little kids. But the girls had some hiding place. When they emerged, they turned out to be her worst enemies.

"John! Shirley's looking for you! Shirley! John's hurt his finger and he wants you to — suck it!"

She had no idea why this made every other kid fall about with laughter, made more raucous still by the look of disdain and puzzlement on her face.

She didn't know how John felt. She suffered. Somehow the nice warm feeling was being infused with shame. It was confusing. In the end it was too much.

When they left school, against the background of catcalls and taunts, John would go on with his younger brothers and some other boys; Shirley would look around for some girls or walk by herself. Usually she walked partway with Betty Farber, who was younger than she was and who, off the school ground, seemed to feel some sympathy.

Then, on the other side of the hill past the Farbers, John would just happen to drop back or she would just happen to catch up, and after awhile they would be having a nice talk again, shoes scuffing on the dusty road, goldenrod in the ditches and bluebirds, in those days, everywhere. The sun would beat down and it seemed like four miles to his house, although really the whole trip, from the school to her place, was only a mile and a half. Neither of them would ever say a word about what was going on with the kids at school.

One day, she didn't know why, perhaps wanting to sound sophisticated and smart, perhaps just in a lapse of awareness that can happen at the end of a long day, she failed to make the transition. She lifted one shoulder as she had seen the other girls do and, with a grimace straight from recess, asked:

"Do I have to walk with you? Don't I have a choice?"

John walked faster. He did not reply.

Immediately Shirley was out of her depth. Miserable, she had no idea what to say. If it had been a girl, she would have thought to apologize. But this was a boy, and she couldn't trust her feelings, and she didn't know the rules.

John walked with the boys after that, and although she still sometimes played with her sister Beth and his sister Jane, he never spoke to her again.

She knew no way to make it right.

Violet's mother invited the choir to a trousseau tea. All the women brought cups and saucers as gifts and trooped up the squeaky stairs in the mother's small frame house to exclaim over Violet's underthings — rayon panties, bras and slips from Woolworth's; one set all in pale green, matching her going-away dress, a pale green knit pinned up on the door. The underwear was laid out prettily on a bed — the actual bed, as it turned out, where Violet and Herbert were going to sleep as a married couple, because after the wedding he would just move in. Violet would continue with her job at the bank.

The choir threw a shower, and a lot of people came, including wives or mothers of the men who joined the choir only at Easter and Christmas. Shirley was as usual the youngest there. She wandered about as Violet opened her gifts, examining all the cake plates and embroidered linen and minor household appliances — there were three toasters — displayed on card tables in the next room. She also read the cards: her view of the universe included the presupposition that everyone carefully chose the messages printed on their cards.

This is how she found the card with the roses. The verse in it had a lot to say about roses: how they represent love and bring beauty into the world and seem so right for this bride.... She was caught up in the image of the church pianist as the gentle, loving bride. How much more appropriate all these words would sound, she thought, if instead of "rose" they said "Violet." And so she found a blank piece of card that had been used as a spacer between two sets of bowls, and she borrowed a pen from Thelma Baird and she found a corner where she believed she was unobserved, and she recopied the poem so that it became a hymn of love and praise to lovely Violet. She disguised her handwriting by imitating the script in the original card. Her heart was pounding as she wrote. It seemed to her that these were the perfect words. This was the secret she had felt growing in herself: that dowdy, dreary Violet was lovely, to be loved. She slipped the card in among the gifts, and returned the pen.

Some time later one of the women found the card, and read it out.

"Who wrote this?" she asked.

Something in Shirley knew better than to indicate by so much as a blush or a gesture that the poem came to her as anything other than a complete surprise. She felt, though, like fainting. There was a draining feeling at her lips and a buzzing in her head as she said nothing. She played at looking about herself as if for the person concerned. No one asked her directly, although Eleanor glanced sharply her way, and Thelma Baird snickered. Violet reddened and looked vaguely pleased. The moment passed.

Twenty years later, Shirley saw Violet again. It was on her trip home to tell her mother that her second marriage had come apart and once again someone, herself this time, was filing for divorce. As she came into the vestibule of the senior citizens' housing where her mother lived, there was Violet, looking exactly the same, sitting with Violet's aged mother, playing euchre in the sitting room with two friends. After a moment's hesitation, this much older Shirley went over to them.

"You probably don't remember me," she said.

But Violet did. To Shirley's surprise, Violet's mother said that she did, too. The mother had recently moved into this residence, and Violet and Herb had a house in the village nearby. Herb helped out with the general store, delivering the groceries, and with an aging population there was more and more call for his services. Violet had retired the previous summer from the bank. She didn't mention any children. She held her cards in a tight fan, close to her, and Shirley noticed the engagement diamond, and above it the worn gold wedding ring.

Her own mother, when she got there, was feeling subdued. She loved her daughter, she said (but Shirley thought her hug had been perfunctory. Maybe it was just her mother's bad back, but what Shirley needed right now was a lot of reassurance), but she couldn't understand what it was young women wanted nowadays. She and Shirley's father had understood that marriage is a matter of give and take. "And there's another sad thing," she said.

Shirley felt angry. She wished her father were still alive: she felt as if he would have understood. But she managed to reply courteously. "What is it, mother? What else is sad?"

"That John Wilson," said her mother. "You remember John, Shirl. I went to his funeral last week. He shot himself in the head. It's very hard on his mother, and he leaves a wife and two children. This world is moving faster than I care to know about."

The two women sat in silence in the darkening room. Shirley thought of making some bizarre little joke, like: "Hey, I was his first girlfriend, Mum. He should have stuck with me."

Then she began to wonder what John's problem really had been, what his life had been like. Was he a Pretty Boy, after all, she wondered, and what, then, was she? How early did she begin to overlay her real encounters with people with constructs of romantic lust, and now that she is adult, and has stopped looking about for the rules, why does she go on wishing there was some way to make it right?

JOKES

Harold sets down the business section of *The Globe and Mail*. He hears a clink in the kitchen. For a moment he takes for granted that Angie is making them both a cup of Ovaltine. Then of course he remembers that Angie is not there, and that the noise he hears is the cat, walking around on the dishes again.

"Get down from there! Ssst!" he hisses from the living room, then gets up to make sure that he has been obeyed. What a mess. The cat has knocked over a cup of cold coffee, and brown fluid is running all around the cabinet at the edge of the sink, just now breaking the meniscus — high school physics: he has not forgotten the word — that was holding it back, and spilling over the edge of the cabinet and onto the floor.

"Shit."

He finds a cloth, pushes it into the spill, and looks around for the cat. It slinks under the dining room table, apparently believing that he can't see it, and when he bends to scoop it up, moves faster in a sneaky way and tries to escape. He captures it easily, though, and carries it back to the kitchen, scolding as he goes.

"Listen! You know better than that! I'm not going to tell you again! Dishes are off limits! Look what you did! You want to go on living with me? Bad! Bad cat!"

He holds down her soft furry neck and rubs her nose back and forth in the spilled coffee. The animal cringes, tenses. He gives her a bat with his hand as he releases her. She springs away and slinks under the table again. While he's down there, he notices that her food dish is empty, and wonders how long it has been that way. There's still some cat food left in the bag. He pours it in; a few bits spill into the cat's grungy water dish. With an air of virtue, Harold rinses the water dish out and refills it.

There's a brown carpet in this kitchen, something that was here when he and Angie moved in, so it's hard to see now where the coffee landed. He decides to scrub the general area anyway and takes a few minutes to wipe up most of the rest on the cabinet, rinse the cloth — it's actually the dishcloth — and rub at the place on the carpet. He becomes aware of a number of other spots. He's going to have to rent a cleaner from the grocery store one of these days, get this place looking good again, probably better than it ever was when Angie was here. She was always off to some meeting or other, or out with her women friends.

Her women friends. Some woman would be going with her to the kind of emotional movies she liked to go to, or something to do with Indians or street people or cripples, people who as far as he's concerned are best left to sort things out for themselves.

No doubt the guys he grew up with would say he's been an idiot, but that would be the same guys who would have said he ought to have knocked some sense into her, a foolish and repugnant idea which never had anything to do with what he and Angie were to each other. No, she had to do what she had to do. It hurts like hell and there's nothing he can do about it.

Harold teaches commerce at the local high school, but it's summer, so he's home. Other summers he took an upgrading course, but not this year. He finds it hard to get going these days: he needs focus. Needs a woman, too, but although he's had a few good fantasies, the thought of really going back into all that, especially now, with all the new complications of VD and AIDS, has been too much for him. He's caught himself eyeing the girls on the corners downtown and wonders if maybe that wouldn't be the best way: they have to keep clean, don't they, in order to stay in that line of work? He doesn't know for sure: there have been stories in the paper of a prostitute who deliberately spread AIDS. Some confused young woman, angry at men. He can hear Angie saying to him that if he knew more about that woman's life . . . ! But he doesn't know. And what did Angie know about a whore's life, for that matter? The ones he sees downtown look to him as if they like their job just fine. He bought a box of safes one day in a pharmacy — felt like a fool, and half-expected the girl at the checkout counter to make some smart-ass remark, but this is the modern age: she just checked them through as if they were toothpaste or Preparation H, both of which he also bought at the same time.

That was the first he'd bought condoms himself since university. After they were married he always got Angie to do it. She used to complain sometimes; once or twice she tried to send him for a box of Tampax. But there was no way he was going to do that, and it got to be a kind of joke between them. When they were in bed and he'd get aroused, he always found a condom under the pillow, and Angie would have a clean towel under hers. She must have wanted it, or why did she get ready like that all those years? And she'd put a little vaseline in between her legs, too, when she was coming to bed. She didn't do that just sometimes; she did it every night. Sometimes just the sound of her unscrewing the lid of that jar was enough in itself to turn him on. He would lie there with his hard-on, waiting for her to finish letting down her nightie and come into the bed. He had to go slow — he liked to, in fact, after the first few years — she needed a little touching and cuddling first, before he slipped in there on that vaseline welcome mat —

Harold has to decide what to do with his hard-on. He's up and dressed, has been watching TV, and he's getting hungry for his breakfast, so he just lets it subside, which it does as soon as he smells the bacon frying. He washes a few dishes while the egg's cooking, but not the pans from last night. He sets them in water to make them easier to clean when he gets to them. He tries not to notice that every pan in the house is now sitting around the kitchen full of water.

Harold eats his breakfast. He's worried about cholesterol, and so lately he has an egg just every other day. On the in-between days he has bran flakes. A good source of protein — if you add enough milk. Harold chokes up a bit as he chews on his toast. That was another old joke between him and Angie — about the way cereal was advertised as being a good source of protein, if you added enough milk.

He discovers he is looking forward to lunch with that woman Doris. Her phone call out of the blue yesterday really knocked him for a loop, but now he finds it's cheering him up. He hasn't been looking for friends, especially not women friends. And he had been several minutes on the phone just trying to place her. At moments like that he really misses Angie. DORIS SURLES? he would have written on the whiteboard over the phone in big black letters, and then given her a beseeching look, and Angie would likely have laughed in that way he wished she wouldn't, as if he must be pretty stupid not to remember *that*, but anyway she would come over to help. She would have written CALGARY CONFERENCE on the board and if he still looked confused maybe RED HAT? and TOP SALESWOMAN and even, looking annoyed if he hadn't looked enlightened by then, HAD DRINK IN HOTEL BAR. Except that Angie couldn't have known any of this stuff, because Angie had left him by the time he met Doris last Easter break in Calgary at a convention that he went to out of sheer loneliness, sheer want of a place to go, because what does a commerce teacher need with a sales conference? He had told himself that he had to keep in touch with the real world of business, but common sense suggested that he would have done better taking the manager of the local pharmacy or something out for a beer. Instead he had endured the crowded airlines to get to that conference, and he had enjoyed every bit of the hype and flash and jargon to do with the world of SALES! Angie would not have understood this at all: "Madison Avenue" was practically a swearword for her. But he had liked it. Sometimes a little superficiality and slick talk are what a man needs to make him feel part of the time he lives in. Angie thought she understood how he felt about this, but Angie was trying to live in some future utopia she was hoping for, not the dog-eat-dog, competitive world that's really out there, with E-mail and downsizing and stock market fraud....

He'd joked to her once that he should have been a stockbroker: it would have given room, he'd said, for his natural bent toward larceny and sculduggery and she could have been proud of him. Had he really thought that she wasn't proud of him, then, or was it just a joke? Harold hesitates over the question, and then decides that he really doesn't want to know. What he wants to know, and to remember, is that he said something that made her laugh and that it was a nice moment. He remembers more: he'd started a little dialogue and she had played along; every once in a while she was willing to play his straight man — or straight person, are they saying nowadays? — and it always delighted him when she did ... What a fool he has been ... or maybe not. ...

Hello, dear, I'm home!
Angie (falsetto): *Oh, hi, dear. What did you do today?*
Harold: *I – I – well – Oh yes: I had lunch with John!*
Angie (sweetly): *How is he?*
John? Oh, John's fine, just fine. ...
And how is Sarah?

(It was when she did that, played along a little bit further, that he had felt the burst of delight:)

They both seem very well. You know, it looks as if the – the – well, the indictment – has been dropped. They're both really happy about it. ...

Angie had laughed hard. It was nice of her to laugh at his foolish jokes. But if she liked them that much, why isn't she here now?

Harold struggles to remember Doris. He's fairly certain about the red hat. A little beret thing, that was what it was. Looked quite smart. Maybe hats are coming back in. Brown hair. Wavy. A business woman, probably with no ideas inside her head other than profit and loss and whether the r-word is turning into the d-word. Still. It could be a refreshing change, talking to a woman like that. Angie never knew the first thing about the economy. Maybe he had listened to Angie too much.

How had this Doris woman known where he was? He must have given her his card in Calgary. Imagined that, if she showed up, Angie could invite her to supper, forgetting that Angie wasn't going to be there anymore, and they could show her some hospitality in a strange town. Damned awkward now that she's here and he's on his own. He'll have to take her to a restaurant and which one? Can't take a guest to the place where he and Angie always went: Cap's Fish and Chips. Maybe he and this Doris could meet in the restaurant in the Eaton Centre. She could probably find the Eaton Centre. The restaurant in there was a bit classy and not too expensive. He remembers going there once with Angie, when they came here the first time as tourists and were spending too much cash.

This lunch with Doris isn't really firmed up: she's supposed to call back sometime this morning. It all came at him too fast yesterday. He'd let on that he might not be able to tear himself away, that he needed to take care of a few things to do with the house. She'd been over to his school, no doubt on business: she was in some kind of software, as far as he can remember. That'll be how she got his home phone — from the school. So she's supposed to phone this morning, and probably he'll suggest the Eaton Centre. If he really wants to go.

He doesn't, really, want to go.

He could stay here and finish up plans he was working on last night. He's thinking of building a boat. What does he want to go off for and make conversation with a woman in a red hat? What will they talk about? Besides the stock market, he means.

Harold is besieged by erotic images of the woman he had met at the conference in bed with him, her red beret off on the pillow, her breasts like pillows, she's going to a lot of trouble to get hold of him, maybe she wants it really bad, maybe he's got the upper hand here, maybe she would be a much softer person than the woman who had pulled out her notepad and had worn that uptight business suit. In his mind she has taken off that suit, she is all over him . . . . Where is this taking place? Back here?

With dismay Harold notes his second hard-on of the morning. He'd better take care of this, hadn't he, or he'll be attacking her over lunch. Or at least he might stray from business. It occurs to him that she might not even be aware that he no longer has a wife. In Calgary he probably wasn't talking about it. The girl in the office at the school might have told her, if they got into conversation, that his wife has left him. Wonder how women talk about that. Maybe an alarm goes off: this other woman left him, maybe there's a reason. On the other hand . . . .

Thinking of this woman Doris maybe coming after him because somebody has told her he's on his own, thinking of how maybe she's extremely available, Harold has gone back into his bedroom and is just at the point of coming into an old silk nightgown of Angie's when the telephone rings.

Fuck, he can't answer now.

The telephone rings four times and then the answering machine comes on. He always meant to change that message, but he doesn't know where Angie put the manual. Behind his shuddering and thrust, Harold hears his wife's bright voice, inviting the caller to leave a name, a number. Angie loved getting messages. The voice finishes and for a moment there is silence. Harold zips up his fly and thinks about picking up the phone. He feels obscurely, though, that he'd sound foolish, coming in after the message like that. While he waits, whoever is at the other end hangs up.

There is a click.

The message tape rewinds.

николая

This little boy, see, he comes in here regular, red hair, freckles, or he did. He watches where I'm working, redoing furniture. He likes to bring along his plastic lunchbox from school and eat what's left over while we talk. And I like him. He's a good kid. Different. He wants to know the names of everything, what they're for. I don't mind explaining as I go along. I have to tell him to keep his fingers off what I'm doing, though.

There was trouble at home. That's why he was in here as much as he did. Now they weren't throwing dishes or nothing, but those young folk his parents can't've been getting along. You'd see her, his mother, coming down the street with her shopping bag. When the boy he was in school — he's at kindergarten now, he told me — some days he was here and some days he warn't — she smiled at neighbours as normal, tried to pass the time of day, but there's something was not right. Don't rightly know how to put it. If you caught sight of her when she's not noticing, there was a sadness. Yet if you met him he smiled and says Good morning, Mr. Douglas, nice day. He'd be wearing that business suit, and he knows from nothing about furniture, although he let on that he does. To look at them two, you'd never think nothing was wrong.

I'd noticed there was an arrangement for the boy to stay at

Mrs. Armstrong's across the street when the mother went into town to the college. She's taking courses there, though Jesus knows why: women these days seem to have to keep on going back to school. There's where I made my mistake, I told her, not staying in medical school. She's got a nice laugh. Whatever, it wasn't working out; just as you'd think it's okay, the boy comes in all upset. I always could tell.

This one day he come in and he was more than upset, he was in a rotten stinking mood, which I never seen in him before. Cranky, getting into everything, messing with the pieces I had set up ready to put in place. You're acting like a kid didn't get enough sleep, I said.

He looked at me like I must know everything. I was up to midnight, he said, trying to look proud of himself. Nobody'd put me to bed. Mommy had a exam and Daddy was mad.

What was your dad mad about then? I asked, making it my business.

I don't know, he said, looking bored. Maybe cause Mommy had a exam. Stan's not really my dad anyway. What's this for? He had an upholstery needle.

You put that down now, Richard, I said, but I told him what it was for all the same, showed him where I was going to use it next. He listens like a grownup ordinarily, better'n most grownups, but this time he could not keep still. Finally he just got into too much stuff and it started to get on my nerves, so I told him I was busy and tried to shoo him out. Then he started to cry.

This never happened before neither. He's only four but he's always been cheerful. I don't think he puts on a good face, maybe, like his mother: I think by nature he's just a cheerful kid.

I can't go home, he said. Mommy told me I can't go home.

So? She wants you to play outside awhile.

But I want to go home. I'm tired and I'm grumpy and I don't like Stan.

I saw then that the father's car was in the driveway. Hadn't noticed that before.

I guess they need some time to talk, I told him. I could see he was really tired, and so I started to talk to him kind of coaxingly. Can't you go over to Mrs. Armstrong's? You're a big boy, Richard, my lad. Why don't you go over there and just lie down for a little while? I think you need to have a nap.

Richard? You in here? It was his father. I didn't care for the way he was looking at me at all. Sorry he's bothering you, he said.

He's not bothering me, I said. I wasn't going to tell on my young pal that today I'd been just shooing him out just when his old man turned up. He's learning the trade here, I said.

The boy'd went out as soon as his dad called and was staring down at the ground. His dad put his hand on the scruff of his neck and steered him towards home.

I thought you was supposed to be at Mrs. Armstrong's, I heard him say.

We're an old neighbourhood down here, so I suppose you can believe me that when I see single sheets out on their line five days in a row I don't need the wife to tell me that some young person over yonder has taken to wetting his bed. Twice I saw the boy go by with his mom, or doing something in the front yard at the Armstrongs, but he never come over here. He looked to me like he'd lost his bounce. I noticed his father bought him one of those motorized sidewalk cars that must cost a small fortune. Richard drove it up and down in front of his place, but there aren't any other kids around here to show it off to so he looked kind of lost.

November was coming up, and I'd been saving bits of broken wood and torn cloth in a trash can in the backyard. Where I come from they have bonfires at Guy Fawkes, the fifth of November, and I figured I'd get away with a short one back of the store and invite the lad and his mother and his dad if he wanted to come, to come over and toast marshmallows. Missus has some unbent wire hangers left over from when we had our own kids. So we're all set, and then I don't get to see the boy at all.

Finally I catch him just when he's getting off their mini school bus.

Richard, I call to him, can you spare a minute?

He come over to me with the same sunny look as ever, and I realize I'd missed him.

How was school, I have to ask him, just like he was one of my own. And then I tell him we're going to have a bloody big bonfire the next night and how we're inviting him and his parents and if he had any friends they're welcome.

He backs away all of a sudden when I make mention of his father. He glances at me in a sullen way and stares at his running shoes.

I don't think I can come, he says, mumbling.

Perhaps I can ask your mother, I say.

He perks up.

Yes, he says, could you call my mother?

He knew his phone number — we always taught it to our kids young, too — and so I wrote it down and later in that night I had the Missus give them a call.

I can't promise, she says when she come off the line. What does that mean, I wonder?

Her old man thinks I molest little boys, I say as a joke, and then something goes thunk inside me. I realize that was exactly what he did think. I try to remember what Richard and I had been talking about that day his dad might've been listening in at the door. Made me damned mad to think of a neighbour thinking those thoughts about me. His lad and I have had some good times together and my own grandkids are all in Wisconsin. My daughter married an American.

So are we doing Guy Fawkes or what? says my wife, and I think she's asking for the second time.

We'll burn it ourselves, I say disgustedly. It's got to go out in the garbage otherwise.

The next day I add a ruined chair frame to the pile, and just before seven at night I pour just a little barbecue starter in there, not enough to cause trouble, but just enough to get her started. I don't want to have to wait around.

I guess you might have heard how that story came out. I must say I blamed her some. But that young man of hers, as it has turned out, must have had problems we didn't know about. He come back late in the night that night, and next afternoon we seen the police cars down there and it was cordoned off. He died by his own hand, they say, and from what else has been in the paper — that boy they found in the woods near Bancroft — I think young Richard and his mom, where they'd got to, was not the first thing on his mind. You never can know what goes on behind another's closed door.

What I do like to remember is the look on that lad's face, when he and his mother come around the corner of the house just as I'd lighted a good paper torch to start the thing off. I turned the handle of it around and held it out to Richard. I saw his mom look worried but he didn't hesitate one second: he took it. He held it straight out from him but he wasn't dropping it, no sirree. He held it where I pointed at the bottom of that scrap pile and that stack went up like shot from hell. I grabbed the torch away from him and tossed it in, because I think he'd forgotten he even had it. I've never seen a kid look so god-damned pleased with himself: he was like a bonfire himself, lighted clear through from inside. We had a nice neighbourly time of it while the fire died down, with the toasted marshmallows and the neighbourhood jokes, but what keeps coming back to me now is that moment when Richard started the fire.

We all had to back up from the blast of the heat. For a minute there was firelight in every last corner of our yard, and down the drive. The Missus and I were busy with our fire and we certainly didn't look, even then, up the driveway where everything must have been red with light, or we would have seen those two little suitcases, one for her and one for Richard, which we know now, because they never went back into that house, she must have left standing right around the corner from my shop, packed.

The Poem

Elizabeth is walking down the middle of the street. It's 2 AM. Most houses are dark, but up at the corner she can see a light which her father has left on for her. She'll be glad to get there: it has been a long walk. Downtown there were cars out in spite of the hour, and some people on the sidewalks, but here near home it's mostly quiet. Not entirely, though. A car roars up to the intersection behind her, squeals its tires and turns in her direction. She strides to the edge of the street. Two guys yell at her as the car speeds by. Likely these nerds are going to go around the block and come up behind her again, but if she hurries she won't be there: she'll be inside. There's a man approaching on the sidewalk on her right. He looks okay, likely a student coming home from a party or a girlfriend. She teeters a bit on her heels. She wore them to show off to Win, and she knew that Steve was giving them all a ride over there later and so she'd thought — if she'd thought at all — that Steve would bring them back too. But he left early. Right after she said she didn't want to buy any coke. Piss on him.

The man leaves the sidewalk and is crossing the street at an angle that means they will meet, or nearly meet. She pauses and slips off her shoes. Drops one into her satchel and carries the other in her right hand, heel forward. Felice says it's a good weapon, there was a movie with that in it. The man does nothing — passes silently before her as if she is invisible. She gets goosebumps and glances over her shoulder to see if he's circling back, but he's walking steadily on. The asphalt's not too hard on her stocking feet, but there's the odd piece of sharp grit.

She steps back into the shoes and runs up the stairs into her house. The front door of the apartment is locked and for a minute she can't find the key. Then there it is, in the little Nicaraguan change purse Felice gave her. She lets herself in and remembers to relock the door.

"Lizzie?"

It's her dad. He must have been sleeping light.

"Hi, Dad. Go back to sleep. It's just me."

"Did you lock the door?"

"Yes. I'm going to bed now."

But at breakfast he wants to know more.

"You came in awfully late last night."

"It was only two."

"Two! Where were you till then? I thought you said you were babysitting for Alicia."

"I was, but they came home at eleven, and so I went down to the Bistro and met my friends and we went over to Hull. The buses stop at midnight and so I had to walk back."

"You walked all the way from Hull!" She can tell he is partly admiring her. "How long did that take you?"

"It's not so far. Maybe an hour."

"Lizzie, you mustn't do that again. It's too dangerous. I don't want you out after midnight by yourself."

"Why not?"

"You know why not. It's dangerous. You'll get raped."

"It's not dangerous. I walk down the middle of the streets." She decides to lie. "And I was with friends until we crossed the bridge, and then they had to go the other way. It was just from there to here. Nothing happened. Nothing will. I travel in groups whenever I can, and I take care of myself. Rapes happen to little girls in broad daylight, you know, on their way home from school. I'm safer in the middle of the night than I am at five in the afternoon. Or babysitting at George and Alicia's."

"I hope you lock the doors over there."

"In the evening? In a suburb? With people out walking their

dogs all up and down the street? Get real, Dad. Listen, don't worry — I can take care of myself. I just don't go into unsafe places. I'm fine."

He's letting his coffee grow cold as he looks at her, worry lines furrowing his brow.

Elizabeth checks the kitchen clock. "Holy shit, Dad, aren't we both late for school? It's a quarter after nine!"

"Oh. No — I've got leave of absence to — work on a curriculum."

Now who's lying, she thinks.

Her father looks at her. "But what about you?"

"My first class is at ten. So if I rush I'll make it."

She rushes. Once out of the house and out of sight, she stops under a tree to light a joint. What to do with the day. Now that for some reason her father is staying home. She's not going to go to school an hour late: too much flack. She'd be sent down to the office and have to fill out forms. Much better take the day off and bring in a forged note tomorrow saying she's been sick.

It's always notes from her mother that Elizabeth brings in: she enjoys writing them. She knows just how her mother would say things and it makes her happy as well as sad to listen to that voice in her head, making loving excuses for her kid. Their handwriting is quite similar, and she has practised with a real letter from her mother until she has learned enough about her way of writing p's and r's and capital T's to make the note look different from her own writing. Nobody at the school knows that her mother is gone. Her friends know, of course. Felice knows.

She checks her pockets for coins and finds she has enough for lunch and maybe five dollars over. She'll go down to the Black Cat and buy a coffee. The long poem she has been working on is in with her English notes. She'll work on that.

At the restaurant, the waitress recognizes her and comes right over with the pot of coffee. Soon Elizabeth is lost happily in her poem. Her long dark hair falls across the page and absent-mindedly she brushes it back from her face, her head dancing with jazz riffs from the bistro and voices and zydeco rhythms from the bar in Hull the night before. She tries to catch it, to give it a shape, to make her poem like dancing. Once in awhile her father's voice comes in, a thud breaking the rhythm, or more humorously, a querulous, rising, puzzled bit. She giggles. She looks out at the still water of the canal, and at the leaves turning colour. Then she thinks of her mother and bends her head quickly.

Saturday night, 2 AM, Elizabeth is walking home again from Hull. This time she has on the right shoes, Felice and Mark are with her and they've all kept clear of that jerk Steve. Her friends take off for the co-op house they live in in Centretown, the one with the cockroaches, and she comes down her quiet street, walking soundlessly this time, still taking the middle of the road.

There is a sound like a dove cooing. It gets louder. She sees two figures coming this way, also in the street, a tall one and a short one. The short one is a child, a little boy, and he is weeping softly. A young woman has him by the hand. They all stop when they meet as if the woman had intended it.

"Hush, Richard," says the woman.

"Is something the matter?" asks Elizabeth.

The woman speaks tiredly but in a straightforward way, and she is not drunk. "We don't have a place to sleep. The boy's father kicked us out earlier today and I've been looking for a place but nobody will take me with a child." She stops speaking and looks into her eyes. "Do you live around here?"

"My father will throw a hairy fit," says Elizabeth, "but come home with me."

The boy, who looks about four or five, stops crying. He wipes his nose with the back of his hand, sniffs and asks in a voice that is almost a whisper, "Is it far?"

"No, it's right here." She looks from one to the other of them. "Okay, he's Richard. I'm Elizabeth. Who are you?"

"I'm Rose."

"Hi, Rose." Elizabeth leads them to the door under the light, and up the stairs. As she fumbles for her key, the door opens, and there is her father in his blue pyjamas.

"I was just out of bed to get a drink of water. I thought you were already home, Lizzie. You've — brought some friends?"

"Yes, Dad." She keeps it brisk. "They just need a bed for the night. They're going to sleep in my bed and I'm going to sleep on the couch."

"Not so fast. Not so fast." His gaze takes in the woman's dress and the boy, who has sat down on the carpet in the hall and seems about to fall asleep right there.

The woman starts her explanation again. Her short humiliating story has a practised sound. There is no emotion in her voice. Elizabeth feels that she has said it many times that evening, to many faces.

Her father stands in front of the woman. His face wears an expression of intense anxiety, as if he is suffering.

"Have you tried the Sally Ann?"

She nods. "They wouldn't take me with a child. They said come back tomorrow, and I will, but right now we need to sleep." Her eyes roam past him to the kitchen, to his open bedroom door.

"You need the police, then. There's a pay phone out there on the corner. You call them now and they'll take care of you. Do you need a quarter?"

Elizabeth tries to step past him.

There is a movement of his body, almost imperceptible. Suddenly he seems larger and there is a sense of danger.

He looks directly at her. "This is too much to deal with 'this late at night, Lizzie. Let her call the police. That's what police are for."

The young woman's face hardens. Her lips twitch downwards.

"Hey, it's okay. We don't stay where we're not wanted. I wouldn't have bothered you if I hadn't been invited." She stoops to the child, who is now sound asleep against her legs. As his weight comes into her arms, she staggers slightly. Elizabeth grabs hold of his jersey and helps shift his body closer to his mother.

"I'll just go out with them to make sure they're okay," says Elizabeth.

"That's not necessary, Liz." He lays his hand on the arm of her coat, but she shakes him off and runs down the stairs to open the outside door ahead of the woman and child.

"I'll be right back."

And she is. As she comes back across the street, she sees his face at the window. He meets her at the door, looking relieved, and clicks the lock into place behind her.

"That's over, then," he says. "Where was I? Oh yes, getting a drink in the middle of the night." He shambles into the kitchen and turns on the tap.

"Good-night, Daddy."

She goes into her room and shuts the door. For a moment she stands there, listening, then realizes that the sound of her pulling some blankets out of the cupboard will sound like normal going-to-bed noise. The hangers in her closet clink as she drags down her sleeping bag as well. She hears a door close. Cautiously, she opens her bedroom door and peeks out. Her father is in the bathroom. She can hear him farting in there. She slips into his room and extracts two twenties from the wallet beside his bed. Then, picking up the pile of blankets and sleeping bag, she carefully closes her own bedroom door and lets herself out of the apartment, resetting the lock.

In seconds she's out of sight of the house, around the corner where the woman and boy sit huddled beside the pay phone booth.

"Wasn't sure you'd come back," says the woman.

"It'll just take two calls," says Elizabeth, "one to my pals and the other for a cab."

Saturday night, 3 AM, Elizabeth lies stretched out in the dark on cushions from the living room couch in the house where Mark and Felice and some of their friends live. Near her she hears the deep regular breathing of the boy, the lighter breathing of Rose. She stares at the rectangle of light where streetlights shine in at the window. She hopes that itchy feeling isn't cockroaches getting into her sleeping bag. In her imagination, her father comes out of the bathroom, glances with satisfaction at her closed bedroom door, double-checks the outside door one more time to be sure it's locked. She thinks he will not call out to her or check on her before morning. She sees no reason to go to school tomorrow, no reason to finish her poem.

It will be a different kind of life. But if Rose can survive, so can she. She is not afraid.

Sandspit

I have a plan. I'll share it with Ruby tomorrow when we are out getting sand, and I'll swear her to secrecy. We're used to secrets here. Our lives are based on keeping things from one another, especially from folks in the village who might seek to penetrate our barriers of barbed wire and, in the water surrounding our fishing grounds, our secret system of mines. When our men left for the war, they were themselves boys from the village. When they came back, my husband, Gerry, brought secrets. Secrets have maintained five of us out here for more than fifteen years. The secret of the mines was kept hidden from our son, Jan, until just before he left: we wanted him to think of the world as more safe than it is. The fact that Jan has gone into the village has so far been kept secret from Gerry's war buddy, Steve, and Steve's wife, Ruby: they think they have just missed seeing him around. And Ruby and I know there are many things the men keep secret from us: we have never been told exactly what they look for when they gut the fish, check inside, and cast most of them into heaps, to be buried in the sand along the east shore. We see only the ones they have declared safe to eat. The fewer people who know, the better, they tell us, and we have accepted this. It means we don't have to do the tedious job of gutting, but it also means that, if anything ever happened to the men, we couldn't survive out here. I think sometimes that Steve has told Ruby more than I know, but if so she has kept it from me. We work together on the sand, she and I, and find plenty to talk about without betraying our men. Loyalty and secrecy are important where we live: it is a matter of survival.

At least that is what we have all had to believe. But after Jan left, I began to see things differently, and after what I found on the beach today suddenly I have a plan. It's funny in a way how long you can live one way and never see what is going on, and then in one moment it all comes clear. I never had a plan before. I never saw the need. I guess I really couldn't face the idea of taking apart all we have out here. I imagine the villagers pity us, wonder why we choose the life we have. But I pity them. They've been starving, literally, while we've been eating well. They are forbidden to fish the harbour, because of the pollution. The secret of finding safe fish has never been brought to them. And years ago, when our men came back from the war and brought Ruby and me out here on the sandspit as brides, we were warned we must never let that secret out. If we do, everyone will fish and there will no longer be even enough for ourselves. Better they should scrabble at that sandy soil and laugh at us, watching for signs of the fatal poisoning and feeling our hostility, keeping away. Better we should all live separate, and manage best we can. There've been times in the spring run when we had much more than enough for ourselves, and it broke my heart to see good food shovelled under sand, but I understood the situation, I knew it wouldn't last, and I had to think of ourselves, and our two friends and our son. A baby was a powerful reason to keep me in line. That little boy had to live, and there was nothing out here but mother's milk and seaweed and fish. He was poorly at first, too, but he throve, and grew to delight us and to delight in us. We told him nothing of the mines and the men kept from him, too, the secret of identifying fish. There was plenty for him to play at, and plenty later for him to do to be of help, lending the men a hand with the boats and nets, shovelling sand, collecting shells with Ruby and me for the jewellery we make to sell once a year in the city.

Mostly the villagers leave us alone. They are trying to turn into farmers but it takes a different breed: they scratch at the barren land without conviction, their eyes on the open sea. Once in a while a young fellow ventures out at night to see what it is we catch in our nets, and disappears. We hear a muffled explosion; I always used to tell young Jan it was thunder. One lad made it back to shore with his leg torn off, and apparently talked of sharks before he died. They tend to stay away. Once or twice over the years, paddling on the west shore with our son, we have had to move quickly to prevent him from seeing a body, or parts of a young man's body, washed up on the sand. But we have always managed; things were buried; he grew up strong and innocent. He, no more than the villagers, knew what our men do in the evenings, their silhouettes against the setting sun, so picturesque, the little fishing boat, the lifting and checking and mending of nets, the bobbing floats marking the mines they have set, just under the surface, beginning at our shore, along the perimeter of our bay. We have to play it cool, look as if we just like privacy. On the water we keep our voices down.

"Shh," says Gerry, patting me, and I shush: sound carries on water.

He and I like to row around the point together of a calm night. There is an inlet like another lake; it holds light after the sun goes down. We wait until the stars are out, make wishes, make love sometimes before we come back in the dark. When our son Jan was home, he would smile affectionately at us when we came in, as if he knew what we'd been up to. He had the usual teenage restiveness but as a family we've been very close: we had to be.

Before Jan left, he and his father walked over to that inlet for a man-to-man talk. Jan came back looking serious with the weight of adult secrets but not rebellious about what he had learned. He understood that it was this had kept his life safe for him out here during his growing years. It is the way of the world. But he had to be told, I insisted on it, so that he could be safe in his return.

That was two months ago. Jan had thought he'd spotted nets out on the far side of the village, and it's possible they have started again to fish. If the pollution count is down, if the world is changing, we wouldn't know. He and Gerry spent a long while looking through the binoculars, discussing the matter in low tones.

"There's something out there," announced Jan at last. "I've got to go and see."

I was surprised Gerry agreed, but he did. There was a time when he and Jan didn't get along so well as they do now. There is a closeness there as our son becomes a man. More and more I've had to turn to Ruby to have anyone to talk with. Maybe that's the way it should be. Ruby and Steve have no kids; Ruby spends her time alone. She was glad when I suggested years ago that we could go together to get sand. We could use our old truck, and go farther, not just dig near the houses. So we do that: Gerry and I go over to their place of an evening and the men row out in the boats to "check the nets." They think we spend the time planning our next trip for sand. Men make such a project out of the simplest things. We laugh about that, Ruby and I. It takes us one minute flat to plan the next day:

"We'll go north this time, okay? Up where that scrub pine has taken hold."

"Right."

Then we turn to other topics. Bit by bit, checking our way as women do, we've built a bridge of trust. I think of it as like a real bridge, one I saw on our way to the city once, when there was a flood and we had to take a different road. It was woven out of vines, each strand fragile, but the structure as a whole able to bear. Each time Ruby and I meet, we weave a little more, trying to understand now what happened to our men during the war, what it did to them, what exactly is the nature of the bond it forged between them and — this part is very tricky; we start into it and draw back — what manner of women we must be, what we have in common, to have become so entangled with these two men, our husbands, to love them and want to live with them out here in this peculiar existence, isolated on our long spit of sand. I want to know what she will say tomorrow when I tell her about the girl, and whether I really will dare to discuss with her my Plan. Laughingly, of course, making fun of myself, saying, hey, it made me think of doing this: what do you think? And she will laugh too, be outrageous, we will paint it all in vivid colours as we jounce across the sand dunes with the shovels rattling in the back of the truck. When we get back, we will say to the men: we had a great time.

I wish Jan would come back. I have been mortally afraid that he is dead. He left two months ago — did I say that already? He left when the smelt were washing in on the west beach in their annual death run, flopping and dying and smelling like their name along the village side, so we have to swim and wash clothes over the dunes near Steve and Ruby's where the beach stays clean. It was then Jan left, one evening after dark. Gerry and I went with him as far as the barbed wire, helped him lift it and skin under it with his little backpack. I hugged his slim frame one more time, too hard.

"Oh, Mum," he said, "don't be like that. I can look out for myself. Don't fuss."

And disappeared down the beach, a pale glimmer, then nothing. And hasn't come back. There's a lot for him to find out, Gerry tells me, I gave him a whole list. He can spy out all the new traps, maybe even steal some supplies. At the end of the first month, Gerry took my hand one evening, led me to the end of our beach, then looked a long while through the binoculars, quietly.

"There," he said at last, and passed them to me. "Check over there, on the point, between the two pines. Do you see a light?" I looked, adjusted the glasses, looked again, and then I saw it. It looked like a campfire.

"That's him," said Gerry. "He's all right."

So I was comforted. But the second month has gone by now, and I see Gerry glancing anxiously over towards the point.

Yesterday, just after noon, I was shovelling sand from the last load in under the house. It is sinking a bit under the living room: there are cracks starting up the living-room wall. So I was shovelling sand in there, shoring up the boxes the house rests on instead of foundations, pressing it in with the wooden frames Gerry made for the job years ago, when we first came. There are advantages, as he explained to me then, to building one's house upon sand. If you're dirt poor as we were you can get ahead faster. No one wanted these dunes; we could do as we liked. We have loved ever since the violent storms that lash over us, the displays of wind and waves and stormheads lit by lightning in the sky, and then the indescribable calm of other summer nights, the lingering light, incredible sunsets and sunrise, and all the little animals of the dunes, mice, lizards and, in the sparse grass near the water, crickets, watersnakes. Life has been good here in many ways. I wake up in the morning and don't have to ask myself what there is to do. I know we will always need sand. I have grown strong and sunburned and windburned gathering sand, shoring up the house. It's a never-ending job, but it makes sense, too: it has kept a space — for our love-making, shelter from the weather, then shelter for our infant son. Who is now so nearly a man. I have tried not to let myself think about all the harm that could have happened to him where he is. I have tried not to let myself think at all.

Yesterday morning, then, shovelling sand, suddenly I couldn't bear it anymore: I walked down to the shore in daylight, carrying the binoculars, wanting to search all I could make out over there for my returning son. No news is good news, I said to myself. He's on his way back.

On the beach I found Mary, the girl. She couldn't have been more than about eight, with very fair hair and a thin freckled face: she was thin all over, in fact, her narrow arms thrown up to protect her face as she fell. I went to her at once, brought some water in my hand and cooled her face, then thought to lift her up. She was extremely light. I carried her into a shallow cave carved out of the sand at that spot by the tides. I took off my skirt and dipped it in the water and cooled her skin. At first her breathing was harsh. Then she began to come to, opened her eyes, and smiled weakly at me as if she were not surprised to find kindness. She told me her name, and said she had come from the village to see who lived out here, but hadn't known it would be so far. Might we have a carrot, she wondered after a while, or a piece of bread? It was going to be hard to get all the way back home.

Well, it was a conundrum. She had no idea what a problem she was in my mind. I was pretty sure I'd better not let Gerry see her, and yet to send her back in that condition was impossible too. Her presence here broke so many rules it was laughable (Ruby will laugh at this part too) but to her it was all so simple: the long walk out of curiosity — what a strong, animal drive curiosity is in the young! — overdoing it, but the expectation of simple human succour now she was found.

"Stay here," I commanded her, and put my wet skirt back on, so that from a distance I'd look normal going into the house. There was chowder left from the night before; I got her a dish of that, plus an old straw sunhat I don't use anymore and which Gerry would be unlikely to miss. I looked around for something else, decided I could take her drinking water in a can. So I did. I did those things. I succoured the child, the stranger on our land. I fixed her up. She needed very little to revive: children are amazing. I left her building moats and castles in the sand, in the shelter of the little cave, and with strict instructions not to wander very far. I told her there were sand monsters that would bite her if she went out, and that anyway she had to stay out of the sun. Her eyes widened, and then she giggled, as if I had told her a story she enjoyed but didn't believe. I showed her a bruise on my arm where I had hurt myself working under the house, and I told her a sand monster had done that. She seemed to accept it. We talked a little about her life in the village, and then

I told her I'd come back at dusk, help her through the barbed wire, send her on her way when she couldn't be seen.

I went back to the house, keeping an eye out for Gerry, hugging to myself the great treasure she had brought me, the reason I knew I was going to have to tell the story to Gerry, once she was safely gone, in spite of knowing I should shut up.

"Is there anyone new in the village?" I had asked her, trying hard to watch what I said.

It was the way her eyes lit up.

"There's Jack," she said. "A big boy. He's helping my uncle with the nets. And we play sandcastles and he tells me stories."

"What kind of stories does he tell?"

"Stories about where he comes from, over the mountains." She pointed. Her thin arm with blond flecks of hair. "There are real castles over there, Jack says, and a queen and a king. He's going back someday. But he said he had to find out first what was here."

When she was bigger, she said, she wanted to travel over the mountains too. "Next time I'll wear a hat."

So Jan was alive two days ago. Two days ago he was telling stories to this little kid.

Gerry stayed away longer than usual. When it was past dusk and the moon was rising and he had not yet come in for supper, I decided I would see to the girl. I would tell him I had just run down to the shore to get a little kelp. In fact, I had done just the opposite, as I slipped some into my pocket to take to her, not wanting to send her off with nothing but that sparse lunch. Then I turned back again and picked up a shell bracelet as well. I thought she might like it. It has been so long since I have talked with a child, and we never had a girl.

When I came to the cave and found that she was gone, I did not know for a moment what to do with my feeling of loss.

Then I saw the signs on the moonlit sand. And then I understood.

When I came back to the house, Gerry was already there. He was just putting away a bowl in the cupboard. He took a cup and drew some precious drinking water, then sat at the table and looked at me.

I looked at the bowl he had just put away, and I looked at my old sunhat, back on its hook.

"Gerry," I said, "there was a little girl wandered in here today. I found her fainting on the sand."

"She was a spy," Gerry said.

"No," I answered him, "she was too little to spy. She just made a mistake." Carefully, then, I told him the story about Jan: how those people in the village, with so much less than us, have taken in our boy.

"Of course they would send a child," said my man. The candle I had lit glinted red in his beard, but his eyes were sombre as he listened to me.

"You fed her?"

He knew that I had.

"She was so hungry. I couldn't have sent her back the way she was."

"She was pretending to be hungry. Of course she would. They would tell her to do that. You fed her fish?"

I had left the bowl of chowder with her when I had abandoned her on the beach.

Again I tried to explain, to make him see. Her youth. Her frailty.

"She wouldn't have remembered it was fish," I said, but heard her myself saying, "This is very nice!" and knew it might have stuck in her mind.

"She was a spy," said my man. "You played their game. How could you take that kind of chance? And our own son risking his life out there!"

"They're being kind to him!" I cried. And then: "He's spying too!"

He has never struck me, and he didn't strike me now. What I saw in his eyes was harder to take than violence: disappointment, hurt. He had thought I was with him and he had found out that he had to handle it all by himself. I had been a woman, that's what. Weak, when he needed me strong.

He went out to the truck without inviting me along. I knew he was going over to Steve's, to check the nets. The mines.

I sat alone in the house. This place we built with our hands. I sat on a stool we made together when we and the world were young and he was just back from the war, before even Steve joined us.

My heart broke those times we had to bury good fish along the beach when I knew in the village babies like my son were crying for food. I know how sand looks when something has been freshly buried. It is easy to erase signs of struggle and there would not have been much of that. I remembered her trust, the way her smile darted into mine. It takes several hours before sand that has been disturbed dries to the same colour as the rest.

So I had known what had happened even before I checked,

before I knelt on the sand and reached in until I uncovered once more, and then reburied, that thin freckled arm.

How Ruby and I will laugh together going out for sand! — And then you light your campfire, she'll say, wait, while you're at it, why don't you really fire the house? And this will seem very funny, with the sun beating down and the sand spraying back in our faces in the wind. — No, okay, your bonfire, a big one, eh, you can make the excuse you've found that leg that boy lost, in his boat, and you're going to have roast meat! — You're sick, Ruby! I'll shout through laughter and tears, but I'll make a big fire! And that will be the sign then, we'll both agree, not certain if we mean it or not. That will be the sign that I've really gone and done it!

I know how to string the mines. I have even found out how to mix the gunpowder so nothing too serious will happen, they likely will live to tell the tale, they'll lose a finger, maybe, an eye, and definitely the boat, they will have to swim to shore. It will be enough to stop them, enough to give us time to get away. Understanding what pain feels like is only part of what those men are going to have to find out. At first they'll only relearn what they think they know now from the war: that they're under attack. It's later, when they get home and find the messages that we'll leave, the warnings, and they really understand that they're out there without us, and they have no way of knowing now where the mines are, either in the water or the land, so they can't get out, that maybe they'll have to begin to see.

At any rate, that's my plan.

It will be dirt-easy to string mines across the middle of our bay, one night while Gerry's gone over to Steve's. And Ruby for sure can take care of the truck: she knows the insides of that engine better than the men do themselves. When the flames start up over at our house, the men will find out that they can't come back by truck. Take our boat, Ruby will tell them. You can get there twice as fast straight through the middle of the bay.

And then, if it all works out, she'll put whatever she took out of the truck back in and drive like mad for my place. I'll let her through the barbed wire in the one place I've left open, we'll stop long enough to dig one last hole in the sand, plant gunpowder one last time. By the time the men hit the line she and I will be halfway to the village, and to finding out what has happened to my son.

We will tell each other that it's thunder, and hope for the best.

Because someday we might want to go back.

Miss H.

The obsession came upon Janet as she was riding a bus. The way it happened was this. She had come to Victoria, British Columbia, only three months before, accompanying her husband, Keith. They both were now graduate students in the English department at the university, only Janet was a year behind Keith and still had her master's thesis to do.

They had moved across the country, and were at that phase where they believed they knew no one at all in their new place. In fact eventually they were to meet all kinds of old friends and connections, including Janet's cousins and a high-school buddy of Keith. But at this point they felt like strangers newly arrived in paradise. They came in the spring and, three months later, it still was spring. Hand-in-hand like children, they wandered amazed, looking at tall trees and enormous flowers, wondering how it was that they had somehow managed to leave all their known world so far behind and to have landed in such a beautiful place. At this point, they had actually been married for more than a year, but back home they had been so involved with families and friends that it felt as if only now were they really beginning as a new unit, a married couple.

So it came as a kind of disturbing miracle when Janet picked up the paper and read that her old high-school English teacher, Miss H., the first person to introduce her to Shakespeare, never mind to the moderns and Canadian novelists such as Margaret Laurence, had been knocked down by a car at the corner of, it said, Quadra and Fort, and was in Victoria General Hospital.

"It must be the same woman," she exclaimed, jumping up from her desk and carrying the newspaper across their small living room to Keith at his desk. "There can't be two Mercy Hallams who taught English in Ontario, can there, Keith?" She leaned against his shoulder as he read. "And the age is about right. I remember she refused to take early retirement. She could have been long gone out of the school by the time you and I got there. Mom sent me a clipping when we were in university. They were having a retirement party for her. We could have gone, you know. A lot of her old students went back. But that would make her about 71 or 72 now, wouldn't it? It says here 72."

He agreed that it must be the same woman. It seemed very strange.

Janet realized that she would have to go to see her old teacher. She felt she had no choice.

But first she paused. She went back to Keith, who had just returned to his work. He sighed.

"Keith? You wouldn't want to come with me, would you? It's silly, but she still seems a kind of fearsome person to me."

"Then why go to see her?" asked her husband, reasonably he felt. "I mean, if it's not good for you. She doesn't know you're here. It's not something that you have to do. And she has no power over you now, Janet my love. She never did. Maybe, though, you thought that she did."

"Hey, she could send me to the office!"

"So what was the office? Another room."

They stared at one another for a moment.

"All the same," she said, "I'm going. And I wish you would too."

He turned back to his work.

"I'm not going near the old bag."

"Keith!"

She pulled out her map, which was beginning to wear through at the creases, and traced the route to the hospital. Then she looked at bus schedules and reassured herself about the best bus. Distances still were a pleasant surprise, so much shorter than what she was used to. Once she started for the hospital, she found herself walking through its automatically opening doors less than half an hour later, even including the time she spent waiting for the bus.

Mercy Hallam was in Room 2128. She was sitting up in bed in a scarlet silk bedjacket and appeared very surprised and pleased — delighted, in fact — to see her former student. She still looked much as she had at the front of the class, aside from her hair, which was white and quite long and had curl in it and right now was down about her shoulders. As a teacher she had worn it swept back in a roll. She was notorious for having a comb or two fly out and clatter to the floor as she moved energetically about her classroom, settling disputes and starting new ones as she went. She still had the piercing green eyes and the fidgety, darting manner that showed she could hardly contain herself in her present state, confined to a bed. Her left leg was stuck out ahead of her in a cast and she told Janet that X-rays had revealed two ribs cracked but not broken. More seriously, she was being held under observation because they suspected internal bleeding. All things considered, she felt very well, and was astonished to hear that the accident had been reported in the newspaper.

Janet sat on the visitor's chair. At once the enchantment began that she had forgotten from high-school days, when Miss H. had plunged her students into discussions about what Shakespeare was getting at with Titania's infatuation with Bottom in his ass's head and why Piquette in *The Diviners* had to die. Miss H. had been a terror about homework, but Janet's had always been done. What she recalled now, seeing Miss H. moving restlessly on her hospital bed, plucking at her sheets and momentarily disclosing her good leg, unexpectedly shapely, was her old teacher's energy. She had been death on misplaced commas and apostrophes; she sent some students, Keith's friend Mac, for instance, practically every day to the office for undone work; she used to recommend as supplementary reading any book that made it to the school board's banned list. She wore beads, too. It all came back. Janet recognized the force that had propelled her into pursuing the study of literature at university and brought her into her marriage to Keith and out here to Victoria.

For over an hour she and Miss H. exchanged news and views, one remark tumbling over the next, about what was going on between the covers of books. Patrick Roscoe's first novel had just come out. Miss H. had read all of it and was outraged by parts. Janet hadn't read it, although she knew about it. She was specializing in women authors, trying to make up for a bias she felt in her education so far. Miss H. emphatically agreed that there had indeed been a bias, expounded upon the bias of the curriculum she herself had been required to teach, and listened intently as Janet described a novel she had found on a remainder table. Janet felt it was a novel of the future. Just as Miss H. began to probe for news of Janet's classmates, a nurse came in. Confusedly, Janet remembered that her old teacher was, after all, in a hospital. Perhaps the bright red spots glowing on her cheeks, almost as scarlet as the bedjacket, might not be totally due to the stimulation of the conversation. Janet stood and promised to come back at the first opportunity, and to bring books.

Miss H. held out her hand. Janet took it and found herself held tight. On an impulse she leaned over this much older woman who had always seemed, in spite of her liveliness, totally unapproachable and remote from Janet's world, and gave her a little hug and kissed her cheek. The hand that was held came up between them, pressing against Miss H's breasts. Janet felt surprised and moved by how soft everything was: the hand holding hers, the silky material of the bedjacket, the bosom, the cheek, the soft, straying white hair. She's still young, thought Janet, who had felt nothing but the opposite until that moment.

She took herself off and on the way home on the bus that parting scene replayed in her head. She felt undone by all the softness: she did not know what to do with it. Her whole body was responding to the excitement of the conversation she had just had, the things they had said and the things they did not need to say, because they were women and they had spent so many years in the same city and loved so many of the same things. Perhaps, she thought after she got home, it had to do too with the drumming and throbbing of the bus. Janet had never felt so thoroughly aroused; it was sexual as well as intellectual, and she did not feel like taking it to Keith. She was glad, though, to see him at his desk, and glad to tell him about the conversation, and even to surprise him by telling him there had been a hug and a kiss. Neither of them had ever anticipated such intimacies with any of their teachers.

Keith's specialty was in postmodernism and metafictions and deconstruction. He was labouring mightily to understand Jacques Derrida, and not only to write a thesis about Canadian writers influenced by this new school, but secretly, known only to Janet, to produce his own book. He too had been outraged by Roscoe, but only because the man wrote so brilliantly and chose to use traditional forms.

The conversation between them sparked back and forth as they prepared a meal together, Keith cooking the spaghetti and Janet fixing the salad.

She had trouble paying attention. The body warmth of the red silk bedjacket when she had laid her palm against the woman's back in that hug returned as a physical shock inside her. Without intending it her mind was racing ahead, planning what books to bring next visit and how soon that could be and whether and how she could bring flowers.

He reminded her that many of the students, mainly the guys, had hated old Mercy. His pal Mac whom she kept sending to the office had already gone on to become a successful journalist. Some of these brighter boys had seen Miss H. as a simpering old-maid monster, full of herself and of her elitist view of English literature, totally out of touch with the real world and real young men in it. Everything she presented in class had been on her own terms, take it or leave it. She hadn't been the least bit interested in finding out who her students were and what they liked. She would have called it catering to the lowest common denominator.

Janet tried to keep her temper, but she was upset that he chose this moment to remind her of these things. It didn't matter to her, if in faraway Brinton some immature boys hadn't understood what was being put in front of them. It was true, what he was saying: she remembered kids reacting that way too. Perhaps she herself had sometimes shared some of it. But to the girls Miss H. had also always been vaguely romantic. It was rumoured that the reason she had never married was because her fiancé had been killed in World War II. As Keith rambled on, Janet felt increasingly irritated. And she felt irritated at her own irritation. They came close to having a quarrel. As it was, the atmosphere in the apartment became formal and stiff and they both went off after supper to work at their studies in their respective corners.

In the ensuing days and weeks, Janet spent every moment she could spare — and some moments that really ought not to have been spared — in the delightful company of Miss H. When

Mercy was sent home, still with her leg in a cast, and couldn't get down to wash her floors, Janet offered to go over once a week for the duration and swab down the kitchen floor. While she was at it, she ran a vacuum around the rest of the little house.

Mercy had a cottage not far from the ocean and had cultivated an English garden, with hollyhocks and delphiniums along the fence, and mignonettes and bright red portulaca in the yard. Janet helped her with the weeding, both when Mercy still had the cast, and later, when they both could get down on their knees. Mercy showed Janet things she hadn't known about: when and how to separate bulbs, the collecting of hollyhock seeds, how much pansies tended to spread out. Slowly Janet realized that every inch of the small back and front yards, even the grass, had been landscaped by Mercy Hallam in the five years or so that she had been retired. She was nearing the end of a grand plan she had had for her garden. Soon they talked together as much about flowers as they did about books.

Keith grew restless about the amount of time that his wife was spending at the old teacher's cottage, but at the same time he wanted to be understanding. He realized that his wife was lonely in this new town and had always in the past had women friends. She was still writing long letters back home, eroding still further the time she had for her thesis. He also understood, however, or thought he understood, that she was working something out.

One night he remarked that she never wanted to make love after she came back from spending time with Mercy. Janet felt attacked and defensive about his remark. It seemed to her, inside, that if there was a connection it was almost the other way around. She came back from weeding Mercy's garden feeling fully alive, her head spinning with new information, and a feeling of having been fully met, fully encountered, that she didn't feel with Keith. She was more touchy with him than she would have been if she hadn't felt guilty, and then defensive about her feelings of guilt, because sometimes, when she came home in that state, and if Keith wasn't around, she would lie down on their bed and undress a woman like Mercy in her mind, a woman with combs in her hair and a brassiere and (she pretended) red silk underpants. The orgasm was always quick and deep and satisfying. It also made her weep, but this she attributed to the fact that something about Mercy touched her to the core. She had read enough pop psych to think she knew that one of the signs of a sturdy marriage was that both members masturbate for some of their sexual needs. The idea was that when their needs did coincide it would be from choice to be together, not coercion because of the marital bond. She didn't think that Keith masturbated, but that was his business. As was whatever went on inside his head when ostensibly he was making love to her. There were times when she was certain that it had nothing to do with her and that her body was a substitute for someone else. Sometimes he told her; more often not.

So she became angry when Keith made his remark. She felt it was untrue to start with and that he must be saying a lot more, all of it unacceptable. Her own nagging concerns about the way her thesis was bogged down made her fairly irrational and she felt Keith back off. "I guess you're working something out," he said, thinking he was being very open and really the "new man." To his dismay, Janet became angry at that as well.

One sunny afternoon soon after that exchange, Janet stood in Mercy's back garden, her sneakered feet carefully placed on the path of cedar chips that the two of them had just finished and which wound through the flower beds in such a way that it was easy to get close to all the plants to care for them and water them. Mercy had done all the digging and heavy work. Janet had come along just in time to help rake the chips into place.

It was the moment when they would ordinarily have made their way back up onto Mercy's back porch for a glass of lemonade and a literary and floral chat.

Mercy was wearing her gardening overalls, green like her eyes, and a fetching yellow straw hat. Her soft white hair was caught back in a bun but curly tendrils escaped all around her face and there was a picturesque smudge of garden dirt on one smooth cheek. As she turned and smiled at Janet, she seemed very beautiful.

So it was unexpected when Janet suddenly felt the cedar chips burning her feet. She longed to step onto the cool grass, but that was on the other side of the pansies and anyway she knew the grass was a particularly fragile variety that Mercy was attempting to grow and was not yet ready to be trampled on. The red portulaca scalded her eyes and the delphiniums thundered in blue waves against the fence. Her friend looked like a grotesque painted garden gnome.

Janet's feet moved of their own accord off the burning path

onto the yellow and black pansies, crushing them, twisting them as she danced about with sudden expansive enthusiasm.

"When I have a backyard," she declared, "I'm going to put it all down to grass. I'm going to have a lawn chair and a barbecue and a big old picnic table and a big old straw hat like yours so I can lie out there and read a book." Oblivious to what her feet were doing, she laughed and waved her hands. "This is a garden right out of a picturebook, Mercy, but...."

"You're standing on my pansies, Janet."

"Poor little things," she agreed, dancing on them all the way back to the house. It was impossible to step back on that path. Again she felt she had no choice.

She checked in her jeans pocket for bus fare, and turned to talk again with Miss H., who still stood where she had left her. A frown had appeared between the bright green eyes, but she appeared more worried than angry. It occurred to Janet that her friend was a physically strong woman when she had not been freshly knocked down by a car, and required very little help. The pansies, too, were a hardy breed.

"So send me to the office!" she laughed, making a comic face and feeling lightheaded, as if she might fall over, as if she had had too much to drink.

But they hadn't been drinking, of course. Perhaps it was too much sun.

"Mercy, I have to go now." She wanted to cross back to her friend and give her a hug, but the burning path and the order of the flower beds defeated her.

Instead she went home on the bus, and worked very hard on her thesis. It was accepted. In hard times she lucked into a university job and was suddenly in demand. She worked even harder, giving what she could to her students, being supportive of Keith, whose first novel couldn't find a publisher, and as time passed giving birth to children whom she made of point of often bringing with her to her job. She was a role model. Women students phoned her at all times, including the middle of the night.

She and her husband maintained a sense of adventure about their relationship. In Victoria's long spring they still found time to walk out under the pink flowers and to scuff petals with their children at the sides of the street. The only odd thing was that Janet discovered in herself a compulsive need to read obituaries. Every morning she located the list in the paper and scanned it, especially for "H." To Keith she said she was looking for characters for the stories she had begun to write, and perhaps she was. But always when she put down the paper she felt a sense of relief.

Somewhere in the city, Mercy Hallam still lived. She had never been seen at literary readings; she had opted, it appeared, for her flowers. Early on Janet forgave herself for her own abrupt leave-taking. For quite a long while she mailed off notes to Mercy regularly about upcoming events, but there was no reply. Eventually she stopped. She could have phoned, but somehow she didn't.

One day, perhaps still long into the hazy future, she will pick up the paper and once again find her teacher's name. By then perhaps she and Keith will have their own garden. Perhaps she will be wearing her sunhat when this happens, when she sees Mercy Hallam's name. Janet will be sitting at the picnic table where she and her famous novelist husband like to entertain students and friends. Near the barbecue. She has very clear ideas of how it will be. She will put down the paper, and pick up her lemonade, and nothing will have to change.

An End To Grief

Listen! Do you hear the robin?
Silence.
I don't hear it. And you're not going to hear it again either — there's still snow on the ground!
Just the same, spring is here. I'm going outside to see if the ice is breaking up.
I wish it would.

He hauls a bag of clothes out of the back of the closet and begins rummaging through it. A heavy sweater falls out and he puts it on, and a lined winter jacket. He draws his boots over thick socks, and goes for dubbin to rub them where they have turned white since he wore them last. He tucks in his scarf. A wool cap comes down over his ears and he picks up rough leather gloves. He turns the doorknob and steps outside, pausing a moment on the stoop to pull on the gloves and tug the cuffs of the sweater down over them.

It is a bright day, crisp and cold. His glasses darken as he turns toward the glare from a field of snow. It seems impossible he could have heard a robin.

Then, over the riverbank, he hears a kind of gargle, a thud, then a long groan. The ice is going out.

He sets off across the field. Every year at this time — doesn't he do it every year? — he looks for pussy willows to take back to Bettina in the house.

We imagine this man heading across the field, determinedly, dressed for it, seeming to know where he wants to go. His daughter watches him awhile through the kitchen window, then sighs or smiles and drops the curtain. She knows she has the day to herself.

Every year at this time.

He heads for a place in the bend of the river that he knows, that takes whatever sun there is. He laughs to himself, thinking he is like the cat who searches every door, looking for the one that opens to spring.

He finds what he wants, drops over the bank onto a sunny, muddy clear spot. Some green grass shows. His boots sink in and mud squishes up. They will make a mess of Bettina's floor, he thinks. The pussies have broken out of their shells, soft and horny and sticky at the stem. He gathers a lot of them, then pauses as he sees part of the bank is covered with fragile pink hepatica. He plucks some, a different job from the bending and breaking of the branches of the willow. They make an odd bouquet as he climbs the bank and breaks again through the crust of snow. But it is not so deep here; he moves steadily on.

He comes to Bettina's before dark. As he approaches he realizes he has no idea if she is still there. She hurt herself, he has heard: perhaps she is in the hospital. Perhaps she is dead.

He enters cautiously, pushing the door open, bending his head to enter, holding his bouquet before him like a shield. The voice of an old woman addresses him from behind a closed door.

"You are leaving a mess!"

He looks behind him at his bootprints on the linoleum floor. He calls out an apology, takes off his boots awkwardly with one hand and leaves them beside the door.

He lays the flowers on the table, removes his cap and scarf and jacket and gloves and arranges them neatly on the back of a chair. All this time there is silence in the house. He peers through the gloom, his glasses adjusting after the glare of outdoors.

Probably it wasn't Bettina. He remembers her as younger. Possibly it is some friend. He may not be able to find Bettina again. He is not even sure this is the place where she was living last year. He goes to a pitcher of water, splashes some into a

basin and washes his hands, bends and washes his face as well. He dries on a towel hanging on a nail beside the basin.
   Now he can see.
   He finds a vase and arranges his flowers in water. The old woman calls again, querulously, from the next room, wanting to see him, wanting him out. He is uncertain whether or not he should stay. The afternoon begins to close in. Perhaps he should be moving along.
   But we have run too close to the dream he was in when he woke. We have let him enter a house. With flowers, a mixed bouquet, as in his dream. He has brought female flowers because he knows she likes them. But the people he meets in the house may not know Bettina. Know of her, yes, but without clear direction. They should be hostile.
   In his dream, at this point, a cataclysm occurred.
   The ground shifts, snow slides, the linoleum sags and splits, he is wading in the icy stream without his boots. This is fine in his dream but perfectly without point in his life. We don't know yet who he is: we don't know the nature of his wound or even that he has been hurt. We do hear that Bettina has "hurt herself" but do not know who she is or why he searches her out or why it has been a year.
   We do feel the sense of ritual, of action repeated, each time with deepening and differing sense.
   Is it that he goes to this old woman to get his fortune told? Why in the spring? Is there something sexual in this meeting? There seemed to be when he was choosing the pussy willows and the flowers. How serious is it that he has gone alone, instead of with his companion, his daughter or his wife?
   He might be obsessed with the idea of his yearly ritual, and one of Bettina's daughters might set him straight, remind him of where he has left his boots. If only we weren't using the exact same symbol of the boots, the one from his dream. The jacket, perhaps, is a better symbol of preparation.
   He could go each year armed with a . . .
   He could . . .
   But we ourselves are drifting among dreams. The man and his ritual is searching for us, and there is mud on the carpet of various rooms. We wear socks or maybe bare feet. We are not always prepared.
   The man and his ridiculous bouquet must be accompanied by a cat. Why else are her pawprints on the bank, above where he

went wading so suddenly and uncomfortably without rubber boots?

Could we be involved here with a form of goddess worship or even Mariology? The man goes to pay his respects. He goes obsessively because of a wound: the loss of a mother or a love. Or a daughter.

Some female factor gone out of his life, he is touched at a mystic level and marches off as if compelled —

This could be it:

this red-faced farmer full of concerns about machinery and land and marketing boards and subsidies — a nice guy, with a sense of humour — but once a year he goes strange — it seems he has to. Afterwards, he feels better.

It could be he gets his fortune told. She sets him up for the following year.

But one year it works out differently.

She takes him into her bed.

He finds out she's real: myth and the material world interpenetrate.

He is up to it. He will heal. But we need a better grip on who she is.

Every year at this time Bill Stewart opens his door. Every year as if by clockwork he wakes one morning from a bitter dream, hears a robin call, and knows for sure that the next while will be pure hell. He thinks of it as going nuts. He knows it's part of his grieving for his wife Audrey, now six springtimes gone. But it seems bigger than that. It feels as if it comes from the beginning of time, or his time anyhow. He muses on his mother as he pulls on his clothes, the special clothes he wears for this annual trek. I just let it happen, he explains to himself, and would explain to anyone else if they were there to say it to. He has tried to think of who he knows who might help him work it out a little, but everyone he knows is crazy in the usual ways and wouldn't understand a man who goes nuts once a year.

He puts on the warm winter clothes he was still wearing in the early spring when Audrey died. That way when she sees him she will have less trouble recognizing him. Six years: he hasn't changed that much, he thinks. Then looks in the mirror and sees how much hair he's lost and the new lines at the corners of his eyes and running down beside his mouth. But she will know him all right. He searches out his old boots from that winter, not as good as the ones he has now. But they'll do, they'll still do. It's a bright sunshiny day, cold, but ice is melting on the road. It will be muddy on the riverbank, where he goes to look for a gift. He never even knew for sure if Audrey liked pussy willows all that much. She loved them, perhaps, because he brought them to her. She would make a fuss, getting pink in the face, smiling at him, arranging them in the grey vase. After he sees her today, he might go back and pick some more for himself.

He stands in the kitchen a moment, looking around. The stove is off, the cat is fed. There are some papers on the counter, beside the kettle, that came in today, having to do with the Farmers' Association. He will have to call George Henderson later on, but that can wait. They wouldn't say that it can wait, but he's the secretary and he gets the mail, so they don't know yet what the issue is. Weird. He can feel the pull of all that, his normal world.

A man's dream comes from his need. He grieves and the dream gives him some sort of reply: a cataclysm, a joke, some kind of image he can use. But our need, too, must be addressed: it's unpleasant when the ground shifts constantly beneath one's feet. It's unfair when characters change their names. We could be led in, perhaps, with some universal experience: "Do you remember how it feels when you fall in love?" No, much too philosophical. What is needed here is the sound of his voice. Let's say he's found somebody neutral to talk to about this. He's not the type to go to a psychiatrist; he might open up to the family doctor. Or maybe he is talking to the woman in the blue parka, the one he is going to pick up at the mall.

―――――

Every year about this time I look for her. It's a little ritual I have. I can't see that it hurts no one so long as they don't know. The neighbours see me walking along the road and heading in to Reid's maple bush, and if anybody happens by on a skidoo or in a car they say, "G'day, Harold." If I had to I'd say I was going on back to check the fence or some darn thing, but it hasn't ever come up. Probably never will. It's usually not hard to walk back to the sugar bush in March: the snow is pounded down by skidoos. It gets right messy back there about then if we have a warm spring.

Cheryl died six years ago. So there's not much use to go looking for her, and I know this. But something comes over me and then for a while it seems to make perfect sense. I don't know anybody else around as I could explain it to. The point is, there is a part of me that never stopped looking for her. Could be I did something wrong at the time she died. Probably I ought to have went in to see her the way the police wanted me to, to identify her, like, before she was prettied up by the undertaker. But her brother had to do that job. I was shook up.

I've thought maybe because of that I never quite grasped that she was dead.

I'm not sure about explaining even to you about this. Not sure, for instance, that I really want to be fixed — I mean, what's wrong with remembering somebody? It's the way it comes over me that you might find a little nuts. First off there's a dream that I can't quite remember. Then I wake up and I'm definite: today is the day I go and find her. As if: this has gone on long enough. I drop everything. This makes it more real, I guess, helps fool myself. Sometimes I'll phone up the garage, like, and say: "I can't bring the truck in today, Charlie: something's come up" — change the appointment to another day.

Then I put on the clothes she would remember me wearing: my old rubber boots instead of those Cougars I left at your door just now. My jacket and that from that winter.

I open the door and I head out.

There are several places she could be. The maple grove's a good place to start. She always liked it there. We tramped back there in March more than once. She always liked those seed things, dried weeds — I agree with her that some have nice shapes. This year I took my jackknife with me and cut her some pussy willows and some bright red sticks that are growing back there. Sumac. I thought they looked good together. Checked around to see if she was just back there, maybe sitting on a stump listening to the trees the way she used to like to. Stood and looked around me on purpose, really checking. So I can tell you she wasn't there. There were some rabbit tracks, and a hole in the fence where the snowmobiles have gone through, and yellow and grey seed pods poking out of the snow. You understand I didn't really expect to see her.

I figured next I'd go over to her dad's and then maybe to her friend Mary's, who married Jack Phillips and lives on the second concession. She could've tooken the car and gone over to either one of them places. I also thought about going in to the mall, in case she'd done some shopping. She'd sure be surprised if she came out with her arms full of groceries and I just turned up beside her and offered to help carry the bags.

None of this chokes me up — it just seems like a normal day's plans. Although I don't plan in any errands if I go to town; I drive right past the places where I get my mower blades sharpened or pick up various parts.

At the mall I always see several women who look quite a bit like Cheryl but I always know right away it ain't her. I don't follow along of them or nothing. I just look around, and especially I check out the Dominion Store for a little lady in a blue parka and pushing a cart with a week's supply of food.

If I can't find her there, I head on over to her dad's. Him and me always get along anyhow, and he's usually glad to have a hand with something when I turn up. I don't forget myself enough to come out with something dumb like — Cheryl ain't been over here, has she? — but I look around real sharp. When I turn in at the driveway I look for our old blue Chevy to be sitting there, and even when it's not there, I think — Oh well, maybe he picked her up at Murray's, and I go up the hill and maybe I find him working in the shed or in the house. I excuse myself to go up and use the bathroom, so I can take a look into the room she had before she married me. Her dad has made it into a storeroom nowadays; I look around just the same.

No Cheryl.

But I feel better, as if I've just missed her, know what I mean?

Our hero could now just head for home. He can set up the pussy willows on the kitchen table, remembering to use the grey vase. He is careless in the way he puts the bouquet together, and the vase tips over and shatters on the kitchen tiles. He sweeps up the pieces and tosses them out. He locates a mason jar and starts over again, putting the water in first this time and arranging the branches. Then he watches some TV, goes to bed, wakes up next morning dreamless, and gets on with his life. In which case we have here a little essay on loneliness, a bit schmaltzy, and you know he's going to do the same thing every spring, maybe even for the rest of his life. They'll find him face-down in that muddy spot sometime when he's in his eighties, wiped out by a heart attack when he tries to climb the bank.

And we haven't been told what kind of woman Cheryl was, or

Audrey or whoever, although we noted that part about her listening to trees, and getting pink with pleasure over the pussy willows. There is the possibility that she isn't even dead, but has left him for another man. We don't know how much of all this he has made up.

We could have a twist in the story right about here, which might be the best thing, story-wise. It turns out that the search he makes is actually a recurrent dream. That's why the names change and details shift. The dream that he can't remember is his real life.

But maybe instead the guy will figure out something else all by himself. He could discover the folk wisdom of searching for her everywhere by caring about many others. And really finding comfort in that. Hard to write that without making him sound a bit of a saint, although if you added in some of the raw sexual loneliness he is feeling, it might humanize him sufficiently, and it would be a useful moral tale.

More likely he does see a woman who reminds him of Cheryl, suddenly takes fire and goes after her, and then discovers she's really different and that his feelings are hurtful to her, not really what she needs at all. She suspects that they belong to someone else.

So then what — he returns to his house, throws out the pussy willows and fires the grey vase after them, starts a new life without Cheryl.

I'm going to find her a lot of places from now on, and no place. In the end if there is going to be a woman around the house here again I am going to find her the exact same place I found Cheryl: just where you'll least expect. So nothing to do but get on with it. Don't see myself waking up one morning and going through that nightmare again. I'm giving those clothes to the Sally Ann and the rubber boots are already at the dump. That's all in the past. It's more, if you follow me, that every day now she's the spice that keeps me going — what she was to me: somebody who could look me in the eye and care about what the hell happened next. I believe now that's out there to find again. I believe I can wait.

There's mail come in from the Farmers' Association. I'm the secretary, so I'd better look at it. And I checked the old mower today. A blade needs sharpening. I'll have to take it into town. It's spring: the ice is going out in the river, even though there's still a lot of snow on the ground.

Listen — do you hear the robin?

LINE OF STONES

Journey Dream Story
Story Journey Dream
eggstone

On my sister's verandah, close to her front door, is a large pink granite stone, perfectly rounded. Enclosed in it, showing at one side and rounded and smoothed into the lines of its container, is a smaller white stone. Quartz, someone said. The effect is of a two-coloured egg, or perhaps the human eye. She and her husband found it on one of their "Easter rambles." They liked it and so they lugged it home. It's not an Easter egg. It's not a symbol of anything. They just like it.

Inside their house are many other objects that they like. A feather mask from New Orleans lights up one place on the living room wall. A green mask made by their son hangs in the hall. In the children's bedrooms are large wooden structures made for them by my sister's husband, who took over the fathering of these kids at the usual point in second marriages of change and pain.

My niece was six when she received her dollhouse. She is fifteen now and still it dominates her room. Inside it she cares for babies. Every room has its tiny cradle, crib, playpen or highchair, complete with babe. My sister says her daughter has become a collector of miniatures. When they go for trips together, they look for stores that carry tiny furniture and exceedingly small books, rattles, toys, cups and saucers, even a minuscule roll of toilet paper. All to scale, more or less, except in the living room a gigantic seated mother brushes the ceiling with her head. In her arms, a gargantuan baby, dressed in long white clothes.

My nephew's room has the castle. Superheroes guard turret and balustrade. When we go on our trip to the medicine wheel, chosen heroes accompany us in the back seat. Behind and under the larger journey, my nephew and his heroes go about their whispered business, their death-defying leaps.

On the night before we were to visit the medicine wheel, we stayed in a cheap motel at Lake Kenosee. I was the reason for this trip.

I slept in a room by myself and dreamed I was clinging to the side of a dangerous castle moat.

I intended to dream: it was written into the schema I'd outlined already on three different blackboards: *Journey*, I wrote (the original trip to the Gatineaus near Ottawa with a group of friends, slogging around in the March bush, breaking through ice, stopping to listen to wind in the trees. We were: two married couples, each with tensions; a recently divorced and very beautiful young woman; a twelve-year-old girlchild; an older woman who, when I broke through the ice over my boots, looked back and, before she turned to lend her hand, hesitated).

Journey. Then: *Dream*. I had dreamed of sacred land. A woman in green leads a group of affluent yuppie tourists over contoured terrain. She unfolds an aerial-photo map and shows us that the land has been deliberately altered to resemble a temple and amphitheatre from ancient Greece. I take her to be a guru, perhaps a goddess. I wake and think: it's true — we were on sacred land. Each of us involved in an inner trip, scarcely able to make one another out through the fog of internal myth. Only the child danced through the day in the real Gatineaus, in real snow, under the shadow of a real hill. ("Don't be so sure," say friends I tell this to, remembering being twelve.)

So in *Story* (next in my schema) I eliminated the child, amalgamated the two quarrelling married couples, and paid attention mainly to the two other women. The younger one seemed outside all their tensions, observing, treading her own path, yet surely not easily: so much going on in her own life. In the story I made the young woman the recorder, and had my group travel to the only truly ancient sacred place I knew of in Canada: a prairie medicine wheel.

There was no money to travel there myself, and so I researched it secondhand. I interviewed a Cree friend and local poet, looked up maps and the meaning of Saskatchewan names in the library, discovered a very useful article had been saved in a scrapbook by a New Age friend (synchronicity, we both believed), made phone calls and accepted xeroxed articles and photos and personal accounts from my sister in Saskatoon who has an eggstone at her door and masks on her wall, but rarely remembers her dreams.

Perhaps, I offered, you don't need to remember them because you bring so much of this stuff into your everyday life.

We both felt shy. Well, I know that I felt shy. The fires in my sister that I had felt flare soon after my arrival tamped down. I remembered that we always go through this rough bit, feeling close, then jarring against difference.

I pulled out the gift I'd brought: a grey stone. I had picked it up on Galiano Island when I visited there with my husband two years before, and had kept it ever since on my dresser, a reminder of my sister and a reminder to bring it to her whenever I found my way to Saskatoon. In some ways it was an ambivalent gift. I had felt quite bad about it, yet determined, when I plucked the stone out of salt water. A lady limpet had been sweeping along its smooth surface, trailing her long fanned skirts. I was enchanted, wanted to keep her. Would have preferred to have kept her alive. But as the rock dried and the limpet became still, I had to accept — I was a long time letting myself know this and would even now rather not be told for sure — that, if restored to saltwater, the creature cannot revive. The limpet died, slowly or quickly, tight to her rock, conserving to the end whatever moisture she had inside her skirt. I wrapped her and her deathstone gently in tissues in my suitcase, but I needn't have worried: the limpet adhered to her stone. She and it became one.

It's a limpet.

Oh — what is a limpet.

Don't you remember? I used to call you that name. When you used to ride on my back! I liked the sound of "limpet" — with the "pet" in it, too.

It sounds better than barnacle!

But really she is pleased, and goes and places the stone in front of the photograph, the gift from last time, a fuzzy old photo taken with my very first camera, a picture of my little sister in a white nightie, freezing in bare feet on the front porch. This was before flashbulbs, at least in our house, but not before mothers. My sister is caught in near-flight, about to run back into the house as our mother cries in the background, her warning caught in the picture in the turn of the child's bare foot "You'll catch your death of cold!" You'll catch your death of foolishness, she used to say, too. Mother, I'm straight into foolishness now, in pursuit of my life.

Limpet stone in front of the photograph seems to have been always there. To this house of living plants and beautiful dead weeds and paintings of prairie landscape and sky, with the eggstone out front, I have brought the right gift.

Story, I write on the blackboards. I wrote the story. The child danced back in, changed into a Cree lad who holds more keys to the mystery than does any guru in green.

Next I got a grant, and asked for extra money to visit the wheel. (*Grant*) I write on the blackboards, parentheses because I feel apologetic about this component of the internal/external flow of the writer's life. But now because of the grant I have come to Saskatchewan to visit the medicine wheel and also some family places. BUT REALLY TO VISIT MY SISTER. IT'S A KIND OF SCAM SO I CAN VISIT MY SISTER. Truth in its own peculiar way turns out to be both true and not true. My sister has fallen in love with our family roots, the history and prehistory of Saskatchewan. She and her prairie husband are delighted to take me on this trip. They want me to come back another time and visit the petroglyphs, the badlands, Big Muddy and. My sister shows the paintings she has made, trying to capture the earth colours of the prairie. I gaze at her paintings and later, as we travel, at the fields and, surprising me, the hills and wooded valleys of the prairies, flowing by. I try hard to pay attention.

Paying Attention, my Cree friend back home has informed me, is the essence of native religion. It is what the Amerindian would have been doing up on that windy hill three thousand years ago.

The same friend told tales from her girlhood in a Catholic

residential school where you were in serious trouble if you spoke your own language to anyone after you came there at the age of six. At the solstice, she said, we'd skip school and we'd go up into the hills. The nuns thought we were practising secret rituals up there, but we were paying attention. Now it is spring, we would say. We spoke to one another in Cree. We looked about us. At home, in the spring, we knew the Mounties would stop any native religious ritual. But in the spring we almost always had a wedding. Now, a wedding! She laughed, as she does instead of sounding angry. Everyone understands a wedding! So we'd have a wedding on the twenty-first of June, and we'd have a dance beside the lake late into the night. And we'd dance, we'd dance all night in the light from the lake.

Well.

Things we have lost. It's not a symbol of anything, that limpet on its rock, the water receding from under its skirts.

Journey Dream Story (Grant)
eggstone limpetstone blackstone whitestone two-coloured stone for throwing away. When does your love become a pointed grey pimple clinging to a stone that is older than the hills. If restored to saltwater will your love spread her skirts and skim once more across the surface of this hard, hard earth.

On the lee side of the medicine wheel, sunwarmed, we sisters traced an old line of stones. We wanted to see how far it would go.

"You start imagining things," she smiled at me. "But I love this." We pointed out stones to one another, stone stone stone another stone. When at last we could not persuade even ourselves that the line continued up the hill, we agreed that perhaps it didn't matter anymore: we were in a sightline now for one of the great wheel's spokes. Its small end cairn lay directly ahead. We looked back and marvelled at how far we had come: the line held all the way from the teepee rings laid out below the hill.

I, too, am following a line of stones, as I did with my sister that October morning, and as the ancients did, painstakingly placing the stones they gathered one by one by one. They made two concentric circles and then five lines, across the summit of their highest hill. Their intention, it is believed, was to discover

LINE OF STONES

the moment of solstice, spring and fall. Mine, too, is to find a point of transition, a coming or fading of light.

When I applied for a grant to complete a manuscript of stories, I included a request for money to visit my sister, although I said it was to research a story. I intended to climb a hill among the Moose Mountains, sit with the wind in my hair looking out over land that is much the same as it was two thousand three thousand years ago, when small dark people, perhaps joking among themselves, laid out these lines of stone. In England, other people who also didn't know that they were prehistoric toiled and muttered and no doubt joked some too as they hauled at gigantic menhirs, first bringing them across water on barges and then across green fields. Today you can stand at Stonehenge and trace the line of deeper green where their stoneboats gouged a path. To this day it holds more water than the surrounding countryside, grows more green. Does this make sense? Wouldn't all those centuries of ploughing and harrowing have long since flattened out that ditch? I remember the line of green. I only know what I was told. I believe that if on Moose Mountain medicine wheel I had reached out my hand and overturned a stone, I would have been the first to commit this sacrilege, the first two-legged creature in three thousand years not to hold sacred the earth and the bright eyes of the human beings who spring from her and return to her and who have held this place sacred, have honoured the line of stones.

When you have said that, you have said everything there is to know about this place. It is here, it is fragile, human beings washed over it for three thousand years and for all that time it has not been destroyed. A man with a pickup truck could remove this wheel in less than a day. In some parts of the province, this has happened: wheels identified in the seventies have disappeared. But this one is on grazing land and it is on native land.

A fieldstone warm under my hand, I thought I saw that in forcing our attempt to understand ourselves, we devalue and destroy the parts we cannot understand. Some of the few farmers who remain on this prairie land, riding high-removed from it in agribusiness machines (each one costing more than a house), have uprooted stones like these, cast them from their fragile moorings, sent them adrift again across the prairie sea, in fence rows, foundations, crushed in gravel or cut into facing for city bungalows, patterns new and possibly not even wrong. Each in our own way we search to find our place, our grid pattern of streets, roads, fences, backyards: privacies from which we take our bearings and to which sometimes we can return.

The thing is that we run into a gap in what we know, hiatus in the lines we trace on our experimental trails. Someone removes the clues. Hard-won tenuous insights shift and we have to win them again. If only someone had stopped and laid a mandala of stones, to hold in place the little we know. If only the bulldozer or the giant combine had not come by. But then, in three thousand years stars themselves shift. Only the smell of prairie grass must be the same. Perhaps this small yellow flower.

My sister was in charge of our journey, and she led me first to several family spots: the site of the hospital where I was born fifty years ago; a pink granite gravestone, Selena and Thomas, Indian Head; the house in nearby Kendal where Selena, without much help from Thomas, cared for our father. I was taken to visit that house when I was three, and carry faint memories from that time.

I am slow to add the pink granite headstone to my line of stones. It was a stone of my journey, but one shaped, smoothed, shined, engraved. On it Selena, my namesake (I am Margaret Selena, after two prairie grandmothers) — Selena has no surname of her own, her history dissolved into what remains of Thomas. In life it was not like this. Selena was broad, big-armed; she ran a boarding house. Besides her own daughters she raised as her own a neighbour's son. Four trees were planted in memory of her beside this stone, by this son, our father as a very young man. When I was three, I left a wishbone behind on the big Kendal woodstove. All through my growing years I imagined that someday I would go back. Now at last I am here. The idea seizes me that somehow the wishbone may have survived inside this decrepit, boarded-up frame house. For a moment I dance on the sidewalk, wanting to get in. My sister brings me back to earth with a look and a question:

"Why?"

In saner mood, trying to explain the writer's life, I wrote on the blackboards *Journey Dream Story (Grant)* and underneath that, *Journey* again. I am on that second journey now, and waken next morning in a motel room in Lake Kenosee, where we have spent the night before we go to see the wheel.

LINE OF STONES

Enjoying being alone, I arrange paper and lamp on the round table provided and write down my dream. This time I am clinging to a precarious wooden trellis or drawbridge which is collapsing into a moat. As I fall I make a little joke, and hold on tight to pieces of trellis still attached to the sides of the moat. A dark-haired girl like my daughter or my niece pushes through the trellis to be with me, and together we thrust our heads through the railings at the top and clamber out into life. There is more to the dream: a telephone message that can't get out, children, an angry friend who resembles my mother and hesitates, then moves mysteriously in the dream from left to right. The dark-haired girl returns to help me look for a gown I have lost. We find it draped over a light.

Later in the week, back in Ontario, I find the gown where I left it, on a hanger, put it on and sit down to throw the I Ching. It disappoints me with Clinging and Fire. *Perseverance* furthers, it says — it always says this — and also: take care of the cow. I experiment with changing lines and am referred to the hexagram on Family, Clan: wind comes forth from fire. I don't understand any of it, but I like wind and fire and family better than taking care of the cow. Perseverance *of the wife*, it specifies, will pay off.

I recall the trellis that I clung to in that dream, persevering, even making a little joke. I try to get something out of it. The trellis was black. It had snow on it. Nothing flashy. No guru in green. Just hang on and pay attention. There is a time, perhaps, for superheroic leaps, and a time to hang tight and climb with care from darkness into light.

Alone in the motel room, I write out my dream, dress and walk outside to the lake. Its borders have receded twenty feet. The docks have extensions built onto extensions, and still they end up high and dry. As I approach the water, I pick up five interesting stones, one for each of us. I am uncertain about these stones: they may be gravel, brought in from other places to this beach. I decide to go to the water's edge and retrieve stones new-birthed from this retreating water. The image pleases me. I know that a lake can represent the unconscious; later I learn that passage from left to right in a dream can signify passage from unconscious to conscious, darkness to light. And will find hope in the fact that my lost gown was found on a light. My identity, is it, enlightened? I don't know.

You'll catch your death of foolishness: the voice of my

mother, that part of my mother that is me now, my own disapproving voice inside my own head. What is all this nonsense about left and right, gowns, lights and lakes? Kenosee is down because there's been a drought. The limpet sticks to the stone because it's dead. You dream of a wooden drawbridge because last night in the dark in real life you slipped on the boards of an old dock and had to sit down for fear of falling off. You clung and saved yourself and went to bed and dreamt a hodgepodge of distortions out of your daily life, synapses firing randomly in sleep. This black stone you lift from the water, disentangle from seaweed, symbolizes nothing. Or if it does, because it comes to your hand from the water of a receding lake, it signifies drought.

My real mother is not like this; perhaps she never was. My real mother would be with me beside the lake, telling me the names of the stones.

Five stones I gather from the lakewater, put them in my other pocket, smile good morning at a man walking three dogs, and meet my young nephew, the superhero, coming down to find me, and then his mother my sister with a camera, who takes a photograph of my nephew and me walking along companionably. I am a little wide in the picture, the pockets of my jacket filled with stones.

Before we leave, I wash the stones in the motel room sink. There is a crumpled black stone, grey granite, pink granite, and one that is two colours, yellow and white. My nephew and I admire how pretty they are when they are shiny with water. I tell him how, with my husband, his uncle, when we were first married, I picked up little stones all the way to Newfoundland. Our first possession as a couple was a green tent. Our second was a Volkswagen van. We sat in the tent in the evenings with the van outside loaded with our books and clothes and wedding gifts, and we polished stones. We made love, too. This part I do not say out loud. We had bought the finest grain of sandpaper and before we made love we talked and paid attention and polished stones. We had been one summer together and seven months apart and one month of family preparations for getting married. There was an enormous amount still to say.

Soon we will be thirty years married and sometimes he says, over breakfast or perhaps over a muffin and coffee in the afternoon, That's it, then, is it? After all these years? We've run out of things to say?

We laugh and take up the threads: he tells a dream, I tell family news. Sometimes I talk to him cheerfully about how my obsessive emotions are travelling mysteriously from the left to the right and losing their spell. You smashed my window, he says then. You smashed my window and I don't know why you did that.

On the medicine wheel, I choose the black stone. It is folded in on itself and at first I think it might be coal. I hold the black stone in my hand and look out over the land of my mother and my father and my two grandmothers — my namesakes — and my grandfather who ran the post office in Kendal and my grandfather who turned virgin prairie sod and built himself and his brothers their first home.

From the end of each of the five great spokes I gaze across brown hills. The wind lifts my hair. I feel nothing and everything. Other women have stood here, other men and young children. My nephew and niece have gone off by themselves and are sitting down and being still. No one told them to do that. The folded black stone warms my hand as if with its own heat. There are no flashing neon signs, no strange rites. One has only to pay attention.

I find that so difficult to do.

My mother pays attention easily. One day we went for an evening stroll, my mother and my husband and me. At the corner of Wilbrod and Chapel we stood for what seemed to me much too long, while those two gazed at a bird on a telephone wire and tried to determine which it was, a pigeon or a gull. I don't care, I said to myself. And then: why don't I care?

I tell my sister this tale later on, and she laughs and opens the glove compartment of their van. There is a book identifying wildflowers. Another identifying birds. Yet another identifies planets and stars. There is a book identifying trees.

When they have come down from the hill and are back in the van, I bring out the stones and show them to my nephew and niece. They choose one readily. Neither asks why: what is the use of a stupid old stone? They put their choices away carefully in their pockets. Aunt Margaret washed them off this morning, remarks my nephew. He and I remember how shiny they were. He pulls superheroes out of other pockets, and starts an adventure in the back seat.

eggstone limpetstone (gravestone) blackstone whitestone

White stone is manna stone, the vanishing, the Other. Once I had a stone that looked like the white fudge which is called "divinity." It was squarish and sugared-looking; one longed to sink in one's teeth but the stone resisted. The hollows in its square sides were made not by human hands for human needs but by water in a prehistoric lake. I felt drawn to it, yet alien; it could not be bitten or hollowed to my needs. It stayed as much as a year or two in my jacket pocket. Finger it, look at it, feel frustrated by it. Then it disappears. I find a reference in the front of Joy Kogawa's novel *Obasan* to Revelation 2:17 and the white stone with one's name on it, a white stone that like manna brings nourishment only for a time, and on its own terms.

Thou art like the white stone, I said when I fell in love.

The white stone was my own symbol, and I lost it years ago, but just near the parked van, as we return from our visit to the wheel, my sister stoops and picks up a stone.

It is exactly the shape of the hidescrapers she has in the pictures in her books — she has books for identifying native artifacts, as well as birds and trees and stars. The hidescraper has a curved edge for the scraping, and a smooth edge to fit into one's palm. It has the telltale place where a chip has been hollowed out, suitable for the placement of a human thumb. Women scraped hides, so this was made for a female hand. But it is small. It has been made for a little girl, hardly big enough to sit by her mother and learn woman's work. It is almost a toy.

"Here."

My sister hands me a white stone.

It had not been on the hill: it lay by the public road, in earth churned by beef cattle who had been run into a corral.

What are the ethics of moving a stone? Stone set down by a tired small girl, or lost out of her pocket as I lost that divinity stone so long ago. It was right for the ancients to place stones in a line, sighting from earth to stars in the sky, catching and marking the first rays of summer sun. It was right all those years for humans to hold those lines sacred and to sit quietly there, or to pitch teepees and sing loudly, pounding on their drums. To dance.

I borrowed the white stone; I took it home.

I don't know what to do about this, my sister said earlier, looking troubled and holding out a large white stone. It fit in her hand as if made for it — unbalanced until she scraped it as if across hide. "I found this when I was there before; I wonder if I ought to take it back." She held it tenderly, brought from the careful place she keeps it. "If I were a romantic like you," she said, "I'd say it was like holding the hand of the woman who used this stone."

"I think you should borrow it a little longer."

This is the sister who refuses to remember dreams. When a reference to child abuse comes up, her tamped-down fires flare. "I cannot talk about it: I am irrational about this. Isn't this the sane reaction?" she cries. "Why be rational about a subject like this?"

It is as if she herself had been abused.

But we were there together. I loved her. We all loved her. I called her "limpet" and carried her on my back. Nevertheless. Something lit that dark fire. Something told her it must not be looked at in the light. Something drew her to the eggstone, the gravestone with its four trees, something gave her an eye for following lines of stones, and for discovering, first, this white stone made for the hand of a woman, and now, in a swift stooping movement, this small version of what she already cherishes at home.

"Here."

We could hurt each other very easily. She in her anger and tension over emotion, over rituals. I in my arrogance, acting as if there is only one path up the hill. Psychoanalysing a dollhouse and a castle, failing to notice the colours of the prairie or the fire behind the sociological jargon words with which my sister reports on the reality of children who are hurting.

Toward the end of the visit, we exchange a few words about the state of our hearts, the fierce inner journeys we guard jealously yet want, when we are together, to share.

From my remaining collection of prairie stones I select the one with two colours, a fragment broken from some larger structure that also had a stone encircled by a stone. I turn it in my hand. Worrystone. I plunge into the enigma of my foolishness.

Stone of two colours, yellow and white, fragment broken from some larger dream.

"Shit," I cry to my sister as we near the airport. "I intended to throw this away when we were behind the art gallery. I forgot."

"What is it you want to do?"

Awkwardly. "I just wanted to throw this away. A small personal ritual."

"No problem," she says. She who was so tense about rituals on the hill.

She pulls the van to the side of the road and smiles. Self-conscious but determined, I climb out of the van. The two-coloured stone flies from my hand, returned to a prairie field. Worrystone, good-bye.

I get back in.

"You never know," I say.

She starts the van again. "You never know."

We take three more pictures with airplanes in the background. Then she rewinds the film in her camera and hands it over.

The journey is done, and one dream. Now there is a story to write.

Journey Dream Story

Story Journey Dream

eggstone limpetstone blackstone whitestone worrystone for throwing away

When we buried the ashes of our father, the family formed a circle of hands. The hole in the earth was filled in and we sang a verse of a hymn that he had loved. Overcome by her loss and the presence of her children and perhaps the opportunity to give us one last helpful hint, our weeping mother began to sing Blessed be the ties that bind. My sister broke the circle and ran down the hill. Another sister pelted after her. My body ached in the broken circle, but I finished the verse before I ran. Three sisters tangled down by the garage. All through our Christian upbringing, our sister had hated hated it; the old hymn harmed her.

I've brought stones, I said casually as we climbed the hill to the wheel. In case we want to do some ritual up there.

Fire leapt: I felt scorched.

What's wrong with what we are doing? Why can't we just go up there, just poke around? Why do you have to add to it?

All right, I said. It's fine. I can just do something for myself.

I love this, she says later, wind lifting her fine fair hair, face alight in the sun. You start imagining things, don't you. I love to follow a line of stones. Let's see how far we can go.

MARGARET DYMENT is an accomplished short story writer and poet. Her fiction has appeared in *Quarry, Canadian Fiction Magazine, Queen's Quarterly, Fiddlehead, Best Canadian Short Stories* (1983,1989,1991) and *The Journey Prize Anthology*. Based in Ottawa for many years, Margaret and her husband Paul ran the much-loved Scholars' Bookstore. Margaret was the founder of the Booksellers for Peace organization and was a tireless worker and organizer for the Peace Movement.

Margaret and her family moved to Victoria, BC in 1990 where she is an active member of the Federation of BC Writers and the Victoria Literary Arts Festival Society. Margaret teaches creative writing and writes a monthly literary news column for the *Times-Colonist*.

Over 50% recycled paper
including 10% post
consumer fibre
Plus de 50 p. 100 de
papier recyclé dont 10 p.
100 de fibres post-
consommation.

M - Official mark of Environment Canada
M - Marque officielle d'Environnement Canada.

PRINTED IN CANADA